The Long Road to
Longbourn

Renata McMann
&
Summer Hanford

Cover by Summer Hanford

Acknowledgment

With special thanks to our editors, Joanne Girard and Betty Campbell Madden.

By Renata McMann and Summer Hanford
The Second Mrs. Darcy
Georgiana's Folly (The Wickham Coin Book I)
Elizabeth's Plight (The Wickham Coin Book II)
The above two books have been published in a single volume as:
Georgiana's Folly & Elizabeth's Plight: Wickham Coin Series, Volumes I & II
The Scandalous Stepmother
Poor Mr. Darcy
A Death at Rosings
Entanglements of Honor
From Ashes to Heiresses
The above two stories have been published in a single print volume as:
Entanglements of Honor with From Ashes to Heiresses
The Fire at Netherfield Park
Courting Elizabeth
Her Final Wish
Believing in Darcy
Foiled Elopement
The Widow Elizabeth
The Forgiving Season
Hypothetically Married
Caroline and the Footman
Mr. Collins' Deception
Mary Younge
Lady Catherine Regrets
The above four stories (and two additional stories) are collected in:
Pride and Prejudice Villains Revisited – Redeemed – Reimagined A Collection of Six Short Stories

Table of Contents

Chapter One

George Wickham used his turn as dealer as an opportunity to study the three men seated with him. The late hour rendered the Meryton Inn's common room empty of all but his table and the weary innkeeper. A haze of smoke, the product of cheap candles, firewood and cheroot, hung about the room. Wickham's companions watched his hands through blurry bloodshot eyes, fixated, looking for any indication he was cheating.

They could look all they liked. They'd find no wrong doing on his part. For once, he didn't even need to consider cheating. He was winning. More than he ever had before. Enough that he could pay off all his IOUs or all his debts in Meryton. Better still, he'd played with different men all evening. With him winning so much, no one had remained long. It would be days, if ever, that anyone gathered enough gossip to have an idea how well he'd done tonight.

Only one hand remained, one more fleecing of these last few desperate fellows. Then he'd go. He'd already told them as much. This sort needed that warning. They either wouldn't, or couldn't, walk away from a game of cards, sorry sods. Wickham had learned long since that the best way to handle men like them was a drawn out, oft-mentioned departure.

He dealt the cards, picked his up, and flashed an evil grin, quickly suppressed. In truth, he had nothing. His luck had finally run out. They didn't need to know that, though.

"I fold," the one to his right said and slapped his cards down on the table.

Wickham looked to see the man across from him studying his face. The one to his left seemed too drunk to know if his hand would play or not. Wickham slid a few coins into the middle of the table.

The man across from him cursed. He slapped his cards down and pushed back his chair, pent up anger sending the rickety bit of furniture skidding away. "I've had enough," he declared and stomped away.

Wickham shrugged. He turned back to the man on his left. "You in?"

"What?" The mumbled question was accompanied by rapid blinking.

"You playing that hand?" Wickham pressed.

"He's not," the fellow to Wickham's right said. "Come on, Walt, let's get you home so your wife can have at you." He offered Wickham a nod. "No hard feelings. We'll win it back tomorrow."

Wickham grinned, nodded, and gathered up the cards. He waited for the other three to be well gone before standing from the table. Feeling generous, he tossed the half-asleep innkeeper a coin as he headed out into the night. Or, if he was any judge, the early morning.

Projecting easy confidence in case anyone watched him with avaricious ideas, Wickham sauntered back to his room. Once there, he locked the door and wedged the cramped space's lone chair against the thin wood. He set about removing the notes he'd won from various places about his person, making a pile on the bed. Then, he sat down to gleefully count.

Once satisfied he had an accurate total, Wickham pulled off his boots. They were special, his boots. For one, he'd commissioned them with a down payment from the funds old Mr. Darcy had left him. For another, he'd stiffed the Derbyshire cobbler, sure Mr. Darcy the younger, Wickham's onetime friend, would pay the debt. Knowing the stuffy, upright, holier-than-thou Mr. Darcy had paid for boots specially made with secret pockets to hold oftentimes ill-gotten gains filled Wickham with glee.

He stuffed all but about seven pounds of his cache into the boots. They barely had enough room to hold it all and still fit back on his feet. He flexed his toes, enjoying the feel of so much money along his calves and ankles. Yes, it was more than enough to pay either his debts in town or his IOUs to his fellow militiamen. Either way, he'd even have a little left over.

He wiggled his toes and tried to choose which debts to satisfy. Logically, he should pay his IOUs. The regiment would soon be headed to Brighton. If he stiffed the merchants of Meryton, he'd never be welcome there again, but why would he ever want to return to such a countrified backwater? Better to have the men of his regiment think him honest and willing to gamble with him more.

An evil smile crept across his face. Why part with any of his winnings? He'd earned them, after all. He'd played fiendishly well all evening, for hours, while lesser men threw themselves against his skill and broke, like waves. Waves of winnings.

Wickham gave his head a little shake, reflecting he could have done with a touch less to drink. Still, the idea was sound. He shouldn't give up any of his hard-earned coin. Instead, he would leave. Part with all his debts and keep all his money.

With quick, sure movements he went about the little room and gathered his possessions, stuffing them into a carpet bag, which overflowed. He put the few things that didn't fit into a sack. Then he moved the chair, unlocked the door, grabbed the bag and sack, and crept from the room. In moments, he was back out on the street, no one the wiser. The sun hadn't yet risen, but the sky was a bit lighter in the east. A glance down the street showed the stirrings of morning. A shabbily dressed man with a ladder was putting out the few guttering streetlights the town boasted. A supply wagon had pulled up alongside the inn.

Neither of those were of use to Wickham. He walked a bit farther, pace quick, toward the edge of town. He'd keep walking if he had to, but he'd prefer a faster, less strenuous option.

Two streets down, he found a somewhat squat man, with rough-cut hair and nondescript workman's garb, loading a wagon. The man wasn't tall but looked strong. They'd be even in a fight, if no one cheated.

Wickham plastered an amiable expression on his face and sauntered over. "Where are you headed?"

The man shot him a quick, assessing look. "Southeast."

"Mind if I join you?" Wickham asked. "If you let me ride with you, I'll buy you a bit of food on the way."

The man shrugged. "Put your stuff in the wagon," he said and went back to hoisting sacks.

Wickham threw his luggage in the back of the wagon, then went around to climb up. While he carried all his money on his person, he didn't like the idea of his possessions in a wagon he wasn't onboard. Besides, if the fellow wanted help loading, all he need do was ask. Wickham would be happy to negotiate the service.

Apparently, the man didn't want help loading. He was slow enough about tossing in the small pile of sacks that Wickham started to sweat. He didn't want anyone to wake early and see him about to depart.

Finally, the fellow loaded the last sack and came around to climb onto the hard bench beside Wickham. "Name's Smith. Yours?"

Wickham saw no reason to lie. Especially since, if the man had been around town at all, he might already know. "Wickham."

"Where you going to?" Smith flicked the reins and set the team moving.

Truth very often bred trust. Wickham gave an exaggerated wince and offered a dollop of honesty. "It's more a matter of going from. I'm in the militia and many of my fellow officers hold my IOUs."

Smith looked at him askance. "They can't put you in debtor prison for that."

"No, but they can make my life miserable." Wickham let out a longsuffering sigh. "I won enough last night to pay a few of them off but not all of them, and everyone will want to be paid. It occurred to me, well, it's easier to leave."

An avaricious glint that Wickham recognized well sparked in Smith's eyes. "How much did you win?"

"Six pounds and a couple of shillings." Wickham made sure to sound proud, like he was boasting. In truth, he'd won much more. He'd put six ponds and change in his wallet, though.

Smith's interest dimmed. "Don't forget you offered to pay for lunch."

"Yes, but I didn't say you could have whatever you like," Wickham countered.

They reached the edge of town and headed southeast. The horizon glowed like an open flame, but the golden orb of the sun still lurked below, out of sight. Smith's team, well past their prime, plodded forward at a slow pace.

They took turns driving and stopped often to rest the team. Wickham wasn't really worried about being followed. No one would realize he'd left for quite some time. Still, each delay made him nervous. He didn't see why the quarter full wagon, the sacks turning out to be cabbages, necessitated such slow going.

The sun still lingered just low enough to be in Wickham's eyes when Smith, who was driving, turned them down a farm lane. Wickham's worries returned. Could this be as far as the man meant to go? Wickham would have trouble flagging down a new ride and they were still uncomfortably near Meryton.

"Your farm?" Wickham asked, endeavoring for a casual note.

"Just a little more cargo."

Wickham relaxed in relief. He even helped Smith and the dour old farmer load the small collection of sacks, leeks this time, into the wagon. They climbed back in and resumed their course.

The next time they rested the team, Smith didn't request a change of driver. Wickham didn't mind. Driving was more work than riding, after all. When they set out again, Smith went only a short way before turning down a narrow trail, hardly wide enough for the wagon.

New concerns sprang to life in Wickham's gut. They were going east now, toward the sea, which glittered on the horizon before them. The trail was steep, much more so than a man would risk for any honest purpose. Did Smith mean to accost Wickham for his possessions and seven pounds, then toss his body in the water?

The trail sliced through a hill, the wagon occasionally grating on the steep walls. Wickham looked about for a possible weapon. A large rock or a branch. Anything. They came out onto a rocky cove. Smith drew the wagon to a halt.

A ship was anchored in the narrow bay. It had the look of a wealthy man's private vessel, built more for speed and comfort than for cargo. A small boat was beached beside stacked casks, presided over by two somewhat rough looking men. At the sight of Smith and his wagon, the two men each hoisted a cask and headed up the beach. Smith jumped out and started removing his meager stacks of vegetables.

Smugglers, Wickham realized. From the look of the casks, he guessed brandy. French contraband.

"Give me a hand," Smith called.

Wickham craned his neck to look over his shoulder. Somehow, his bag was now on the ground, pinned under one of the vegetable plies. He glanced back at the two approaching men. Neither they nor Smith seemed to be armed. He could leave his possessions and run.

But why? Smuggling brandy wasn't a real crime. Not like robbery, kidnapping or murder. Most magistrates drank the stuff, after all. Wickham climbed down and went to help Smith remove the rest of the sacks.

Once the wagon bed was empty, Smith pulled up the bottom to revel a secret compartment, deep enough for the casks. The two men reached them, both eying Wickham.

"Who's he?" one asked while the other deposited his cask.

"He's all right," Smith said.

While that didn't answer the question, it appeared to be enough for the man. He nodded and stowed his cask as well. Both men trudged back down the beach toward the stack of casks.

"Come on," Smith said and headed toward the sea.

Wickham shrugged and followed. When he reached the pile, he hefted a cask to his shoulder. He tried not to reveal the effort it cost him. Smith lifted his with ease, just like the other two. Wickham reflected that maybe they wouldn't be evenly matched in a fight after all. Certainly, he couldn't take all three. He imagined he was faster than any of them, though, light and lean. Hopefully, he wouldn't need to find out.

When all the brandy was loaded and the vegetables and Wickham's possessions back in the wagon, the four of them met halfway up the rocky beach. The two men eyed Wickham again, as if assessing his continued value now that the wagon was loaded. He offered an ingratiating smile.

"Jeb find any new buyers?" one of the men asked, turning to Smith.

"Not yet." Smith's tone held annoyance. "Says the parson he works for isn't called on by anyone but some old lady and her spinster daughter, and they're too sanctimonious to buy smuggled goods."

"But you got someone in London for this load, right?" the other man asked.

"Aye, all lined up." Smith nodded. "London's getting full up, is all. Competitions driving down the price. Ain't hardly worth the trouble."

"Well, tell Jeb to make himself useful," the first man muttered. "We need a new buyer. I ain't risking my hide for pennies." He turned and marched back toward the small boat they'd beached.

Wickham wagered the little vessel, a rowboat of some sort, only held two men. Or one man and brandy. Out in the bay, the larger vessel bobbed in time with the waves. He hadn't noted anyone on it as they loaded the casks but that didn't mean it was empty.

The remaining man nodded to Smith. "See you--" He broke off with a glance at Wickham. "Next time," he settled for. He followed the first man to the boat, which they pushed out to sea.

Smith turned to Wickham, arms folded across his chest. "I'm off to London now. My brother usually goes with me, but he's otherwise employed. I could use an extra set of hands. Keeps anyone with unlawful intentions at bay."

Wickham watched as the other two men got through the crashing waves, one rowing vigorously. "So, I'd be an asset?" Wickham suggested, forgoing mention of the irony of Smith's wish to avoid the unlawful.

Smith's gaze shifted toward the other two as well, likely with the same thought as Wickham. They were back to one on one. It would take the other two men a bit of time and effort to return to the shore. He turned back to Wickham with a grudging shrug. "I'll pay you a shilling a day and feed you."

"Day's nearly over," Wickham noted. He didn't fancy a long ride in the dark, just so Smith could get the most out of his first day.

"I know someplace a couple miles from here."

"Meals and drink." Wickham wasn't going to sit on a trove of brandy and go thirsty.

Smith gave a curt nod. He turned and headed for the wagon.

Wickham figured that meant negotiations were over, so he followed. "Your brother, Jeb I assume, left because the money isn't good?" he asked as they climbed aboard.

Smith flicked the reins and set about turning the team. "Got himself a woman, and she got a job at the parsonage, so Jeb got a place there too," Smith said, his focus on his driving. "He's supposed to use his position to find us some rich folk what want stolen brandy. Thought he might find something worth stealing, too, but I don't think he has. Maybe up at the fancy lady's house. Old bat would probably never notice. What's an old lady and a spinster need with such a big house, I say. They probably don't go in but ten rooms, if that." He set them back up the narrow trail, the team noticeably straining.

Wickham leaned back and watched the team work. His day was getting better by the moment. Not only had he gotten a free ride this far, he'd be paid to go the rest of the way. Even the destination was fortuitous. He wouldn't mind going to London at all. He could check in on some friends and deposit most of his winnings. Despite his specially made boots, he didn't care for keeping so much of his money on his person.

The old team plodded up the hill, making it look like enough work that Wickham was happy he didn't have to walk the steep trail. His day was definitely looking up. In fact, his whole week was. Maybe even his year. Yes, from here on out, things were going to go well for him. He could feel it.

Chapter Two

Large as his aunt's favorite parlor was, Darcy still found the room stuffy, yet his wish to leave had nothing to do with the thick air. He wanted to walk, with a particular destination in mind, and to do so unaccompanied. Seated on one end of a long sofa, window to his back, he scanned his companions over the top edge of a two-day-old newspaper. He bided his time until the others seemed well occupied.

Darcy's cousin Anne and her companion, Mrs. Jenkinson, sat before a second window, sewing. As far as Darcy recalled, they worked on garments for a new babe born into one of the families beholden to Rosings, as his Aunt Catherine's estate was known. Anne's gaze was turned toward her work, but her eyes were glazed over. Darcy knew she'd sewn such charitable offerings many times before.

Aunt Catherine, known as Lady Catherine de Bourgh to most, engaged in quiet conversation with her new favorite toady, the rector of the local parsonage, Mr. Collins. His presence was one of the reasons Darcy wished to take a stroll. Darcy's goal was Mr. Collins' dwelling, and he'd prefer the tall, paunchy man's absence.

The room's only other occupant, Colonel Richard Fitzwilliam, cousin to both Darcy and Anne, was Darcy's chief obstacle to an unaccompanied walk. Richard occupied the opposite end of the same sofa on which Darcy sat, likely for the same reason. Light streamed in through the window behind them to make reading easier than in other parts of the gloomy parlor. Richard, too, held a paper before him. He seemed to be doing a much better job of reading than Darcy.

Darcy rattled his paper and returned to his perusal of the words. The happenings in the House of Commons lacked their usual import, however. The deeds of parliamentary members couldn't pull his mind from endless contemplation of Miss Elizabeth Bennet and her comments of the evening before.

He'd put on an unconcerned face when, while seated at the pianoforte, she'd essentially told him the fault was his if he wasn't competent at socializing with strangers. Her words had stung. They'd sparked annoyance, as well. Foremost, for the criticism inherent in them. Second because they were spoken before his cousin, Richard, as if Richard needed more fuel for teasing. Third because of the easy way Elizabeth and Richard conversed and the jealousy that comradery ignited. Lastly, her words pricked Darcy because her criticism was true. If he practiced socializing more, he would undoubtedly excel at the activity.

The aggravating, enchanting Elizabeth Bennet was precisely the person he wished to practice socializing with, but Richard would spoil that. He and Elizabeth couldn't be together without striking up easy conversation. Darcy would be in a terrible fix if Richard were a touch more vehement in his affection for Miss Bennet. Then, the choice of taking her for himself or gifting Richard enough so he could afford to take her would be upon Darcy. Fortunately, though clearly enchanted, Richard didn't appear enamored.

Richard angled his paper more fully into the light and leaned toward the page, a sure sign he was thoroughly engrossed in an article. Darcy quietly folded his. No one seemed to notice.

As casually as he could, he said, "I think I'll stretch my legs," and stood.

Richard didn't look up. Lady Catherine's voice droned on. Mr. Collins maintained every appearance of sponging up her words. Anne's eyes stayed glazed over, her hand rising and dipping with each stitch. Mrs. Jenkinson glanced his way, but she wouldn't speak. Darcy started across the room.

"Darcy, where are you going?" Lady Catherine asked, tone officious.

He kept walking. "To stretch my legs."

"Anne, go walk with Darcy," Lady Catherine ordered.

"I'm sewing, Mother," Anne protested.

"So, put your sewing down and walk with Darcy," Lady Catherine said. "You're to marry him. You must spend time with him."

Darcy, nearly to the parlor door, halted. With a grimace, he pivoted back, turning in time to see the annoyance on Anne's face. Richard still scrutinized the paper. As well he should. He'd heard their cousin and aunt argue over Anne's marrying Darcy well-nigh two hundred times.

"I am not going to marry Darcy, Mother. We've been over this," Anne snapped.

"And I am not going to marry Anne," Darcy added quietly.

"That doesn't mean you can't walk together," Lady Catherine declared. She shot Mr. Collins a prompting look.

"Quite right. Walking together is only proper and good for the health," Mr. Collins offered.

"And you two will come to realize you must marry," Lady Catherine stated.

Anne leveled a flat stare at her mother. "No. Just because you and Darcy's mother thought it would be nice for us to wed doesn't mean we feel the same."

"Of course, you do." Lady Catherine swiveled her formidable, jowly visage toward Darcy. "Right, Darcy?"

Richard's paper rattled as he folded it closed. "I say, Darcy, I'll walk with you. I could use a bit of fresh air."

Darcy shook his head, irritated on all counts. He addressed his aunt. "I will not marry Anne, and I will take a walk," he stated and all but stomped from the room.

He heard Richard stand as he left. The sound of a folded paper plopping down on a tabletop followed Darcy down the hall. By the time he'd gone for his outerwear, Richard awaited him in the foyer, similarly attired.

"Shall we?" Richard asked with a gesture toward the door.

The beauty of being known for his lack of social grace was that Darcy could simply nod, his annoyance hidden by his generally laconic nature.

Once through the door, Darcy jogged down the step. He set a brisk pace toward the parsonage. Richard might be with him, but Darcy could still see Elizabeth, at least. Even if she would spend the call chatting with Richard and leave Darcy to engage in stilted conversation with Mrs. Collins and Miss Maria Lucas, Mrs. Collins' younger sister.

Once they were well on their way, Richard cleared his throat. Darcy shot him a quick glance, realizing his cousin had something on his mind. He slowed his pace, interest piqued despite himself.

"I was thinking, since we've extended our stay here," Richard began. He cast Darcy a quick, assessing look. "Well, should we invite Georgiana to join us?"

Darcy frowned, surprised by the suggestion. "She doesn't care to visit Rosings." His shy, meek little sister, only fifteen, was generally bowled over by their aunt.

Richard cleared his throat again. "Yes, I realize she finds Aunt Catherine daunting. It's simply, after the incident in Ramsgate, I can't help but worry each time she's left too long on her own."

Understanding unfurled in Darcy. "Georgiana wouldn't make such an error again," he asserted.

In truth, she hadn't followed through with her ill-conceived plan the first time. She hadn't run off with George Wickham. She'd told Darcy of the plan instead, and he'd put everything right. Chased off Wickham, fired Georgiana's old governess and hired a new one. Though nearly disastrous, his little sister's near-elopement with Wickham was now safely behind her.

Richard stopped walking. "Are you certain? She seemed rather, well, resentful to me. As if she wished she hadn't confessed to you."

Darcy stopped as well and turned to his cousin in surprise. He hadn't realized Richard and Georgiana had spoken on the issue. He'd informed Richard, of course. As Georgiana's co-guardian, Richard deserved to know about her near-elopement. "I'm sure she's happy she confessed."

Richard shrugged. "I think she's still enamored of Wickham and regrets she didn't go with him. And you never know where that villain will turn up. Mark my words, Darcy, he's not out of your life yet."

"No, Wickham and I are through. I paid him for the living my father left him, at his insistence. I paid his debts in Derbyshire, under very firm orders he's not to be given any credit there ever again. I sent him fleeing Ramsgate after he attempted to elope with Georgiana. He wouldn't dare trouble us again." Darcy shook his head. "He was forced to join the militia to make ends meet. They'll keep him out of trouble. With his regiment stationed in the countryside, Georgiana is perfectly safe in London."

"I guess I want to assuage my guilt over how vastly we almost failed her," Richard finally said.

Darcy nodded and resumed walking. "I understand the urge, but forcing Georgiana to endure Lady Catherine seems too harsh a punishment, even for the crime of almost running off with George Wickham." It wasn't his sister's fault she was charmed by the man. Everyone else had been, from Darcy's father to local merchants to the Bennet sisters.

"I just can't shake the feeling Wickham will come back to haunt you again," Richard said, matching Darcy's stride.

"The militia is going to Brighton in a few weeks. I'll take Georgiana to Pemberley. I doubt Wickham has the money to travel that far. He won't bother us again."

They fell into companionable silence, Richard's gaze abstract, but as they neared the Hunsford Parsonage, his eyes refocused. He glanced about, then darted a look at Darcy. "The Collins'? Mr. Collins, as you know, is not at home."

"What better time to visit?" Darcy said dryly.

His comment earned a wry smile from Richard.

They presented themselves at the door. A maid answered and showed them in. They found Mrs. Collins, Elizabeth and Miss Lucas in the parsonage's small parlor. All three women stood to greet them. Miss Lucas held a ball of yarn, Elizabeth, a skein of it.

"Mr. Darcy, Colonel Fitzwilliam," Mrs. Collins greeted with a smile and a curtsy.

Elizabeth and Miss Lucas also bobbed their greetings. Despite her full hands, Elizabeth managed the act with grace. Miss Lucas fumbled her curtsy, her expression a bit awed.

"Mrs. Collins, Miss Bennet, Miss Lucas," Richard greeted after a pause.

Darcy frowned, realizing Richard had given him a heartbeat to reply, then taken the nicety upon himself. For someone practicing his social graces, Darcy wasn't off to a good start.

"Mr. Collins is out," Mrs. Collins said. "He's calling on your aunt, I believe."

Richard cast Darcy a quick look, then turned back to Mrs. Collins. "Yes, he is. We came out to stretch our legs, and wouldn't you know, they brought us to your doorstep."

Intelligent blue eyes, set in a slightly less attractive than average visage, scanned over Darcy and his cousin. "I see," Mrs. Collins said. "Would you care for tea?"

"We would be most obliged," Richard said. "I daresay we'll now miss tea at Rosings."

"Then do come sit down," Mrs. Collins offered.

Soon they were all seated about a low table. Mrs. Collins, Darcy noticed, was a very adept hostess. Her manners were exemplary, each movement precise and easy seeming. She served them in the proper order, asked all the correct questions, and cheerfully prompted conversation. She was wasted on Mr. Collins.

Once they were all served and the topic of weather exhausted, Elizabeth turned her beguiling eyes toward Darcy. He immediately put down his teacup. He also tamped down his pleasure that she should turn to him and not Richard.

"So, Mr. Darcy." Her eyes glinted with amusement. "Do I dare construe this visit as your attempt to practice social niceties? Are you, in fact, accepting my advice, however cruelly given?"

"You may, and I am," he replied.

"Why, this is terrible, then," she proclaimed in bright, mocking tones.

"Terrible?" Richard asked before Darcy could speak. "That Darcy should practice or that he's taken your advice?"

Elizabeth turned her attention on Richard, to Darcy's chagrin. "Why, that he should practice," she declared. "Now I must abide by my own advice and practice as well. Only," she lowered her voice conspiratorially, "I am too proud. I cannot consign myself to the backroom pianoforte on which your aunt offered to let me practice."

"Then humble yourself," Mrs. Collins advised. "Miss de Bourgh's companion is a wonderful woman. You should be honored to have the use of the pianoforte in her room."

Elizabeth's impertinent smile transformed into a wry grimace. "I stand reprimanded by my oldest friend."

"I would be happy to practice on any pianoforte," Miss Lucas said staunchly.

"Ah, but you were not the one invited," Elizabeth quipped. "Although Lady Catherine would be happier to have you invade Mrs. Jenkinson's room than me, since you would be more grateful."

Mrs. Collins offered her a repressive, if amused, look. She turned to Mr. Darcy. "Did you find the walk over pleasant, Mr. Darcy?"

"Yes," he said, then fell to wondering what he might say next. He refused to look to Richard. His cousin was certain to have a topic, but Darcy was determined to speak. "You must make the walk often," he finally added.

"We do, although your aunt orders the carriage for our return. She is the soul of generosity with her carriage, company and advice."

"Especially her advice," Elizabeth murmured. "And the carriage is for leaving Rosings, but not for coming to Rosings. I'm not certain what message that conveys."

Miss Lucas giggled.

"This parsonage is also a splendid stop while on a ride," Richard stated.

"If you deem it so, then you must by all means view it as such." Mrs. Collins accompanied her words with a smile that made them seem genuine. "We should be delighted to have you two gentlemen visit as often as you like."

"The pleasure will be ours," Richard replied, grin charming.

Darcy wished Richard wouldn't turn that grin on Elizabeth, but he did. Darcy was possessed with the odd urge to scowl at his cousin. He repressed the desire but couldn't make it recede as tea went on. Richard continued to banter lightly with all three women, even drawing Miss Lucas into a smattering of conversation. Darcy didn't manage to get in four more words. Not that he knew what words he would say. He could have thought of some, though, if Richard weren't always speaking.

They rose to leave after a long half hour. Darcy could feel Elizabeth's eyes on him as he bowed to the room but could think of nothing to say other than farewell. No witty words. Not even an appropriate expression. A smile would be too forward. A frown was uncalled for. He settled for calm reserve, an image he endeavored to maintain as he and Richard set off toward Rosings, his cousin chatting amiably about their visit and Elizabeth's loveliness the whole way.

Chapter Three

Despite how dank the subterranean London room was, Wickham deferred the steep steps to Smith and the burly gentleman who'd unlocked the cellar door. By his count, one more cask needed to be removed from the wagon to complete the order. Whoever ascended to the street first would undoubtedly take it down, whereas all the other two would need do was toss the remaining vegetables on top. That work had grown easier, Smith having sold the cabbages.

Sure enough, Smith descended with the final cask as Wickham climbed free of the cellar. He stretched before joining the burly man in moving sacks of leeks. He wondered if smuggling always involved so much labor. Wickham had done more than enough work for a whole day and the sun wasn't even up yet.

The burly man, who'd neither given nor asked for names, eyed Wickham in mistrustful silence while they waited for Smith. Upon his return, a packet of bills was exchanged. Smith gestured to Wickham and they climbed back into the wagon. With a flick of the reins, the somewhat rested team moved away from the mouth of the alley.

"Where can I drop you?" Smith asked. "Only, don't make it out of the way."

"Charing Cross will do." Wickham wanted somewhere he knew and that would be crowded even at this time of day. Despite their travels so far, he didn't trust Smith. Now that Wickham's usefulness was truly over, he wouldn't put it past the other man to rob him.

"Charing Cross, then."

Wickham watched their route closely to be certain Smith intended to take him where he'd asked to go, not down some dark street where more of his questionable associates waited. Traffic picked up as they drew near their destination. The shadows draping alley mouths and storefronts grew less murky with the diffuse light of false dawn. Wickham started to relax.

"I'll be needing more help tomorrow once I find a buyer for the rest, and there'll be a new load to pick up soon enough," Smith said as they waited for a wagonload of crates to pass.

Wickham didn't reply. He knew what Smith was getting at. He wasn't sure he wanted to turn smuggler, but he was sure that making the man ask would begin negotiations in his favor.

"You'll be available to help?"

Wickham shrugged. "Could be."

"I'll keep paying and feeding you."

"I want a pound a day," Wickham declared.

Smith shot him a startled look. The wagon of crates moved out of the way. A nearby coachman hollered a curse at them for holding up traffic.

Smith snapped the reins and set his team moving. "A pound a day is robbery."

It was, but it was a good start to the negotiations. "And food."

"I'll pay you a shilling a day and food, like I was."

Wickham took in the stubborn set of Smith's jaw. He weighed the amount of work he'd done. "Seven shillings a day and food, and we don't always sleep on the road."

"Two shillings a day and I get to decide what we eat," Smith countered. He cast a quick, surly look Wickham's way. "And how much ale I pay for."

"Make that four shillings and all the drink I want, and you have a deal," Wickham countered.

"I'll make it three on my terms."

"Done. Three shillings a day, meals of your choosing, drink and we don't always sleep on the road."

Smith gave a sharp nod. He pulled the wagon off to the side of the street, somewhat out of traffic. They hadn't quite reached Hungerford Market, dense with wagons and carts in the early morning rush to unload. Wickham inhaled the thick London air, at home with the cacophony of horses, men, wagons and rustling wares.

Smith pointed to the corner-most market stall. "Be there tomorrow an hour before sunrise. I won't wait."

"I'll get my luggage," Wickham said.

Smith nodded.

Wickham jumped out and went around for his possessions, not too hurried. Smith wouldn't get anywhere quickly in the press around the market. As soon as Wickham had his luggage, Smith set the wagon moving toward the market. Wickham imagined he meant to sell the leeks and didn't fancy paying for help unloading them. That suited him as he didn't fancy doing any more work that morning.

Whistling as he walked, Wickham went first to an old acquaintance who could be relied upon to keep most of his things without rummaging through them or selling them, for a small fee. The rate was good and sweetened by a little flattery. What she really wanted was the lie that she still held allure. A kiss and a wink, and he'd offloaded everything he didn't need for traveling with Smith, which was a relief. Even the brief walk had been overly cumbersome with his possessions, especially after his early morning exertions.

Next, he found himself a quick meal while he waited for the bank to open. Old Mr. Darcy had helped Wickham set up an account years ago. The hundred pounds the old man had given him to start the account hadn't lasted long, the thousand pounds he'd inherited upon old Mr. Darcy's death, not much longer.

A slow smile spread across Wickham's face. Now, the three thousand he'd gotten out of Darcy for giving up the living old Mr. Darcy had left him in Derbyshire, that had been a tidy sum. Eight whole pounds of that still remained in the bank. The money Wickham carried in his boots, which he wouldn't remove until safely in a backroom at the bank, would in no way replenish the three thousand, but it was a nice addition to eight.

Wickham lingered over his breakfast until the bank opened, then went in and made his deposit, keeping a bit for his boots and even less for his purse. After that, he called on a woman he knew, the green ribbon tying back her curtains a sure sign of welcome. Her husband worked the canals and often left her alone and lonely. Over the years, Wickham had been a comfort to her.

After a brief conversation on her stoop, she bade him sneak around back, out of sight of the neighbors. There, she let him in with a smile but warned he had to be gone before sunrise, which suited him perfectly. On top of her usual accommodating nature, she fed him both lunch and dinner, and helped him launder his spare set of clothes. When morning neared, he crept away with a smile, feeling magnanimous enough to leave a few farthings by her pillow.

With no other prospects and his errands in London complete, Wickham decided he would meet Smith. He'd already smuggled, after all. A bit more couldn't hurt, and Smith didn't make the task too arduous.

Plus, Wickham felt he'd struck a reasonably good deal in food and wages.

Smith met him as arranged, and they went to an even seedier part of town than the morning before. This time, they had to pass the casks through a basement window to men Wickham never saw. That suited him better than the steps and there were no vegetables to reload. Over all, as they left London in the early morning light, Wickham felt he'd made the right choice by going with Smith.

They reached an open stretch of roadway, past the bulk of traffic rumbling into London full of wares for the day. Wickham slumped in his seat, the sun warmer beyond London's fog. He fancied a nap before Smith made him take a turn driving.

Smith yawned. "Tell me about yourself, Wickham. Where'd you grow up? How does a fellow who talks and dresses all gentlemanlike end up smuggling brandy?"

Wickham grimaced but sat up straighter. "That's the crux of things, isn't it? I talk like a gentleman. I look like a gentleman. I have the tastes of a gentleman, but I am not one."

Smith shot him a glance. "No? I took you for a third son or some such."

"If only. Even a third son wouldn't be so ill-used as I."

"And who's been using you ill?" Smith said, tone touched with disbelief. "You look fine enough to me. Fancy boots, hat, clothes. Heavy bag full of things, when you took up with me. I should know. I moved it in and out of the wagon enough times."

"Oh yes, I have all that." Wickham let out a heartfelt sigh. He had a relatively good notion where Smith was going with his questions but didn't mind expounding on one of his favorite topics, the world's injustice toward him. "My father was a steward, you see, but also a great friend to his master, Mr. Darcy the elder. I was also a great favorite of old Mr. Darcy's. I'm named after him and he was my godfather."

"Must be mighty nice to have a godfather who's a gentleman," Smith observed.

The team plodded down the road with an even gait, noticeably spryer with the empty wagon. The gentle sway and predictable squeak of their conveyance lulled, but Wickham would rather educate a willing audience on the wrongs of his life than sleep.

"You would think, but no," he continued with feeling. "Mr. Darcy raised me right alongside his son, the now Mr. Darcy. We were good friends through our childhood. Things didn't go wrong until

Cambridge."

"The gentleman sent you to school?" Smith broke in, clearly surprised. "He did favor you."

"Aye, which is why his son detests me." Among other, not as important reasons. "Now that old Mr. Darcy is gone, I'm left destitute. Mr. Darcy the younger took back every gift the old man bestowed on me."

"You can't take back an education," Smith observed.

"Would that you could. I would be a simpler man," Wickham countered, deliberately misconstruing Smith's meaning. Wickham preferred not to dwell on how he'd squandered the opportunity of Cambridge. Not that he cared. Any employment he could find with that sort of education would require tedious work.

Smith favored him with another sideways look. "Still, you must know a lot of rich folk. Leastwise well enough to know who might want some fine French brandy."

Wickham hid a smile. He'd guessed that was Smith's goal in his questions, more buyers. Instead of getting what he wanted, Smith had fallen into Wickham's trap by opening the door for some of his favorite rants.

He started with the horrors of the aloof, stuffy, supercilious, pompous Mr. Darcy. Next, he moved on to that old hedgehog, Lady Catherine. It wasn't until late in the day, after many stops to rest, changes of driver and lunch, that they reached talk of the Earl of Matlock's estate.

Smith wanted every detail about the estates and their owners. The more Wickham talked, the more questions Smith had. Finally, it occurred to Wickham that he may not have played Smith as well as he'd thought. Yes, Wickham was getting to voice years of complaints to a willing listener, but Smith's questions had a certain predictability by the third round of descriptions. They leaned toward the estate owner's habits and security in a way that began to make Wickham leery.

But what did he care? It was nothing to him if Darcy, the earl or Lady Catherine got robbed. So long as Smith didn't ask Wickham to help carry out the deed, he didn't care what happened to three wealthy people's knickknacks, coins and baubles. They all had more than they needed or knew what to do with anyhow.

"Hmm," Smith murmured, mulling over Wickham's description of Matlock's guardsmen and footmen and their routine patrols inside the earl's homes, outside them and around the perimeters of his estates. "But the old lady who lives alone with her daughter, she must not have so many guards about?" Smith drove again, his hands loose on the reins.

"Don't think because Lady Catherine is a widow living alone that there is less security," Wickham said. The sun was getting lower. He hoped Smith planned for this to be a night they stopped at an inn. All the talking of the day had made Wickham thirsty.

"So you said." Smith didn't sound convinced.

"She is only alone in the sense that she has only one family member in the house, although at this time of year her nephews should be visiting, as well," Wickham cautioned. "She has many footmen, and they don't just stand around. They patrol the place regularly. She is well aware that people might believe her to be an easy target. She would take considerable pleasure in catching housebreakers and having met the lady, I tell you with absolute certainty that she would use every ounce of her influence to see a housebreaker hung."

Smith nodded, silent. Ahead, a building started to take shape on the horizon. Wickham hoped it was an inn, or even a town. He glanced about and realized he hadn't been keeping proper track of their journey.

"Which nephews?" Smith asked. "I believe you said she has three, and one's an earl?"

Smith was considering kidnapping too, Wickham guessed. Well, Matlock would fetch a good sum and be somewhat easier to secure at Rosings than one of his own residences, but he didn't visit there. The earl and Lady Catherine didn't get on. Two goats, they were. "Darcy and Colonel Fitzwilliam."

"The earl's younger brother."

Wickham liked Colonel Fitzwilliam too well to want him kidnaped and ransomed back to his brother, especially since Matlock might not pay. Lady Catherine would be more likely to but that was a piece of information Wickham felt no need to supply. "Neither Darcy nor Colonel Fitzwilliam is a coward, and both would be efficient in a fight. The colonel would be deadly." Thinking it over, he was suddenly glad Darcy, not the Colonel, had chased him away from Georgiana. Colonel Fitzwilliam's response might have been to challenge Wickham to a duel. Both men could best him, but Darcy would never stoop to issue the challenge or be hotheaded enough to forget the impact it would have on Georgiana's reputation.

"Harrumph," was Smith's only reply.

The building Wickham had sighted was indeed an inn, but to

Wickham's dismay, they didn't stop. Once they were out of sight of the ramshackle but inviting enough establishment, Smith insisted Wickham take another turn driving. The questions stopped as Wickham's somewhat unsavory companion fell into a fitful nap.

When the sun disappeared from the horizon, Wickham decided he'd had enough of driving. He pulled them over, intent on getting some rest. As soon as they stopped, Smith woke up.

"Ah, good," he said. By the last violet streaks lingering on the horizon, he dug out a single lantern and lit it. He got out a pole, secured it to the driver's side and hung the lantern out to light their way. "I'll drive."

Wickham dutifully moved over. "How much farther are we going tonight?" He added a yawn to the question.

"Not much."

Smith set out again but soon left the roadway. He took a bouncing trail along the coast. At some landmark Wickham couldn't see, Smith angled the team toward what appeared to be a wall of rocks and trees. There turned out to be a narrow, steep path. The team, docile and tired though they were, balked somewhat. Smith made liberal use of the whip to get them down to the beach, a different one from the first time.

Two men waited, dim outlines against the dark sea until one struck a lamp. Wickham looked up and down the beach. The little rowboat was there but no stack of casks. Smith swore and brought the team to a halt. The two men came up the beach toward them. Smith clambered down. After a moment, Wickham shrugged and joined him.

"Where's the brandy?" Smith demanded as the other two drew near.

"We were boarded again," one of them all but growled. "I think they've circulated a description of the boat."

"Same as last time?" Smith asked in aggrieved tones.

"Aye. We managed to dump the casks off the far side before they got too near," the second man said. "Good thing, too. They searched her stem to stern."

"We won't be so lucky every time," the first man said. "If they catch us with brandy, they'll throw us in prison, or worse. I thought having this ship--" He cast Wickham a quick look. "I thought we was having good luck, but I'm with Jeb now. This ain't worth it anymore."

"You got the cargo off in time," Smith protested. "We'll make up the loss on the next load. Wickham here is going to help me find more buyers."

Wickham raised his eyebrows at that but kept his mouth shut.

"I don't think it matters if we get the cargo off before they board us. Like I said, they must have given out a description of the boat. They were all set to arrest us anyway, but they spotted another smuggler and left. They caught them red-handed. We was watching. They tied up the lot of them and commandeered their ship."

"It's gotten too dangerous," the other fellow said. "The patrols are getting better."

"You could try landing in Scotland," Smith suggested.

"And start over feeling out buyers?"

Smith turned to Wickham. "You know anyone in Scotland?"

Wickham shook his head. "Never been."

Smith turned back to his comrades, expression thoughtful. They exchanged a look. Both appeared obstinate. Behind them, waves slapped the beach. One of the horses stomped a hoof.

"We want to sell the boat and split the money," the more verbose of Smith's two companions said. He glared at Wickham. "Only three ways."

Wickham swallowed. While in London, he should have spent some of his time and coin securing a pistol, or at least a knife. He took a half step back.

Smith turned to Wickham as well. A tightlipped smile cut across his face. His eyes glinted in the lanternlight. "Let's not sell the boat yet," he said. "I have another suggestion."

Chapter Four

Fiona Mary McClintock, who went by Mary to downplay her Scottish origins in this snooty English place, entered the kitchen at the Hunsford Parsonage and took a cabbage and a knife from Rose's unresisting hands. Mustering her best English accent to hide her Highland lilt, she said, "Go on with you, Rosy. Go visit your mum. I'll see to this."

The third maid at the parsonage, Sally, glanced their way with a grimace. Sally also had somewhere she wished to be while the gentrified folk were up at Rosings. Fiona Mary wanted Sally gone, too, but she would be easy to get rid of. Sally would go once Rose, the more conscientious of the two, left.

Rose's gaze strayed to the kitchen door then returned to Fiona. "Are you certain? Only, my mum's so unwell. I really do need to check on her. My brothers won't remember to do it, leastwise not with planting to be done."

"Course I'm sure," Fiona avowed. "The Collins and Miss Lucas'll eat up at the manor. All that's needed is a light snack in case the mister gets peckish later. Won't take me no time at all."

In truth, Fiona detested kitchen work, even though she was good at it. That's why she'd run off with Jeb in the first place. Once her own mum passed, being the only female left in the family, Fiona had to do all the cooking at the inn. Never mind she was the one mum left in charge. It was still cook, cook, cook, day in and day out. Boil, salt, chop, stir, peel, knead. Fiona swore she was half mad by the time Jeb wandered into their remote, lonely inn and took a shine to her.

Certainly, madness would explain her choice of rescuer. He turned out to be unwilling to wed her and part of a burgeoning smuggling ring. What could she do but stay with him, though? Return to cooking at the inn but now with her brothers watching her like a prize heifer? Only, she wouldn't be a heifer much longer. Her condition was starting to show. She counted each lucky day that Mr. Collins was too self-involved to notice and Mrs. Collins too kind to turn her out and Jeb along with her.

And if they were kicked out, where would they go? They couldn't crawl back to Tom and his lot empty handed and expect to be accepted, and neither of their fallback plans for if honest work didn't pan out had met with any success. Little at the parsonage was worth stealing. Their other option, finding rich buyers for Jeb's brother Tom's smuggled spirits, had met with a similar lack of success. They'd thought a parsonage would put them in the way of some wealthy folk to either rob or sell to, but no one called on Mr. Collins save Lady Catherine and her shadow of a daughter. The daughter had no opinions of her own, and the old bag would surely bring in the magistrate at the hint of smuggling.

Rose's sigh filled the tiny parsonage kitchen, reminding Fiona she was still there. Rose reached for the cabbage and knife. "I really should stay. They didn't all go, you know. Miss Bennet remained behind."

Fiona yanked the cabbage and knife back and forced a smile. Jeb's no-good brother and his even less good friends were lurking about, waiting to talk. She'd promised them a few scraps outside the kitchen door to lure them all the way to the parsonage, instead of Jeb going to them. She didn't want him meeting with them without her. She wasn't getting left behind like some sort of discarded baggage. It was a long way back to Scotland, where they couldn't kick her out, even if she would have to endure her brothers' censure. "Never you worry about Miss Bennet. She'll hardly require a thing, so it won't matter you're gone."

Indecision paraded across Rose's face. Finally, she smiled. "I won't be long. Thank you, Mary."

"You know I'm happy to help," Fiona said cheerily.

Expression grateful, Rose untied her apron, left it on a peg and slipped out the kitchen door. Fiona retrieved a large bowl and set to chopping the cabbage. Mr. Collins had a bizarre love of the vegetable. Not that there was ought wrong with cabbage. Only with eating it four times a day.

"I wish I had a sick mum for an excuse," Sally groused from where she kneaded dough.

"Your man acting up again?" Fiona asked with feigned sympathy.

"He's this close to proposing. I know he is," Sally said. "But you know how he gets if he ain't seen me in a few days. His eyes start to wander."

Fiona nodded in time with her chopping. "Oh, aye. I'm lucky my Jeb works right here at the parsonage."

"Your Jeb ain't proposed and don't think I ain't noticed you need him to." Sally dropped her gaze to Fiona's middle.

The jab cut, sharper than the knife she used on the cabbage. "But at least I know where his eyes are," Fiona shot back.

Sally winced and shrugged, mouth clamped closed.

Taking in Sally's hostile expression, Fiona recalled her goal. Her anger vanished. Antagonism wouldn't get Sally out of the parsonage.

"I'm sorry," Fiona murmured, though she wasn't. "Look, there really isn't much work here. Why don't you go see your man? I'll finish the cabbage and dress it, then do the loaves. They aren't needed until morning. We've plenty for today."

Smile wide, Sally was untying her apron before Fiona finished speaking. "Thank you. You'll be alright with Miss Bennet, and you've Jeb about if you need anything. I won't be long." She crossed the room as she spoke and slipped out the door on her final words.

Fiona finished the chopping and dressed the cabbage, then went to the back door and shook out the dish towels, her signal to Jeb and the others they could come to the kitchen. As soon as she saw movement at the edge of the line of shrubs and bramble in which they hid, she went back in. Taking the rest of the day's already baked bread, she set to making Jeb, his brother and their other two companions something to eat. Sally's task she left for the time being. If it didn't get done, Fiona would suffer the other woman's wrath, but it was Sally who would answer to Mr. and Mrs. Collins.

Food in hand, Fiona went out the kitchen door to find the four loitering, speaking in low tones. It took her only a moment to gather they talked of giving up smuggling. Her elation sparked and died in three breaths as she realized their new plan was kidnapping.

"Here you are." She held out a stack of sandwiches wrapped in a kitchen towel.

All four snatched up the food, though none looked as if they hadn't been eating well. She knew for a certainty that Jeb was. He had his lot and what she pinched for him.

"Thanks, love," Jeb said. He gave her a pat on the rear with his free hand.

Fiona shook crumbs from the towel and tucked it through her apron strings. "What are you lot talking about?" she asked.

"The Jonesys here want to sell the ship, split the money and call our little partnership done," Jeb said with a nod to the other two brothers.

37

Fiona didn't know their first names. They said their last name was Jones, which she believed about as much as she believed Jeb and his brother Tom that they were Smiths. Either way, they'd taken to calling the two The Jonesys. "I see. Five ways?"

One of The Jonesys snorted, bits of cabbage and bread spattering from his half-open mouth.

"We was thinking three ways," the other Jonesy said.

Jeb opened his mouth to protest, offering Fiona an unfettered view of his partially-masticated food.

Tom held up a staying hand. "I have a different idea," he said to Fiona. "I came across this fellow, useless sort except for what he knows. He told me the old lady up there is knee deep in funds and a couple of her nephews more so." He turned back to The Jonesys. "Boat would be a perfect place to keep one of them until the others pay up."

Fiona frowned. Smuggling was a crime, true, but it was unlikely a woman would hang for it, or even suffer much more than a fine and public disdain. A man might get time in the stocks, labor or a greater fine. Kidnapping, though, that was a hanging offense, and the wealthier the victim, the more likely you were to swing. Rich folk took care of their own.

"I don't like the idea," she asserted.

None of the men looked at her or even appeared to have heard.

"I'm telling you," Jeb said after he swallowed. "You can't get within a hundred yards of that big old mansion. The old lady's no fool. She won't pay no ransom, either. She's a mean one."

"They must leave the manor," Tom protested.

They did, Fiona knew. The snobbish one, Mr. Darcy, and his friendlier cousin visited the parsonage often. Fiona wouldn't mind if they took Mr. Darcy. He never even looked at her. She'd let him in the door four times in the past week, and she doubted he could pick her out of a crowd. His cousin, the colonel, he was a nice sort and didn't deserve to be kidnapped. Not wealthy, either, for all he was the son of an earl.

"Mr. Darcy's the rich one," she put in.

That earned her a nod from Tom. "Aye. The way the fellow I mentioned tells it, this Mr. Darcy is made of coin. We take him, get a letter to his man in London, and we don't even need to worry about the old lady."

"Mr. Darcy comes this way often," Jeb said. "Sometimes with the other one, military man, and sometimes without. Fiona always lets them in, so she'll know who's here when. Right Fiona?"

Fiona offered a reluctant nod. The men grinned. She grabbed Jeb's sleeve and yanked. He grimaced at the other man's mocking looks but let her lead him off to the side.

As soon as they were out of earshot, she rounded on him. "Kidnapping, Jeb? You'll see us both hang."

He sidled up to her in that way of his that used to make her knees weak. "Come on now, love. Don't be that way. We won't get caught. We didn't get caught with the rum, after all. We were given the boat for a reason and this is it."

"Given? The rich fellow what owned it up and died, and you and The Jonesys tossed his body over the side."

Jeb nodded. "Yeah, but we didn't do the rich fellow in. He just keeled right over on his own. So, that boat was given to us by divine province and all. For a purpose." He cupped her cheek in a large, calloused hand. "Besides, love, once we get a little coin, we can settle down, just you and me."

Fiona bit her lip. She no longer really wished to settle down with Jeb, but in her condition, she needed him, and he knew it.

"Once we nab us one of these rich types and get our ransom, we'll take the boat to Ireland, and I'll marry you and we'll raise the little one," Jeb said. He wrapped an arm about her and gave her another pat on the rear.

On the other side of the house, hooves sounded.

"They back already?" Jeb asked with a worried frown.

"That's not the carriage," Fiona said. "Sounds like one horse. I'll go see who it is. You lot go back into the brush. I won't be a moment."

She pulled free of Jeb's arm and hurried toward the kitchen door. Not stopping, she went through the house to the front. She reached the foyer just after a knock sounded and yanked the door open to find Mr. Darcy.

Fiona dropped her gaze and took a step back. He looked different than usual. Almost frantic. She wondered if something had gone wrong up at the manor. Maybe, in the chaos, they really could kidnap someone.

She drew in a deep breath, amazed she was considering it. But she had to get married. She didn't have a choice. "May I help you, sir?"

"I'm here to see Miss Bennet," he said, gaze fixed somewhere over Fiona's cap.

Her own eyes angled toward the rough wood floor, Fiona bit her lip. No one was with Mr. Darcy. He didn't seem to have noticed Jeb hadn't taken his horse, instead leaving the animal with his reins draped over the porch rail. He was obviously in a state of distraction, and he was very rich. This could be their chance. Their only chance. Her hand strayed to her midsection.

"Right this way, sir," Fiona said.

She didn't offer to take the hat and gloves he held. There was no time. She whirled and led him toward the small parlor where Miss Bennet rested, taken by some sort of ailment. Fiona had no skill in such matters, but nothing appeared wrong with the other woman. She supposed it was one of those ailments the wealthy could afford. Nerves or such.

"A Mr. Darcy to see you, miss," Fiona said as she came to a stop in the parlor doorway.

Miss Bennet looked up with stricken eyes. Fiona wondered if the two were in some sort of amorous relationship. That would be perfect. They wouldn't even need to risk waiting until Mr. Darcy was on his way back to the parsonage. If he had intentions toward Miss Bennet, that would make her valuable. They could take both of them now before the other maids or the Collins and Miss Lucas returned.

"Do you need anything, miss?" Fiona asked.

"No, thank you," Miss Bennet murmured. She didn't even glance at Fiona, which wasn't like her. Miss Bennet was a nice sort.

Fiona felt a pang for what Jeb and his companions proposed but she nodded and hurried away, leaving the two alone together. A good maid would have remained, but Fiona had never pretended to be a good maid. Instead, she hurried back to the kitchen and made a bit of noise. Not enough to attract attention. She simply wished them to believe they knew her location and forget about her. After a moment, she snuck back into the hallway where she could hear what was going on.

"...must allow me to tell you how ardently I admire and love you," Mr. Darcy said.

Fiona stifled a gasp and backed toward the kitchen. Surprise, elation and jealousy warred within her. He was proposing. The stiff, pompous Mr. Darcy was asking for Miss Bennet's hand, when Fiona couldn't get the father of her already growing child to do more than hint at marriage.

More importantly, her guess was right. Mr. Darcy did care for Miss Bennet. He would pay a fine sum to keep her safe.

Fiona darted through the kitchen. Outside, she waved the dishtowel frantically. Mr. Darcy, the sort of man who placed great value on his words, would be longwinded. Still, they must act quickly. There was no way to know how long they had before other maids or the family returned.

The brush rustled, and the four men emerged. They hurried toward her with varying looks of concern and interest, likely seeing her excitement. Jeb's brother Tom reached her first.

"Who was it? Who's there?" Tom asked.

"Mr. Darcy," Fiona replied, working to keep her voice low despite a mix of excitement and fear. "He's proposing to Miss Bennet."

Tom's eyes lit up. "We can take them both."

Fiona bit her lip again. She liked Miss Bennet. Not as much as she wanted her baby to have a father, though. Jeb and The Jonesys reached them, their expressions questioning.

"What's the fuss?" one of The Jonesys asked.

"The richest one of the lot is in there, alone except for the woman he wants to marry," Tom said.

That same avaricious glint brightened their gazes as Tom's.

"We've got pistols in the wagon," one of The Jonesys said.

"Jeb, they got any rope around?" Tom asked.

Jeb nodded, his excitement palpable. "Good girl," he said to Fiona and offered a smacking, wet kiss which she turned her cheek to. He didn't seem to notice her lack of enthusiasm for the gesture as he hurried off.

"Bring that wagon round quiet as you can," Tom ordered The Jonesys.

They hurried away.

Tom turned to Fiona. "When they get back, you lead the way through the house. We'll be a step behind. If you see anyone else, if anyone comes back, greet them loud as you can. For now, why don't you gather up all the food you can carry? We'll come to the kitchen door when we're ready."

Fiona went back into the kitchen, dishcloth clenched tight in her hands. Her insides quaked. More from excitement or fear, she didn't truly know. She set about gathering food with hands that shook.

It seemed only moments before the men appeared at the kitchen door. Steps light, Tom entered first, then Jeb, hands full of rope. After them came The Jonesys, each with a pistol and a grim look. Tom glanced around and grabbed a pile of dishtowels, expression equally set. Fiona swallowed. She added a block of cheese to the pile she'd made on top of a tablecloth then wiped her hands on her apron.

"You can take the food out once we have them tied up," Tom whispered. "This rich fellow, he rode over?"

She nodded.

"You and Jeb will have to ride his horse. We'll want to move fast, and we don't want to strain the team." Tom frowned at her. "You do ride, right?"

She offered another nod. She didn't really ride but she wouldn't be left behind.

"Right. Let's go then." Tom gestured her toward the door leading deeper into the parsonage.

Fiona took a deep breath and turned to lead the way.

The men followed her on moderately light feet. She winced at every creak the floor gave. As they neared the parlor, she could make out first the intensity of the tones being used inside, then some of the words.

Miss Bennet was talking. "From the very beginning, from the first moment I may almost say, of my acquaintance with you, your manners, impressing me with the fullest belief of your…"

The men pushed past her and into the room.

Fiona didn't follow. She didn't want to watch. She heard Miss Bennet cry out in surprise and fear and Mr. Darcy's roar of anger. Raised voices followed Fiona as she ran back down the hall to the kitchen. There, she grasped the edge of the heavy kitchen table and sucked in air. She could still hear yelling, but at least the sound was muted. After a few more breaths, she pushed back from the table and bundled the food. Her pilfered victuals made for a heavy load, but she hoisted the tablecloth in both hands and headed for the wagon.

She stowed the food, then went around the parsonage for Mr. Darcy's horse. Going through would have been quicker, but she didn't want to know what went on inside. There was so much that could go wrong. Mr. Darcy could put up more of a fight than expected. There were four men and two pistols, but he didn't strike her as any sort of coward, no matter his other faults. He could be shot. Miss Bennet could be shot. Jeb, Tom or one of The Jonesys could be hurt. Fiona bit her lip and marched the somewhat reluctant horse back around the parsonage.

She returned to find Jeb and Tom covering the wagon's false bottom. Their smug looks said all had gone according to plan. Tom climbed in back with the food, positioning himself in the center of the false floor.

Jeb had her lead the horse over and use the wagon bed to get up with him. She felt undignified and uncomfortable astride the horse, seated behind Jeb with her arms around his waist. A small penance, she supposed, for her part in their crime. They started moving. She clung to Jeb as he clumsily wielded the reins. Fiona said a prayer for her and her baby and did her best to endure the ride.

Chapter Five

Hands bound before her, tied together and secured to a rope around her waist, Elizabeth couldn't reach the gag they'd shoved into her mouth.

"Allow me," Mr. Darcy whispered.

With some maneuvering, he managed to reach the gag and remove the offending cloth. Freed of at least that much constraint, she concentrated on breathing. Each breath must come in and go out without a whimper or scream. She would not give in to the terror that threatened to overwhelm her.

Panic firmly reined in, she began to assess her situation. The coffin-like under-bed into which they'd shoved her and Mr. Darcy offered minimal light, filtered through cracks in the boards, but once her eyes adjusted she could see outlines. They lay on their backs, shoulder to shoulder, hip to hip. Each bounce of the wagon jostled them, emphasizing his nearness.

A new form of alarm spread through her. She was ruined. She lay beside a man. Worse, one she'd vehemently refused to marry only moments before they'd been abducted. If she managed to win free of whatever terrible fate they were enmeshed in, it wouldn't matter to the world that her virtue was still intact or that she'd been brought to this circumstance against her will. Only the fact that she lay beside a man, alone, would count.

A look askance showed her Mr. Darcy's aristocratic profile, angled toward the ceiling of their little prison. Not enough light filtered through to read his expression, but she could only assume it was grim. His hands were bound before him as well and his gag pulled down, but he didn't speak again. She didn't want to contemplate about what thoughts must be going through his mind.

Something shifted above them. Elizabeth closed her eyes against the grit that filtered down through the cracks and turned her face to avoid the worst of the debris. Someone sat in the wagon bed above, she realized. She supposed that was one way to ensure they couldn't push free.

She wondered if it was Jeb, the Collins' manservant. She still couldn't believe he'd stormed into the room along with the other three, rope in hand. From the little she'd seen of him, he'd been amiable enough. Charlotte had felt sure he meant to marry the maid he'd gotten in trouble, Mary. That's why she hadn't alerted Mr. Collins to Mary's condition. Elizabeth couldn't believe her friend's kindness had been squandered on so unworthy a person. Had he, then, left Mary behind and with child?

She opened her eyes to Mr. Darcy's face, angled toward her. A sliver of light, permitted through by the shifting above, cut across the strong plane of his cheek and down his jaw. His eyes opened to meet her gaze. She read concern there and, oddly, she didn't think it was for himself.

The wagon clattered over something in the road. They bounced together, their noses nearly touching. Elizabeth gasped. She jerked her face away and hoped the dimness hid the heat in her cheeks.

Mr. Darcy's arm nudged hers, then again. She realized the motion wasn't the product of the rutted road and turned back to him. He nodded toward the planks above them and quirked an eyebrow.

Did he mean to try to escape or was he asking if someone was there? She frowned her confusion back. She doubted the two of them, prone as they were, would be able to lever off whomever sat above. Even if they did, they were in a moving wagon, hands bound, and at least two of their abductors had pistols.

His face moved toward hers, fueling the heat in her cheeks. "There's one up there," he said, his voice the softest whisper, barely heard.

Elizabeth nodded.

"If we hear another wagon, we'll both yell, but we don't want them to know we aren't gagged," he continued.

Elizabeth offered another nod. "Can we untie each other's hands?" she whispered back. "Mine are tied in front and to a rope around my waist."

"Mine are tied to a rope around my neck. If I move my hands too much, the rope tightens."

A brief struggle made it plain neither could reach the other's wrists. With a sigh, he settled more firmly against the floor of their prison. Elizabeth pressed her lips together and did likewise.

At first, she couldn't shake her embarrassment at being pressed so close to Mr. Darcy, but there was no room to move away. As the journey wore on, she grew thankful for the comfort and warmth of his presence. Each time they halted, her whole body tensed, a reaction she could feel mirrored in Mr. Darcy's frame. After a time, they'd always set out again, the horses obviously rested.

The form above them shifted often, showering them with dust and changing which boards light filtered between. That light grew progressively dimmer as daylight waned. Elizabeth had some hope they would stop once it was dark, perhaps giving them a chance to escape or for help to catch up to them, but the wagon kept going. The next time the person above shifted, moonlight filtered down and she recalled the moon was nearly full.

They descended a steep slope, the angle sliding her and Mr. Darcy so their heads pressed uncomfortably against the front wall of their prison. The wagon bounced and jostled so fitfully, Elizabeth began to worry, and hope, it might break apart. The idea seemed dangerous, but anything would be better than how they were.

The wagon leveled out again and halted. Whoever was above them stood. Without, the men called to each other. Elizabeth couldn't hear well but it sounded as if the one above them ordered another to get a boat. The wagon bounced as someone jumped out up front but the man above them remained.

Could they be by the ocean? She strained her senses and thought, perhaps, she heard waves and smelled saltwater. She conjured one of her father's maps in her mind in an attempt to guess their location. Belatedly, she contemplated the angle of the evening sun from earlier. Had they gone north, south or east? They couldn't have reached the sea to the west so quickly.

The wagon bounced again and the man above them finally stepped aside. The top was removed from their holding space. A lantern glared down, illuminating a man to either side. She blinked but couldn't see past the brightness well enough to discern faces.

"Don't you two look cozy," one of the men said. He angled his head over his shoulder, then back toward his companion. "When your brother gets back from dropping Fiona on the boat, you row this pretty little miss out."

Elizabeth swallowed hard, realizing what the man had ordered. Row her out? So, they were by the sea. She struggled with renewed fear. She couldn't let them put her in a boat. She couldn't swim.

"Good thing the boat's still here," the other man said.

The man with the lantern shrugged, the movement an outline of brightness and shadow behind the glare of the light. "Where would it go?"

"Someone could have taken it, or the anchor could have come loose and the whole thing drifted away."

"But it's still here, so stop grousing. You're brother's nearly back."

"You can handle him?" the second man asked, gesturing toward Mr. Darcy with a booted foot.

"Jeb and I'll keep an eye on him until it's his turn," the first man said. "You can handle selling the horses and wagon? If you can, sell Darcy's mount as well. Buy some old gelding to ride around on. You don't want to call attention to yourself by riding too fine a horse."

The second man grunted. "Just don't forget to meet me like we agreed."

"You'll have too much money on you for me to forget to do that," the first man said with a rusty chuckle. "You don't forget to show up. Your brother would never forgive you."

The other man grunted. He knelt beside the hole in which Elizabeth lay. "Alright, missy." He reached down and grabbed her bound hands, pulling her to a sitting position. "Come with me."

A low growl rose from Mr. Darcy. He sat upright. His eyes glinted with anger.

"Don't you worry, mister," the first man said. "So long as you behave, nothing will happen to her. We know she's worth more to you unspoiled."

Elizabeth shuddered and let herself be hauled up and out of the hole. She darted her gaze about, seeking a means of escape. A rocky beach stretched to either side of the wagon. There were only the two men on the wagon bed with her and Mr. Darcy. Another trudged up the beach toward them. She could make out a rowboat just above the surf behind him and a ship of some sort in the moonlit bay. A fourth man, one she recognized as Jeb from the parsonage, was tying Mr. Darcy's horse to the back of the wagon.

The man who'd hauled Elizabeth out of the sunken hold turned and jumped down, then held out both hands to her, as if he might catch her. Not hiding her disdain, Elizabeth marched to the side and jumped down as far from him as she could. She nearly twisted an ankle when she landed in the rocks, her bound hands making it difficult to balance, but managed not to.

The man eyed her up and down. "Come on, missy, and don't get any brave thoughts. The same goes for you, you know. Behave and your lover there will get through this with all his bits and pieces attached, though I hear he's rich enough, you shouldn't mind if we cut off a finger or two."

Elizabeth glared at the man, angled her chin in the air and marched toward the rowboat. She hoped her bravado hid her fear. Men like these thrived off inspiring that emotion.

The rocks in the bay were slippery, forcing a slow pace, but she didn't ask for assistance. Her body ached from her time in the hidden compartment. She was likely bruised head to toe from jostling on the hard wooden planks but she would evidence no weakness before these men.

As she neared the rowboat, rumbling waves rushed up the beach toward her. She looked out over the dark water and swallowed a hard knot of fear. To take her mind off the approaching sea, she mulled over what the men had said. She nearly issued a bitter laugh when she realized they thought she and Mr. Darcy had an understanding.

Was that why they'd taken her? After all, they could have waited until Mr. Darcy stepped outside if they wanted only him, which they must. Elizabeth's family didn't have enough money to make her worth kidnapping.

Or had the man called Mr. Darcy her lover simply to mock her? Could that be the case when it seemed she was there to ensure Mr. Darcy's good behavior? That would require quite the assumption about his personality, but it was one she willingly made, so their abductors may have as well. Despite Mr. Darcy's self-centered, egotistical nature, his highhandedness and snobbery, Elizabeth had no fear he would engage in behavior that would cause her harm.

Then again, in denying her friend Mr. Wickham the living he'd been promised, Mr. Darcy had harmed him. He'd harmed Elizabeth's sister Jane as well. Jane suffered a broken heart thanks to Mr. Darcy's manipulation of Mr. Bingley. It was unforgivably cruel of Mr. Darcy to press Mr. Bingley to leave Jane's side and not return. So perhaps her trust was misplaced.

She shook her head, gaze on the ever-nearing shoreline. Despite those things, and Elizabeth's hearty rejection of his proposal, she couldn't conjure worry that Mr. Darcy would let her be harmed were it in his power to prevent it.

Nor would she inflict harm on him. Although she never wished to look on Mr. Darcy again after his treatment of Jane and Mr. Wickham, and his insulting proposal, she wouldn't do anything to jeopardize his fingers, toes, or any other part of him. That in mind, she clamped an iron will about her fear of the ocean and dutifully climbed into the rowboat, soaking the bottom third of her skirt in the process. The man pushed the little boat out and climbed in with her. The craft, hardly large enough for two, dipped low. Waves knocked against the sides as her abductor took up the oars, further soaking her dress.

While the kidnapper rowed, Elizabeth scanned the shore, heart pounding in her chest. She saw no lights at all. Wherever they were, it was remote. Even if she wished to risk reprisal on Mr. Darcy, there was no reason to scream.

In less time than she expected, they reached the side of the larger vessel. Her abductor pulled in the oars and grabbed a dangling rope. He used it to tie them to the base of a ladder secured to the ship's side, then turned back to Elizabeth.

"I'm going to untie your hands, so you can climb up," he said. "Don't forget, I have a pistol and I'll be right behind you. You've nowhere to go, missy."

Elizabeth nodded and held out her hands. "You don't have to do this," she said as the man worked at her bonds. "Mr. Darcy is a man of honor. If you agree on a price with him and let us go, he will pay you." She had no idea of the truth of her statement and didn't care. She suspected Mr. Darcy very well might pay, right before he had them arrested.

The man shook his head. "You let us take care of who makes what deals, missy." He pulled the rope from her wrists and hands. "Up you go."

Praying she didn't tip the boat, for she was sure they were out in waters over her head, Elizabeth stood. The little craft trembled beneath her, each movement amplified. She turned with care and latched onto the ladder. Rowboat and legs shaking, she half fell, half jumped onto the bottom rung.

The man let out a curse. She dared a look over her shoulder to find his arms splayed as he worked to stabilize the small craft before he spilled out. He shot her a glare. Each step hindered by her heavy wet skirts and by having to cling to the ladder with both hands, Elizabeth made her way up. At the top, she grabbed the side of a break in the railing and pulled herself up the final steps.

When she finally spilled over the edge onto the deck, her abductor was right behind her. Belatedly, she wished she'd kicked him into the water, though all he would have had to do was grab her foot and both would tumble down. He wrapped a hand around her upper arm and marched her to a set of narrow steps and down. Hardly enough moonlight spilled into the short hall for her to make out the doors, one to each side and one in front of her face.

One of the doors had been rehung and had a bar across it, the shabby but effective construction suggesting the outward swing of the door and restraint were new additions. The man lifted the bar, yanked the door open and shoved her into complete darkness. She stumbled, a hand before her face, but didn't run into anything. Behind her, she heard the bar drop back into place.

Heart pounding, Elizabeth stood for what seemed like an eternity. She took back her earlier wish never to see Mr. Darcy again. Better the reassurance of his strong, if antagonistic, presence than to be locked away alone in the dark. He'd likely order her about, but he'd know what best to do and would keep her safe if he could.

Taking deep breaths, she slowly gathered in her fear. She bundled that debilitating emotion into a tight knot and shoved it down. Out of her head, out of her throat, away from her thudding heart and deep into her gut. It rested there like a lump of raw clay, but she managed to get the trembling in her limbs under control.

The ship rocked beneath her, creaking in time with the waves. Surf pounded the beach, still audible. She took a step backward, then another, until she reached the door. She felt around it, tried to press it open, but to no avail. Ignoring the surge of panic that caused, for she hadn't expected it to open, she felt along the wall the door was set in until she reached a corner, then slowly along that wall.

She found nothing but pegs, likely for hanging clothing. She reached the outer hull, fingers skimming over rough wood. There, she encountered a shutter. Hope surged in her. She fumbled to find the latch and yank the slatted wood open.

Moonlight streamed in, illuminating a window too narrow for her to fit through, even if she could swim. Cold air seeped in as well, icy and damp. Elizabeth stuck her head out the window but there was little to see but a long, choppy streak of moonlight knifing across the water toward her and the moon itself, high above and unfeeling.

On the other side of the cabin, the bar slid free. She whirled, taking in shadow-filled bunk beds built into the wall she had yet to explore, and watched the door swing open. Mr. Darcy stumbled in, as if pushed. The line of moonlight in which she stood stretched across the floor to illuminate his boots and offered enough light for her to read the relief on his face when he saw her. Relief surged through her as well, not to be alone. She resisted the urge to go to him and throw her arms about him.

"Miss Bennet." He rubbed at his wrists as he crossed the small space to stand before her. "I trust they kept their word and you remain unharmed?"

"I am as well as can be expected," Elizabeth managed in even tones. "And you, Mr. Darcy?" Her eyes dropped toward his wrists. "Did they hurt you?" She held out a hand.

He grimaced and proffered wrists that looked raw even by moonlight. "My own doing, I'm afraid. I worked at my bonds the entire journey here, to no avail."

"I applaud your determination," she said.

Mr. Darcy shook his head. "Folly, I suppose," he said, voice pitched low. "The ropes were hardly loosened by the time they untied me to climb the ladder."

"You always suffer from your own stubbornness, Darcy," a familiar voice said.

Elizabeth whirled toward the bunks. Booted feet swung from the shadows of the lower one and into the moonlight as a form sat up. A torso followed. The man ducked slightly to avoid hitting the upper bunk and slid to the edge of the lower.

"Mr. Wickham," she gasped. Anger and joy wared in her. A familiar, amiable face was nothing short of a boon, but he'd been there the whole time. All but spying on her. He must have recognized her, though she was sure she looked a sight.

"Miss Bennet." Mr. Wickham nodded toward her. "Darcy."

"Wickham." Mr. Darcy acknowledged, tone colder than the sea air streaming in through the open shutter. "Is this your doing?"

Moonlight slanting across his profile, Mr. Wickham winced.

Elizabeth whirled back toward Mr. Darcy. "Why do you accuse him? He's locked in this room, just as we are." Could Mr. Darcy really be so jealous of Mr. Wickham, so snobbish, that he'd harangue the man even here and under these circumstances?

"Well?" Mr. Darcy pressed, gaze locked with Mr. Wickham's. "And keep in mind that I always know when you're lying."

Mr. Wickham cleared his throat. "I'm afraid Darcy's right for once, Miss Bennet."

Elizabeth's eyebrows shot up as she turned back to Mr. Wickham. She took in his rumpled clothing and couple-day-old beard. "How so?"

He shrugged. "It all began when I decided to leave Meryton because of my gambling debts."

From the corner of her eye, Elizabeth saw Mr. Darcy shake his head. Whether signaling a lack of surprise or for Mr. Wickham's bluntness, she didn't know. For her part, she found his frank acknowledgement that he was running out on debts of honor shocking.

"On my way out of town, I ran into a man getting a wagon ready to leave," Mr. Wickham continued. "I decided to join him for the free ride." He offered another shrug. "Before I knew it, I found out I was with smugglers."

"So, you tried to part ways, and they locked you in here?" Elizabeth guessed. She frowned. "How did that see us kidnapped?" Had he tried to exchange information for freedom? That was low, but perhaps he felt he could reach them before they came to harm.

Mr. Wickham looked between her and Mr. Darcy, who now stood with his arms folded across his chest, chin up and eyes glaring. Mr. Wickham shrugged. "Not precisely. They offered to pay me to help, and I did."

"Just like that?" Elizabeth gasped. "You simply took to smuggling?" How could he? He always seemed so cheerful. So amiable and genteel.

Mr. Wickham offered another shrug. "It was only brandy."

"And then?" Mr. Darcy prompted in those same cool tones.

"And then they hit a spot of bad luck," Mr. Wickham said. "So... they wanted to try something else."

"Kidnapping," Mr. Darcy stated flatly.

"I didn't realize that was their goal, at first," Mr. Wickham protested. "You have to believe that, Darcy. The one, Tom, he asked me a lot of questions while we traveled. I thought he was simply passing the time."

"Really?" Mr. Darcy's query dripped sarcasm.

Mr. Wickham ducked his head. "Well, to be honest, I thought maybe he wanted to rob you, or that crazy aunt of yours, or even Matlock." He looked back up, expression defensive. "I swear I'd no idea they planned to abduct anyone. As soon as I found out, I told them I wouldn't be a part of it. That's when they locked me in here."

Elizabeth stared at Mr. Wickham, incredulous. She blinked several times. Perhaps the terror of the journey and the moonlight were combining to play tricks on her. The man seated on the bunk, disheveled, unshaven and speaking so casually of running from debt, of smuggling and robbery, he couldn't be the same dashing dance partner and enjoyable conversationalist who'd been her frequent companion in Hertfordshire.

"You would have seen Mr. Darcy or Lady Catherine robbed?" she blurted.

His shrug grated on her. Did he think the gesture shed his crimes like one might shake snow free of a cloak? He employed the motion often enough that any power it might have had vanished.

"Darcy, his aunt and the earl can all spare a few trinkets," Mr. Wickham said. "Likely, they could be robbed and not even notice. There are whole rooms at Pemberley I doubt Darcy ever sets foot in. Maybe whole wings."

"That's no justification," Elizabeth cried. Had the man no honor?

"You set their sights on Lady Catherine, or did you expect me to be there at this time of year?" Mr. Darcy asked. "How long have you been plotting this?"

Mr. Wickham held up his hands, palms out. "I haven't been plotting. I swear. They already had some people at the Hunsford Parsonage. That's why they were quite so interested in my stories about you all. On my honor, Darcy, if I'd known where their interest would lead, I would have kept my mouth shut." Mr. Wickham turned to Elizabeth. "And I doubly apologize to you, Miss Bennet. I'm not sure why they took you."

Elizabeth darted a look at Mr. Darcy, who glared at Wickham. Even under the circumstances, she wouldn't voice the idea that their abductors thought she and Mr. Darcy had an understanding. She hoped the moonlight didn't illuminate her blush.

"Possibly for leverage over me," Mr. Darcy said but didn't elaborate.

"Ah yes, the noble Mr. Darcy," Mr. Wickham said. "You'd never let a lady come to harm. They likely gleaned as much from my stories." He snorted. "It's a good thing I didn't tell them how much the two of you dislike each other. I should have. It's an amusing tale, you calling Miss Bennet here ugly and saying you'd never stand up with her."

Elizabeth's face grew hotter. This time, she didn't dare even glance at Mr. Darcy.

"I said no such things," Mr. Darcy snapped.

Mr. Wickham chuckled. "Really? It was the talk of Meryton how, the very day you arrived in Hertfordshire, you said the second prettiest girl around wasn't handsome enough to tempt you."

Beside Elizabeth, Mr. Darcy stiffened, but he didn't speak.

Mr. Wickham chuckled again. He swung his feet back up onto the bunk and lay down. "Darcy, you're the largest. Perhaps Miss Bennet and I can share," he said.

Elizabeth didn't know if Mr. Wickham joked or not, but his words made her wish to drag him back out of his bunk by his shirtfront and slap him. Share with him indeed.

"Miss Bennet will take the top bunk," Mr. Darcy said.

"Suit yourself," Mr. Wickham said. "Close that shutter before we all freeze to death. I'm going to sleep."

Mr. Darcy turned to Elizabeth. "Take the top bunk, Miss Bennet. I'll close the shutter once you're ready."

"Oh, and Darcy," Mr. Wickham called. "Mind your head. There are spots low enough you'll have to duck."

"Noted," Mr. Darcy snapped.

Elizabeth thought about declaring that she would sleep on the floor but decided she didn't have the will for a confrontation with Mr. Darcy in that moment. She was cold and tired, and her skirt was still wet. She opted, especially given the stubborn set of Mr. Darcy's jaw, to accept his chivalrousness. Certainly, his order was infinitely better than Mr. Wickham's offer.

"Thank you," she said and climbed awkwardly into the top bunk to attempt sleep.

The room fell into darkness when Mr. Darcy closed the shutter. Elizabeth listened to him settle onto the floor. She felt comforted knowing he lay beside the bed. Her thoughts returned to how easily Mr. Wickham had accepted that their abductors might take her simply to ensure Mr. Darcy's good behavior. Obviously, even a person who disliked Mr. Darcy, as Mr. Wickham did, could readily acknowledge his chivalry.

Exhausted as Elizabeth was, her mind was too filled with worry for sleep. She was at the mercy of her kidnappers, who could easily kill her. Even if she returned immediately, her reputation was now in shambles.

She pressed her lips into a tight line. She would not worry about her reputation. There was nothing she could do about it.

Instead, she would worry about her treatment as a prisoner. She would worry about the two men imprisoned with her, who disliked each other. She would survive the here-and-now but be attentive enough to take any opportunity to escape that presented itself. A snorting rumble reverberated through the small room as, below her, Mr. Wickham began to snore.

Chapter Six

The door flew open. Elizabeth's eyelids mimicked the action. She started to sit up but caught herself before she could hit her head on the ceiling. She turned instead and looked down the length of the room toward the door. Light spilled in behind two men, each holding a pistol. One was the man she thought must have sat in the wagon bed during their journey. The other was the one who'd come up the beach, brother to the one who'd rowed her out.

Elizabeth couldn't see Mr. Wickham. A glance showed Mr. Darcy sat on the floor at the head of the bunk, under the window. Light filtered in around the shutter but slanted past him to hit the floor. Mr. Darcy wasn't looking at her, his attention on the two men.

Still in her cap and apron, the Collins' maid Mary darted in, face downturned. She moved to the end of the bunks. Elizabeth realized there was a curtained off area there that she hadn't noticed in the dark. Mary went in and came out with a chamber pot. She hurried away.

The two men with pistols glared at them, silent. Mary reappeared and replaced the chamber pot. She scurried back out and Jeb took her place. He set a pitcher of water, a glass and a loaf of bread on the floor just inside the doorway, then backed out. He didn't meet Elizabeth's gaze.

She hadn't expected him to. It was obvious he and Mary were more reluctant than the others, not that it mattered. They were equally guilty. The only one Elizabeth had any sympathy for was the one-time maid. A woman with child could be forced to make difficult choices.

"Mr. Darcy," the man from the back of the wagon said. "Wickham says you have an agent in London."

"Most gentlemen do," Mr. Darcy acknowledged.

"Would yours recognize your ring?" the man asked.

"Certainly."

"Give it to me."

Even from above, Elizabeth could read Mr. Darcy's mutinous look.

She held her breath. He looked up at her. His expression softened, and he nodded. He tugged at his ring, making to stand.

"Stay on the floor," their abductor snapped. "Throw it over."

Mr. Darcy tossed him the ring. The man caught it in his free hand. "What's your man's name and address, and keep in mind, Wickham already told us. I only want to make sure."

Mr. Darcy offered the surname Edwards and a London firm so prestigious, Elizabeth had actually heard of it. He also offered the address.

Their abductor nodded along. "Sounds right," he said. "let's go."

He and the other man backed out. The door swung closed. The bar dropped into place with a thud.

Mr. Darcy stood and turned to open the shutter. Mr. Wickham swung free of the bunk. He snatched up the bread, then poured a glass of water, which he drank.

"I assume you mean to share that bread," Mr. Darcy said flatly.

Mr. Wickham rolled his eyes ceilingward. He broke the bread into three pieces and began eating the largest. Elizabeth gave an involuntary gasp. He looked up at her and offered a shrug, a habit of his that she was rapidly coming to despise. She climbed down from the bunk and retrieved the two remaining pieces from him. She proffered the larger to Mr. Darcy.

He shook his head. "You take that one."

"I'm much smaller than you," she demurred. "And I've little appetite."

He hesitated for a long moment. Finally, he took the larger piece. Elizabeth retrieved the pitcher from beside the door and drank a glass of water. She poured the final glass and brought it to Mr. Darcy, who accepted it with a nod.

"Tell me about our captors," he said to Mr. Wickham as he started to eat.

"What good will knowing about them do?" Mr. Wickham asked. "They're going to kill us either way. I should have agreed to kidnap you with them. I can't believe I'm going to die for trying to protect you, Darcy."

"Protecting me would have been not giving them information about me," Mr. Darcy said. "All you did was refuse to directly harm me."

"And what thanks do I get?" Mr. Wickham snapped.

Mr. Darcy opened his mouth to retaliate.

Elizabeth stepped between them. "It can't hurt to know about our captors and it may help," she turned to Mr. Darcy. "We already know two of them." The surprise that flittered across his face sparked anger in her. She should have realized the vaunted Mr. Darcy of Pemberley and ten-thousand pounds a year wouldn't recognize servants.

"We do?" he asked.

"The woman, Mary, she's let you into the parsonage at least half a dozen times,"

"Mary?" Mr. Wickham asked. "They talked about a girl named Fiona working at the parsonage."

"The woman who was just here was Mary." Elizabeth frowned. "She has a slight Scottish accent. Perhaps she also goes by Fiona?"

"She would have an easier time finding work as Mary than Fiona," Darcy said. "Fiona is a common Irish name and I believe it's also used in Scotland."

"Trust Darcy to know an utterly useless fact," Mr. Wickham said.

Elizabeth decided to ignore that comment. "Her man, Jeb, is the one who brought the food." She glanced at Mr. Darcy. "You've more reason not to recognize him. You wouldn't have seen him as often but he's another of Mr. Collins' staff. Both, I believe, selected by your aunt," she added, somewhat vindictively.

Mr. Darcy shook his head, appearing bashful. "I didn't recognize either the man or the maid."

Mr. Wickham chuckled. "Leave it to the great Mr. Darcy not to bother to look at a maid's face."

Elizabeth's anger grew, chagrin surging in her to hear her earlier thought mirrored by a man she was rapidly coming to disdain. "I noticed you didn't so much as glance at her, Mr. Wickham," she snapped. "I doubt you could pick her from a selection of two."

He shrugged. "What's to look at? She's a maid."

Elizabeth momentarily closed her eyes in silent supplication. The man was a hypocrite.

Mr. Darcy cleared his throat and took a swallow of water. "What do you know about this Mary-Fiona, or whatever her name is, and Jeb, Miss Bennet?"

Elizabeth drew in a breath, striving to emulate his calm. "Mary is with child. Jeb's child but he hasn't proposed. They've been working at the parsonage. Charlotte is aware of Mary's condition but has been waiting to alert Mr. Collins, hoping Jeb would do right by Mary."

Elizabeth caught herself about to shrug and suppressed the motion. "That's really all I know."

"Oh, yes, extremely helpful." Mr. Wickham's tone dripped sarcasm.

Elizabeth turned to him with narrowed eyes. "Well, it's something." Not much, though, she knew. "It must also mean something that they haven't killed you yet."

"Yet," Mr. Wickham muttered. He turned to Mr. Darcy. "Look, there's no point in escaping this room. There are two sets of brothers and the woman, whatever her name is. You have quite the right hook, Darcy, but they have pistols. Even if we get the guns, we both know you would never shoot anyone. We can't take the ship from them and if we did, I don't know anything about sailing. Unless you've learned in the last five years, you don't either."

Mr. Darcy moved to the window. He stuck his head out. After a moment, he turned back to them. "They're headed north. This is a small ship. I doubt they'll take her out of sight of land. We already know there's a rowboat. Would they have brought it or left it on the beach? If we can escape this room, we could use that. We may be able to avoid confrontation." He turned to Elizabeth, expression almost apologetic. "Wickham is correct. I will not kill a man in cold blood."

Elizabeth nodded. She wouldn't wish him to. Her greater worry was that he might concoct a plan that required her to swim. Should she admit her inability? She felt he would help her, not feel pressed to leave her behind. Wouldn't he?

"All those years of practice with a pistol, for what?" Mr. Wickham's tone mocked. "You're the best shot I know but that doesn't do us any good because these are men, not ducks."

"Exactly." Mr. Darcy's tone was quiet. "They are men, not ducks."

"You've spent time with these men," Elizabeth said to Mr. Wickham, trying to guide the conversation in a useful direction. "You seem to have told them quite a lot about Mr. Darcy. The least you can do is tell us what you know of them."

"I'm telling you, it won't do you any good," Mr. Wickham said.

"Miss Bennet is correct," Mr. Darcy stated. "Tell us about them." His tone suggested it was an order.

With a shrug, Wickham offered information on Jeb and Tom, who were brothers. More prodding bought her and Mr. Darcy what Wickham knew of the other two men, whom he called The Jonesys. They were also brothers. Of Mary-Fiona, Wickham knew little, but he did believe she was a coconspirator, not a prisoner. Apparently, there used to be more, but the others had left. Elizabeth supposed they'd given up on their lives of crime. Or perhaps moved on to different crimes.

As she and Mr. Darcy worked to get information out of Mr. Wickham, it occurred to Elizabeth that he liked being prodded. He enjoyed having them hang on his words. His reluctance wasn't genuine but a method of prolonging their attention.

"So," Mr. Darcy concluded. "One of The Jonesys is the one they sent to sell the wagon and my horse."

Mr. Wickham shrugged. "If you say so. This morning we saw Tom, one Jonesy, that maid and the one whose face is new to me, Jeb."

"Can you tell us anything else about them?" Mr. Darcy pressed.

Another shrug. "I think they have some dream of taking the ship to Ireland once they have your ransom, and that's all I know," Mr. Wickham's tone held reluctance. "Mostly, I've interacted with Tom."

"Were you ever on the ship but not captive?" Mr. Darcy asked. "Tell me about this vessel. I couldn't see much when they brought me in, even with the moon nearly full."

Mr. Wickham shook his head. "No. It's my turn. Tell me how the rich, well protected Mr. Darcy was kidnapped."

"Mr. Darcy called on the parsonage," Elizabeth said. She didn't miss the annoyance that flickered in Mr. Wickham's eyes as he turned to her. So, he didn't simply want attention. He wanted Mr. Darcy's attention. "Unfortunately, the Collins and Miss Lucas were out. I'm not certain about the other two maids. I hope nothing has befallen them."

Mr. Wickham settled onto the edge of his bunk. "So, they took advantage of the house being nearly empty."

"It seems so," Elizabeth said. "Mr. Darcy was about to depart, I should think, when the four men burst into the room. Two with pistols and two with rope and dishcloths made into gags. They gagged us and tied our hands, then put us in the false bottom of a wagon. One sat on top of the hatch the whole ride to the cove. They also took Mr. Darcy's horse. I've no idea what they'll make of my absence or how long it will be before someone realizes Mr. Darcy is gone." She glanced at him.

"They'll know you're missing, and the man servant and maid," Mr. Darcy said. "But your absence won't have been discovered until late. They would have assumed you went for a walk. As I was out riding, it would have been a similar length of time before anyone questioned that I hadn't returned."

"So, they likely didn't grow concerned until after nightfall." Elizabeth tried to keep a forlorn note from her voice. Would Charlotte write to her father immediately? How soon would Mr. Bennet know she was missing? How long until her mother and sisters realized she must be ruined, one way or the other?

Mr. Wickham let out a chuckle. "If they find you both gone, they may think you ran off together. Darcy says we're headed north. Maybe they'll find us in Scotland after all."

Elizabeth grimaced. She avoided looking at Mr. Darcy. Her neck heated.

"Scotland?" Mr. Darcy repeated. "Is that where they plan to take us? You said they plan to hide in Ireland when all this is over."

"Scotland, Ireland. I don't know," Mr. Wickham said with a shrug. "Scotland's the nearest place north of here."

Mr. Darcy cast Elizabeth a shuttered glance. "Perhaps Richard will think to look there."

Mr. Wickham snorted. "I doubt that. No one who knows you, Darcy, would imagine you'd deign to run off with a backwater country miss with no connections, no fortune and that hideous mother. Meaning no offense, Miss Bennet," he added with another chuckle.

Elizabeth's frayed nerves snapped. She rounded on him. "How can you say that and not mean offense, sir?"

He shrugged at her, still chortling. "Don't blame me. It's Darcy who's the snob. I'm simply stating the obvious."

"Enough," Mr. Darcy barked. "Tell us about the ship. Do they have the rowboat with them?"

Briefly, Elizabeth closed her eyes again, seeking calm. When she opened them, Mr. Wickham glanced from her to Mr. Darcy. Mr. Darcy, bread and water finished, folded his arms across his chest and leveled a stern look on Mr. Wickham.

"Yes, they keep the small boat onboard the big boat," Mr. Wickham said. "But we're locked in this room, if you'll recall, and all we can see from our window is sea. Your theory that we're near enough to land to use the rowboat is only that, a theory. One we can't test unless we get free. Then, with you afraid to kill anyone, where would that leave us if this boat is out in the middle of the ocean?"

"Ship," Mr. Darcy corrected. "We're on a ship."

"It's too small. It's a boat," Mr. Wickham said.

"It carries a boat. That makes it a ship," Mr. Darcy said.

Mr. Wickham scowled at Mr. Darcy. "That so-called boat it's carrying is almost a toy. It's useless unless the water is calm."

"I'll call it a vessel," Elizabeth broke in, exasperated. "It doesn't matter what it's called. Please describe what you know about it, starting with where they have the rowboat."

Mr. Wickham turned back to her. "Why? To help you escape, Miss Bennet? You think you and Darcy can sneak out and grab it? That rowboat will only hold two. I'm not helping you just so you can leave me behind."

"You are the obvious choice to remain." Mr. Darcy's tone held a certain amount of satisfaction. "I would have to get Miss Bennet to safety."

Elizabeth shook her head. "I'm the logical one to leave behind. They're less likely to kill a woman and if Mr. Darcy escapes, he can use his resources to find me." She left unsaid that if she and Mr. Darcy both escaped, their captors would almost surely kill Mr. Wickham.

"The only one they won't kill is Darcy," Mr. Wickham said. "He's worth too much alive. If we get out of this room, which we won't, I'll take you to safety, Miss Bennet." He shot a smirk at Mr. Darcy. "And I'll marry you, because you'll need someone to now. I wouldn't mind. You're pretty enough and, as your being here is Darcy's fault, I'm sure he'll make it worth my while."

Elizabeth stared at him, mouth agape. There was a time she might have accepted an offer from Mr. Wickham. He'd been entertaining, bright, charming. Now, after what he'd done to Mr. Darcy, which seemed even worse than the way Mr. Darcy had denied him a living, and his actions and words since they found him locked up with them, she would sooner die alone. "There is nothing on this earth or in heaven above that would make me accept marriage to you, Mr. Wickham."

Mr. Darcy coughed. Did she imagine the spark that ignited in his eyes? Her face heated. Likely, he took some small satisfaction in watching her turn down another man, and even more zealously than she'd declined him.

"Well, you two aren't leaving me here to die," Mr. Wickham snapped.

"Well, I'm not leaving with you," Elizabeth responded.

"Then it's settled," Mr. Wickham said. "Darcy should be the one left behind. He swims like a fish, anyhow. I can only swim a few yards." He let out a longsuffering sigh. "Darcy always does everything well. He rides well, he knows Latin and Greek well, he shoots well, fences well. You get the idea." He turned to Mr. Darcy. "I'll row Miss Bennet and you can swim behind us. You might even beat us to shore."

"Agreed," Mr. Darcy said, much to Elizabeth's surprise. "And I will beat you to shore and be waiting to see you get Miss Bennet there safely."

They moved on to a more fruitless discussion, how they might escape the room. Mr. Wickham didn't seem to know much. He wasn't certain how often they would be given food and water, or if two men with guns would always appear.

While they talked, Elizabeth studied Mr. Wickham. Divested of his uniform and with a day or two worth of stubble, and obviously in poor spirits, he held none of his original charm. In truth, the more she saw of him in the cabin, under such poor circumstances, the less she cared for him. She began to wonder if all the things he'd told her about Mr. Darcy were true. At the time, each slight and slander had been a little bit of gossip that she'd gobbled up and added to her list of reasons to dislike Mr. Darcy. Now, she was embarrassed to have been so taken in by Mr. Wickham. Everything he'd said was suspect.

Eventually, they tired of making plans that would likely never bear fruit. Mr. Wickham went back to sleep. At one point, after the sun had moved far across the sky and departed from direct view of their eastern-facing window, a fair amount of commotion sounded on the deck. Mr. Wickham woke up long enough to say they were likely unloading and then loading the rowboat. Elizabeth recalled that one man had gone to sell the wagon and horses, including Mr. Darcy's, and that someone would be sent back to London with his ring. She hoped Mr. Darcy wasn't too fond of either for it seemed unlikely he'd see horse or heirloom again.

When the next delivery of food arrived, as well-guarded as the first, Mr. Darcy retrieved the bread and water the moment the door closed. He divided the loaf into three pieces that were much more even in size. He offered the choice to Elizabeth. Hunger made her reluctant to take the smallest piece, but she did so. Mr. Darcy then offered the choice to Mr. Wickham, who took the largest piece, leaving the middle-sized piece for Mr. Darcy.

Their next food delivery included cooked fish and more bread, which was notably stale. Mr. Darcy again retrieved the food first, but this time gave Elizabeth the job of dividing. She was surprised at how readily Mr. Wickham accepted Mr. Darcy's authority. She divided the food as equally as she could, though she still took the smallest share. She reflected that if they weren't offered better portions soon or, better yet, able to escape or be rescued, all three of them would grow rather thin.

Chapter Seven

The days ticked by. With their view of the rising sun and ocean, it was impossible to gauge their progress up the coast, but Elizabeth began to wonder how many days it should take to sail to Scotland or if that was even their destination. If the sun didn't rise every morning to mark their northward passage, she would think them off course.

Gazing out the narrow window at sea and sky, she once again conjured her father's books and maps in her mind, this time with an even greater pang. Mr. Bennet would be aware she was missing by now. He would be frantic to find her, yet there were no clues. Only that Mr. Darcy, whom no one likely knew was at the parsonage, as well as a maid and a manservant were also missing. What would her father, or Mr. Darcy's cousin Colonel Fitzwilliam, make of that?

What must her family be thinking? Her father would be worried and grieved. Her mother... well, her mother would blame someone. She would probably claim that she hadn't wanted Elizabeth to visit her friend Charlotte Collins in the first place. Elizabeth's older sister Jane would be terribly upset but wouldn't show it and would care for her mother, new troubles and grief piled atop her sorrow over Mr. Bingley's lack of a proposal.

A twinge of anger shot through Elizabeth. She resisted the urge to turn a glare on Mr. Darcy. He was to blame for Jane's sorrow over Mr. Bingley. The cramped cabin and their role as prisoners made for a poor time and place to confront Mr. Darcy over that, though.

Elizabeth drew in a breath to calm her anger. She loosened her grip on the windowsill, sorry that the window was too small for anyone to climb through. If it were a bit larger, Mr. Darcy could slip out and swim to shore, if they ever saw a shore. Once there, he would be in a position to arrange for a search, since he knew something about their captors. She cast a quick look Mr. Darcy's way. With him gone, though, the kidnappers might panic and kill her. She shivered. Knowing her life hinged on the protection of a man to whom she'd issued a humiliating refusal and didn't even like filled her with disquiet.

Deliberately, though it pained her no less than contemplating her circumstances, she turned her thoughts back to her family. Her next younger sister, Mary, would be nearly as upset as Jane. Oh, she would have some moral quotation that would almost apply to the situation, but behind that she would worry and grieve.

On the other hand, her two youngest sisters, Kitty and Lydia, would not be particularly concerned. They had a terribly naïve, sheltered view of the world and would assume all would come out well. Likely, they imagined she'd run off with a gentleman and would return wed and pregnant. Also, likely, if word had gotten out about Elizabeth's disappearance, as she assumed it must, they would be using the notoriety of the scandal to gad about town, guests in every parlor as Hertfordshire sought gossip.

Elizabeth let out a long, low sigh. In her mind, she conjured an image of her home against the backdrop of endlessly rolling sea. She missed Longbourn. Even when she'd enjoyed herself visiting her friend Charlotte, she'd sometimes missed the physical presence of her home. Now, she craved it as a near-physical ache. The familiar. The safe. Oh, how she longed for Longbourn.

She grimaced slightly at her unconscious play on words. She longed for Longbourn. Before, she'd considered the name of her home as sort of a pun on the fact that she had no brother. That her parents waited a long time for a son to be born. There never was a son born, making her mother desperate for Elizabeth and her four sisters to wed, so that when the estate went to Mr. Collins on Mr. Bennet's death, they wouldn't be destitute. Now, the name of her father's estate took on a whole new, even sadder meaning.

She shook her head. No, maudlin thoughts wouldn't do. She refocused on the horizon in an attempt to see something, anything but more sky and water. If she recalled her father's maps correctly, the only place they could be headed, if not Scotland, was somewhere on the continent.

But why? Why tell Mr. Wickham they wanted to retire to Ireland but then head up the east coast of England? That would be the long way around. It couldn't be out of a desire not to risk the channel. They'd been smuggling French contraband, after all. They must know the channel well.

On the other hand, why take them to Europe? That made no sense.

Was it because so much of Europe was allied with Napoleon? Mr. Darcy was very wealthy. Just how much did they mean to ransom him for? Enough for treason to be involved?

Elizabeth shook her head and turned from the window, deciding her break was over. She'd taken to walking back and forth along the open space between bunks and wall for several hours every day. She worried that continuously lying about would make her weak. Her exercise also gave Mr. Darcy an excuse to rest in her bunk, to be out of the way so she could walk.

She cast a glance toward the upper bunk, her gaze tracing his strong profile. She liked to think forcing him into the bunk was a boon, as he spent nearly all his time on the floor. Then again, he couldn't stretch out fully in the bunk. Or if he did, his feet must be propped over the edge and pressed into the curtained-off space, which didn't look comfortable in the least. Those few hours each day were the best she could do for him, though. She considered it unfair that he slept on the floor, but he not only did not complain, he acted as if it wasn't any trouble.

"Must you persist in that?" Mr. Wickham grumbled. "All that swishing about is making it difficult for me to sleep."

"Really?" Elizabeth shot back. "You don't seem to have any trouble sleeping. It's all you do."

"Better that I should save my strength than engage in pointless circling."

"Miss Bennet's circling is not pointless," Mr. Darcy said.

"Says you," Mr. Wickham muttered.

"Yes, says me." Mr. Darcy turned his head to regard her. "It could, however, be improved on."

Elizabeth met his gaze and raised her eyebrows in question. "How so?"

"You turn the same way every time," he said. "You aren't exercising your legs evenly."

"Darcy always knows better," Mr. Wickham observed. "He's so critical."

"But correct," Mr. Darcy threw back at Mr. Wickham. "Miss Bennet, if you do a figure eight, it will be better exercise."

"There isn't room to do a figure eight," Mr. Wickham said. "And no shape will disturb my rest less."

It took scant consideration for Elizabeth to realize Mr. Darcy was correct. As soon as she reached the wall, she turned the opposite way she had been. After a few laps, she took to turning left at one end of the room and right at the other. After all, if and when they escaped, they might have to walk some distance. She didn't want to hinder them or, far worse, be left behind.

When she estimated another hour had passed, she went to the bunk to find Mr. Darcy's eyes closed, his breathing even. Though she had to stand on tip toe to do so, her gaze skimmed across his smooth brow, down along angled cheek bones. His straight nose, strong lips and firm jaw, now thick with a growing beard.

She frowned slightly. Mr. Wickham's beard hardly seemed more grown in than Mr. Darcy's. He'd only stubble when they arrived, as if he'd shaved not that morning but perhaps the one before. How long had he actually been a prisoner? She doubted they'd been letting him shave but curtailed the activity once she and Mr. Darcy arrived.

"Had your fill of Mr. Darcy's perfection yet?" Mr. Wickham muttered from the bunk below.

Elizabeth stepped back to scrutinize him through narrowed eyes. Was he even a prisoner, or a spy? Someone to keep an eye on them and discourage any attempts to escape? "He's asleep. I debate waking him."

Mr. Wickham kicked upward, jarring the upper bunk. "Your turn, Darcy. Show off your muscles."

Mr. Darcy's eyes opened. For a moment, Elizabeth read an anger bordering on hatred simmering there. Then he dropped his lids. When those dark eyes, lined by thick lashes, opened again, he was calm.

"Thank you for waking me," he said and turned to slide from the bunk. "I beg your pardon, Miss Bennet."

"There's no pardon to beg." She climbed back into her spot, still suffused with Mr. Darcy's warmth. As cold air was a constant if they wished the window open, and she did, the heat left by Mr. Darcy's body was welcome. The blush which stained her cheeks was not, but Mr. Darcy had already launched into his stretches and Mr. Wickham couldn't see her from his position below.

From stretches, Mr. Darcy moved into squats, then pushups, then sit ups. Each day, Elizabeth tried not to stare but she was endlessly fascinated. Without his coat, which he'd left hanging on a peg on the wall when he first ascended to the bunk and never wore while exercising, it was easy to see that not one inch of his long, lean torso or broad shoulders was augmented by padding. Fortunately, he never glanced her way, maintaining a look of concentration, so there was no risk he'd catch

70

her staring.

From those more mundane forms, Mr. Darcy moved into what she must assume were fencing exercises. Arm extended, he lunged, parried and dodged as best as the tight quarters allowed. She noted, now that she knew to look for it, that he practiced each set of forms using first one, then the other side of his body, though his imaginary blade always remained in the same hand.

"Could you spare us the acrobatics for one afternoon?" Mr. Wickham muttered from below Elizabeth.

"I'm keeping in shape." Mr. Darcy didn't pause in his exertions. "You might consider trying it."

"Why? So you can lounge about in my bunk?"

"Hardly," Mr. Darcy said without pausing.

"While you're at it, why don't you get out a fake pistol and practice imaginary shooting." Mr. Wickham's voice dripped with a mixture of scorn and humor, as if he thought his words actually funny. His arm snaked into sight below Elizabeth as he illustrated his words by mimicking a pistol with his hand.

"First, there would be little exercise in that," Mr. Darcy replied, as if Wickham had spoken reasonably. "Second, I would never shoot a man."

"Would you shoot a woman?" The words were out of her mouth even as it occurred to Elizabeth that their time closeted together would go smoother if she didn't antagonize Mr. Darcy.

He shot her a quick, tight grin. "I would not."

"Darcy doesn't have it in him to kill." Mr. Wickham's tone held derision.

"As well he should not," Elizabeth exclaimed. "He's a gentleman."

Mr. Wickham snorted. "A lot of good him being a gentleman would do us if we got the chance to escape."

Mr. Darcy stilled. He turned toward the bed. His gaze, hard and assessing, sent a chill through Elizabeth even though it wasn't aimed at her. "Would you kill a man, George?"

The bunk creaked as Mr. Wickham squirmed under that stare. "In a heartbeat," he muttered, the declaration robbed of merit by the fear and uncertainty in his voice.

"You see then, Miss Bennet, being a gentleman doesn't determine if a man will turn murderer," Mr. Darcy said.

Elizabeth stared at him, unsure how to take the statement. Was he viewing Mr. Wickham as a gentleman who had lied a moment ago, or as not a gentleman and taking him at his word? Either way, she had the deep suspicion that if ever there was a true reason to do so, Mr. Darcy would shoot a man and Mr. Wickham would run. She shivered.

"Would you care to wear my coat, Miss Bennet?" Mr. Darcy asked. "I won't require it for some time."

She shook her head. "No, thank you."

He nodded and returned to his fencing forms. Elizabeth returned to watching him, Mr. Wickham once more silent below. After a time, he shifted restlessly.

"I say, Darcy, how about you let me take a turn after all?"

It intrigued Elizabeth, how Mr. Wickham deferred to Mr. Darcy. Mr. Darcy's wealth and connections had no power in their cramped room yet, as with the food, Mr. Wickham submitted to Mr. Darcy's will. It was almost as if Mr. Wickham respected him, perhaps was even a little in awe of him.

"Certainly," Mr. Darcy said without a hint of rancor or smugness.

Mr. Wickham rose and began to pace. Shooting a glance at the lower bunk, he made a show of turning the same way each time. Elizabeth lay back. She wasn't tired but had no desire to watch him.

"Tell me, Miss Elizabeth," Mr. Darcy's voice came from below. "What book have you most recently finished?"

Before their abduction, in view of his treatment of Jane and the extremely insulting nature of his proposal, Elizabeth would have answered in clipped, uninviting tones. Now, she willingly launched into a discussion of Anna Maria Porter's Ballad Romances, and other Poems. As they spoke, Mr. Darcy drawing out her thoughts through careful questions, she realized much of her resentment toward him was seeping away and not simply because of their enforced confinement. Regardless of how unfeelingly he'd spoken to her the day of their abduction, since their imprisonment, he was always gracious.

After they momentarily exhausted their interest in Ballad Romances, and other Poems, during which Mr. Wickham retook his bunk, Mr. Darcy spoke about a book by Richard Hoare. Mr. Wickham declined to make a positive contribution to this exchange but sometimes made negative comments. After a time, they both took to ignoring him.

"And before Ballad Romances, and other Poems?" Mr. Darcy asked once he was done describing Richard Hoare's The Ancient History of South Wiltshire.

Mr. Wickham groaned. "No more books. I shall shoot myself with Darcy's imaginary pistol."

Elizabeth frowned. She was beginning to take exception to Mr. Wickham's grumbling. They were all trapped there, not only him. What had happened to the amiable, carefree young man in a red coat who'd danced with every woman at every assembly?

"Would you care to suggest a topic?" Mr. Darcy asked, tone polite, from where he now stood looking out the small window.

"Yes. I suggest not books," Mr. Wickham muttered.

Taking in Mr. Darcy's profile at the window, Elizabeth's mind went to her earlier thoughts when she'd gazed across that endless sea. "Who do you think is missing you most, Mr. Darcy? And would continue to do so, if…" She trailed off. She hadn't meant to be so grim.

He was silent for long enough that she didn't know if he would reply. Books were one thing. The aloof, private Mr. Darcy was likely much more loath to speak of his family. She tried to read his expression but what little she could see of his face was painted dark by the light without.

"My sister, Georgianna," he finally said, tone stiff. Tension rippled across his broad shoulders.

Below, Elizabeth heard Mr. Wickham shift, but he remained silent.

Mr. Darcy cleared his throat. "Richard, that is Colonel Fitzwilliam," he continued in more normal tones. "My staff at Pemberley and in London. Richard's older brother and his wife." He went on to name several other people. Oddly, his list didn't include Mr. Bingley and Miss Bingley or his aunt.

Elizabeth was surprised by how many people Mr. Darcy named. She thought him too haughty and cold to have that many people care about him and his whereabouts. Thinking he might be exaggerating to impress her, she asked him about them. Her goal was to catch him in his ignorance of these people. To her surprise, he answered readily enough, showing a great deal of knowledge about each. She briefly wondered if he was making things up. Twice, Mr. Wickham argued with Mr. Darcy about some fact, but both times he backed down when Mr. Darcy gave more details.

Finally, though Mr. Darcy hadn't included Mr. Bingley, Elizabeth could no longer contain her need to touch on the subject. "You didn't mention the Bingleys. Surely, they must miss you. You seemed quite friendly with them last autumn when you resided with them at

Netherfield Park."

"Bingley would miss me, but he has so many friends that I don't think my disappearance would have any lasting impact on his life." Mr. Darcy spoke without a hint of rancor. "Miss Bingley would look for another rich, well-connected man to pursue, but I doubt my disappearance would touch her heart."

"At least you know your wealth and connections are all they want you for," Mr. Wickham said. "It would be pathetic if you were deluded into thinking they actually like you."

"I don't think hurling insults is profitable," Elizabeth snapped, affronted on Mr. Darcy's behalf.

"I agree," Mr. Darcy said, almost absently. He turned from the window to face Elizabeth and folded his arms across his chest as he leaned against the frame. "Aside from your family, who would miss you?"

"Charlotte," Elizabeth said without hesitation. "That is, Mrs. Collins. After all, I was her guest. But ignoring that, we've been good friends for years."

"Mr. Collins?" Darcy suggested.

"That would depend on Lady Catherine's reaction." Elizabeth offered a wry quirk of her mouth to soften the words. "If she is upset, he will be also. How would she react to your disappearance? I noticed you did not mention her."

"She cares about me for two, no three, reasons," he said. "One, as her nephew. Two, she likes that someone actually visits her. She really doesn't have many visitors."

"I wonder why," Mr. Wickham said sardonically.

"Mainly," Mr. Darcy continued without so much as a glance at the lower bunk, "she considers me a potential husband for Anne. Since neither Anne nor I wish the marriage and my mother only suggested it as a passing fancy, I'm not certain how she became so set on it."

"Every woman wants Darcy for their daughter or themselves," Mr. Wickham said with added sarcasm. "That's well known."

"Not every woman." Mr. Darcy's tone was soft. His gaze, still meeting Elizabeth's, held regret. "Not even every woman with less money or worse connections."

Mr. Wickham snorted. "Find me one such woman in all of England, and I'll swear never to cheat at cards again."

Elizabeth's face heated. She angled it toward the ceiling. Hopefully, in the dim light that reached the upper bunk at that time of day, Mr. Darcy couldn't see the red she knew stained her cheeks.

Chapter Eight

A few days later the sea was no longer calm. Instead, the waters, an icy gray, roiled. Swells crested in frothing white spray. The sky went dark and filled with pounding rain, melding horizon and ocean into one. The ship lurched and bucked. Loud, ominous creaks and moans assailed Elizabeth's ears, growing in frequency and magnitude until she felt the urge to scream. She clung to her bunk, afraid to be tossed out but equally afraid to climb down.

Mr. Darcy pulled himself up from his seat on the floor, under the window. Spray sparkled in his dark hair. Instead of closing the shutter as she expected, he moved to the door.

He stood for a moment, seeming to gage his balance. He leaned back, lifted a booted foot and slammed it into the door. A moment later, he kicked again.

"What are you doing?" Mr. Wickham sat up in his bunk, looking to Mr. Darcy. "If we leave this room, they'll shoot us."

"Not if they're too busy trying to keep afloat." Mr. Darcy kicked a third time. "This may be our only chance to escape." He kept kicking.

Elizabeth didn't know how long she clung to the bunk, gaze riveted to Mr. Darcy's progress. Sometimes, the ship lurched so hard Mr. Darcy was flung sideways and had to reach for the wall to remain standing, but he always returned to kicking. Panic welled in her. The door still stood.

"You'll never break that down," Mr. Wickham predicted.

Elizabeth wondered again if he was actually in league with their kidnappers. She leaned over the edge of the precariously swaying bunk. "Get up," she cried at Mr. Wickham. "Help him."

Mr. Wickham turned a contemplative look on her. Finally, he shrugged and stood. He moved to Darcy's side.

At first, their kicks weren't coordinated. Elizabeth also noticed Wickham's were notably softer than Mr. Darcy's. By design or lack of strength, she didn't know.

A loud grinding sound vibrated through the ship's frame. They lurched hard enough that Elizabeth nearly lost hold of the bunk. The vessel trembled, then seemed to drop in the water.

"We have to get out of here," Mr. Darcy barked. "Kick with me, George."

"Right," Mr. Wickham said, a touch of panic in his voice.

"One, two, three," Mr. Darcy ordered.

Mr. Wickham's kick hit a second behind Mr. Darcy's. Mr. Darcy shot him an annoyed look and counted down again. They kicked. The door cracked. Elizabeth's heart lurched with hope. The two men exchanged a look and kicked again and again.

The door flew open. The ship tipped sideways. Both men tumbled to the deck. Mr. Darcy was on his feet immediately. He stepped over Mr. Wickham and extended both hands to her.

Elizabeth had to pry numb fingers from the wood of the bunk. When she sat up, he reached for her and swung her down. His hands were warm and strong. He steadied her and grabbed her hand, which shook. Elizabeth sucked in a calming breath.

"Come," Mr. Darcy said and pulled her toward the door.

The wood of the door hadn't splintered, she realized as Mr. Wickham scuttled out of their way. The hinges and part of the mechanism for securing the bar had come free. As she and Mr. Darcy crossed the room, Mr. Wickham used the bunks to pull to his feet.

They stepped into the hall to find the one Wickham had labeled as Tom and one of the Jonesys, pistols pointed their way. Mr. Darcy yanked Elizabeth behind him. Mr. Wickham stuck his head out the door, yelped and jumped back inside the room.

"Get back in there," Tom yelled.

"I think not." Mr. Darcy released her arm, dipped, grabbed the bar that had locked their door and stood again before Elizabeth could blink.

"We'll shoot," Tom said.

The ship lurched. A pistol shot rang out. Elizabeth stifled a scream. Histrionics would do no good and might make Mr. Darcy pay attention to her, rather than their kidnappers.

Mr. Darcy rushed forward. The Jonesy aimed his pistol as the ship seemed almost to drop. An ear-splitting crack, wood tearing, ricocheted through the corridor, louder than a pistol report. The ship pitched forward.

Bereft of Mr. Darcy's support, Elizabeth splayed her arms wide. She tumbled to the deck, one palm raking down a wall. In the room, she heard Mr. Wickham hit the floor with a livid curse. Beyond Mr. Darcy, limbs flailed as their abductors tumbled. Water sloshed into the hallway.

Another shot sounded. Heart in her throat, Elizabeth struggled to her feet as Mr. Darcy, the only one who hadn't fallen, rushed forward. He raised the wooden bar. Both men cowered. Makeshift weapon at the ready, Mr. Darcy kicked their spent pistols down the hall. He turned back, his gaze instantly finding her. Switching the wooden bar to his off hand, he held out his other to her. Elizabeth rushed forward to take it.

Mr. Darcy pinned the cowering, stunned-looking men with a hard glare as he helped her over splayed limbs. He hefted the wooden bar. "Move and I'll do my best to knock you unconscious, which I doubt you want to be if this ship is going down."

"Hit them anyhow," Mr. Wickham called out. "They'll only follow us."

Mr. Darcy didn't look back as he pulled Elizabeth with him toward the narrow staircase. Mary, unarmed, materialized out of the driving rain slashing across the sky visible at the top of the steps. Her expression moved from stunned to a caricature of relief.

"Thank God," she cried, water streaming down her face. "We're hung up on something under the waves and the sea is tearing this ship apart. I was coming to release you."

She moved back from the staircase as Darcy and Elizabeth hurried up through the torrent of water coursing down the steps. Already, Elizabeth's hem was soaked, most of her gown wet with rain and spray.

Mary pointed. "Shore is that way. Good luck." She pulled her dress over her head and tossed the garment to the deck, Elizabeth gaped in shock. Not looking back, Mary ran to the gate Elizabeth had come through to board the ship. A moment later she was gone from sight over the side.

Elizabeth turned back to Mr. Darcy. "I don't know how to swim," she cried, trying to keep panic from her voice.

Behind them, men moved. Wickham? Their abductors? She didn't know. Mr. Darcy pulled her to the rail where Mary had gone over. A glance showed the ladder smashed, fragments hanging from the side. Elizabeth cast a desperate look toward the rowboat.

Across the ship, Jeb was trying to lower the little vessel. Elizabeth was aware of Tom and The Jonesy scrambling up from below. They headed toward Jeb. Odds were, none of them could swim either.

Elizabeth turned back to Mr. Darcy, panic threatening. "I can't swim," she repeated.

A wave crashed against the ship, drawing her gaze downward. The water, not so far below as she'd feared, looked cold and angry. Rain pelted them. Through it, the shore was an indistinct haze. Elizabeth cast Mr. Darcy another anxious look. She'd never considered fleeing a sinking ship. The plan had been the rowboat.

Hands braced against the rail, she glanced over her shoulder. Over the surf and pounding rain, she could hardly hear the men who argued by the rowboat. They looked near to blows. She turned back, movement at her side drawing her attention.

Mr. Darcy removed his coat and dropped it to the deck. He pulled off a boot, then the other and shoved his socks inside. Elizabeth watched in surprise as, one at a time, he heaved his boots toward shore, putting the whole of his body into the effort. Rain made it difficult to judge but the arc of the boots showed shore wasn't as far as she'd feared. Both boots landed among the rocks there.

Mr. Darcy turned to her. "We'll jump here. Hold your breath when you leave the deck."

Though she'd prefer not to look, Elizabeth's gaze was once again drawn to the dark churning water. The ship shuddered, battered by water from all angles. She swallowed hard. "I'll drown."

Warm hands clasped her shoulders. With firm pressure, Mr. Darcy turned her to face him. "I won't let you drown." He locked gazes with her. "Keep your mouth closed when you hit the water. It's cold. You'll want to gasp. Don't. You'll go under. I'll come after you, even if we get separated. When I find you, wrap your arms about me. Do you understand?"

Elizabeth realized she shook even more than the rapidly crumbling vessel. She repeated Mr. Darcy's instructions in her head. Jump, don't gasp, hold her breath, grab him. Breath shallow, she nodded. "I understand."

He offered a tight smile. "Miss Bennet, do you believe I would ever lie to you?"

Elizabeth blinked, taken by surprise. "No. Never."

"Good." He squeezed her shoulders. "Then believe me when I say that if you do as I've instructed, we'll make it to shore." He released her and proffered a hand.

Elizabeth took it. Oddly, her shaking was gone. Mr. Darcy led her to the opening where Mary had jumped. Elizabeth clung to his hand as he positioned himself beside her, attention on the sea. Each grasping the rail with one hand, they slid their feet to the edge of the deck.

Wind and rain buffeted Elizabeth. She was already soaked through. Behind her, she could hear their captors still arguing over the rowboat. The ship pitched with the waves but listed to one side terribly. It was clearly lodged on something below the surf.

"Take several deep, rapid breaths," he said. "Ready?"

She nodded but couldn't wrench her gaze from the churning sea to look at him. Beside her, she heard him take his own advice and did her best to do likewise.

"One, two," he counted. His grip on her hand tightened. "Jump."

Elizabeth leapt with him. She squeezed not only her mouth but her eyes tight closed.

Ice cold water slammed into her. Her skirt billowed up to surround her, capture her. She plummeted downward. Panic constricted her chest.

Mr. Darcy's hand tugged hers, pulled her upward. Her head burst through the waves. Her hands, feet and nose already felt numb. Beside her, Mr. Darcy treaded water, his movements encumbered by his grip on her.

"Wrap your arms around me," he shouted, barely heard over the rain and surf.

Elizabeth gasped for air. Her nose and mouth kept dipping below the waves. She tried to kick, but her skirt twined about her.

Mr. Darcy pulled her against him. Somehow, kicking all the while, he got her arms about him. He brought her hands together. "Hold on. I need my arms free to swim."

Elizabeth released his hand to clasp her own. She half lay across Mr. Darcy's back. He set off toward shore with powerful strokes. She tried to keep her body angled away from his, to give him room to kick. She knew she hindered him but could think of no way to help. They were making progress toward shore, but the water bled warmth from her. She could only assume the ocean numbed Mr. Darcy as well.

After what was probably a very brief swim but seemed like a lifetime, he pulled her arms apart and held her up. "I can touch bottom," he said. "Hang onto my neck."

Elizabeth twined her arms about his neck. His came up to wrap about her, holding her higher so her head was on level with his. Though the water was shallow enough for him to walk, he still jumped with every wave. Elizabeth clung to him as if her life depended on it which, she

81

reflected, it likely did. Already, the frigid water had sapped most of her strength.

Soon, Mr. Darcy didn't have to jump any longer. The rain lightened, and a rocky shore came into focus. Beyond, large, jumbled stones piled against a low cliff face. Elizabeth spotted movement near the top and realized Mary had reached the headland. The one-time maid didn't look back as she struck off inland to disappear into the rain and fog. Elizabeth guessed the whole ordeal had likely taken less than ten minutes.

"Miss Bennet." Mr. Darcy's calm tone reached her through rain, surf and the numbness that infused her limbs. "Miss Bennet, I'm going to put you down. You can reach the bottom now."

Elizabeth turned from scrutinizing the shore to look at him. His bearded face was mere inches from hers. His dark eyes shone with concern. For her, a woman who'd berated, decried and refused him.

It dawned on her that he held her. Her arms were wrapped about him. The heat that infused her went a long way toward reinvigorating her cold limbs. With him so near, he must see the pink that suffused her cheeks, even though roiling dark clouds blotted out the sun. She yanked her arms from about him.

He set her down. She could, indeed, stand. She didn't even need to jump, as he had at first. He could have set her down sooner. She wished he hadn't set her down at all. Resisting the urge to cling to him for support against the buffeting waves, Elizabeth tried to gather her cumbersome skirt. She marched toward shore.

Her progress was slow. Her wet clothing weighed her down. Every so often, a larger wave came, and she did have to jump. Mr. Darcy stayed beside her. Whenever she faltered, his arm wrapped about her shoulder to keep her on her feet. Without him, she would never have made it to land.

Finally, she stood on the rock-strewn beach. She resisted the urge to collapse to the ground. Breath ragged, she looked about, attempting to take some stock of their location.

"You'll be well here for a short while?" Mr. Darcy asked, tone urgent.

Elizabeth nodded. She turned to watch with a confused, mild surge of panic as he headed back out into the water. It took her only a moment to realize he was going back for Mr. Wickham, who disappeared beneath the surface but popped up a moment later, only to sink again.

Elizabeth watched for several horrified seconds, then resolutely turned her back. She noted one of Mr. Darcy's boots and went to claim it, then found the other. A quick peek showed Mr. Darcy had reached Mr. Wickham.

Back to the ocean, Elizabeth started to wring out her skirt, though the effort felt futile in the rain. Anything was better than watching the two men swim, her heart in her throat with every approaching wave. If Mr. Darcy faltered, if he couldn't make this second journey to shore while assisting another, she would have no recourse. No way to help him. She'd have to stand on the shore and watch him drown. A tremor went through her at the thought. She concentrated harder on her skirt.

Finally, the two men reached shore. Mr. Wickham walked with a limp, wincing at every step. He sank down onto a large rock. Mr. Darcy knelt to examine his leg. Elizabeth hurried toward them. Mr. Darcy removed his cravat and wound it around Mr. Wickham's left knee. Bright red blood seeped through the white cloth.

Beyond them, Elizabeth spotted the bobbing rowboat, capsized. A head appeared above the waves and moved toward it, then disappeared again. A tearing crash sounded out, louder than the waves. Elizabeth looked to see the ship splinter and collapse into the surf. A body popped to the surface between the ship and the shore. She couldn't see the swimmer or the rowboat anymore. She shuddered and came to a halt at Mr. Darcy's shoulder.

Mr. Wickham, face set in lines of pain, looked up at her. "Did any of the smugglers escape?"

"At least one didn't," she said, unable to suppress another shudder.

Mr. Darcy glanced up from his work to take in her expression, then looked toward the sea. He shook his head.

"Mary made it, though," Elizabeth continued, not permitting a tremble to mar her tone. "She went that way," she added, pointing.

"So at least one smuggler made it to land," Mr. Wickham observed.

Elizabeth had the urge to comment that Mr. Wickham was a smuggler and was on land but refrained from doing so.

Mr. Darcy finished tying his cravat around Mr. Wickham's leg and stood. "Let's not wait around to see if any more survived." He offered Elizabeth his arm. "Miss Bennet?"

Elizabeth placed a hand on his shirt sleeve, which clung wet and transparent to his skin. His vest and breeches were similarly soaked, but the material thicker and dark. Though modesty before these two men was long since lost to her, Elizabeth took a moment to offer thanks that she hadn't been wearing anything flimsy and white at the time of her abduction, but rather older, heavier garments against the parsonage's chill.

As Mr. Darcy helped her climb the rain-slicked rocks to the top of the cliff, she had occasion to wonder if a light muslin, while immodest, would have been preferable. The wool she wore weighed her down and would likely take days to dry. Mr. Darcy made no comment as he patiently assisted her along the rock-strewn beach. Behind them, Mr. Wickham muttered curses while he climbed.

When they reached the top of the low cliff, Mr. Darcy again offered his arm. He led them inland, but at an angle to Fiona's route. Elizabeth was grateful for his continued assistance because the going was rugged, and her clothing felt heavier with each step.

After what Elizabeth guessed to be nearly an hour, they found a small stream. After drinking, Mr. Wickham sat down and rested, only reluctantly coming to his feet when Elizabeth and Mr. Darcy were ready. Mr. Wickham lagged behind them even though Mr. Darcy kept the pace slow. The rain turned into a drizzle and then stopped, but Elizabeth's clothing was so wet it hardly mattered. Meek sunlight behind the clouds gradually faded into dusk.

With the lowering light, it began to loom in Elizabeth's awareness that she would be required to spend the night out of doors and in the company of the two men. She tried to press the thought from her mind. It wasn't as if she hadn't been sleeping in the same cabin with them and her reputation wasn't already ruined. After tonight, though, it would be well and truly in tatters, and there was nothing, not a single thing, Elizabeth could think to do about it.

Chapter Nine

Elizabeth walked through the failing light at the end of the day in a haze of cold and weariness. Her only goal was to place each next step. Her lone solace was the strength of the arm she leaned on. Mr. Darcy's arm.

Mr. Darcy stopped. Elizabeth swayed on her feet. She looked about. Dusky orange and rose streaks stained the western horizon. Soon, it would be full dark.

"That grove will have to do," Mr. Darcy said, pointing.

Elizabeth followed the gesture toward a gathering of pines. She realized the evergreens were the first real stand of trees they'd seen.

Mr. Wickham caught up to them. As soon as he did, Mr. Darcy turned them and set out toward the grove. Mr. Wickham let out a beleaguered sigh and followed.

"That grove will do for what?" Elizabeth asked warily, though she knew the answer.

"To sleep in," Mr. Darcy replied.

Elizabeth could all but feel the tattered remains of her reputation fall away.

"It's about time you picked a place to stop," Mr. Wickham whined, as if they'd been passing places up and not only now found one. "My leg is throbbing. I must have lost a lot of blood, because I'm weak."

"You didn't lose much blood," Mr. Darcy said without looking back. "If you really had lost blood, you would have drunk more water. I wrapped your wound as a precaution. It's merely a scratch."

"So says the great Darcy," Mr. Wickham muttered. "I'm telling you, I've lost blood. I'm weak."

"You are weak because you spent your time lying in bed," Mr. Darcy snapped.

"What else was there to do?" Mr. Wickham asked as they reached the grove.

Mr. Darcy pushed through the heavy branches, holding them aside for Elizabeth. He kept going, Elizabeth on his heels, until they reached a small open space. Behind them, Mr. Wickham crashed about, cursing again.

Mr. Darcy looked around the small clearing, expression dubious. "It's the best we've found," he said, almost as if arguing with himself. "It's nearly dark. We risk injury in these craggy hills."

Elizabeth turned to look up at his face. It was, indeed, nearly dark, and dimmer still within the shelter of the pines. She shivered from cold but hadn't the energy to suppress the trembling. She lightly touched his shirtsleeve, dry now, unlike her dress. He looked down at her, expression questioning.

"I don't know how to thank you for saving my life," Elizabeth said. "You have my heartfelt gratitude."

"You can thank me by forgetting it," Mr. Darcy replied. "It's what any gentleman would have done."

Mr. Wickham pressed through the boughs into the clearing. "Consider it forgotten already. In exchange, I'll go ahead and forget you banged my leg against a rock when you were pulling me ashore."

Mr. Darcy turned to him. "I wouldn't have had to pull you if you'd been smart enough to remove your boots before jumping in. Besides which, in your case, I want you to remember that I saved you for the rest of your life. In the future, I would appreciate your gratitude instead of antagonism, and my choice was to bring you ashore or not. I wasn't going to clear a path for you."

"I doubt Mr. Darcy went out of his way to bang you against the rocks," Elizabeth said dryly. "He saved us both and we should both be grateful." Especially since, by refusing his proposal in angry terms, she'd given Mr. Darcy every reason to believe in her antagonism. He'd risked his life to save her. It would have been far easier for him to swim ashore without her.

"Because he's the great and gallant Fitzwilliam Darcy and you are a pretty miss in distress, he doesn't want your gratitude." Mr. Wickham's tone dripped sarcasm. "Well, you were a pretty miss. Now you look bedraggled."

Elizabeth realized Mr. Darcy's gallantry applied both to saving her and saving Mr. Wickham. Mr. Wickham certainly wasn't gallant. She was glad Mr. Darcy didn't defend her appearance. She was bedraggled. All three of them were. Looking at her companions, she was glad she didn't have a mirror.

"Assisting Miss Bennet was in no way a trial," Mr. Darcy countered. He turned eyes on Mr. Wickham that, even in the dim light, glinted with a notable disdain. "Rescuing you, on the other hand, was difficult. Mostly because a part of me wished to let you drown. Then you would be out of my life completely."

Elizabeth stifled a gasp at that heartfelt declaration. She hadn't realized quite how deep Mr. Darcy's dislike for Mr. Wickham ran.

Mr. Wickham smirked. "No, I wouldn't. If you'd let me drown, your father's ghost would haunt you. After all, I was his favorite." His tone taunted. "Besides, I'm here because of you. If I'd agreed to help kidnap you, they wouldn't have imprisoned me."

Mr. Darcy's look molded into disgust, but he smoothed his expression and refocused on Elizabeth. "We need each other's warmth, so we will huddle together to sleep," he said, voice touched with apology. "Miss Bennet, as your garments are still quite damp, I suggest you be in the center. Both of us will have our backs to you for propriety."

Elizabeth's face heated but she nodded. "Thank you."

With no food, water or light, there was little else to do but arrange themselves for sleep. Soon, Elizabeth settled onto a somewhat soft bed of deeply-piled pine needles. She tried not to think about what might be crawling in them as she lay down, each of the men taking a place beside her. Though the last light to reach into their enclosure was gone, preventing sight, she could all but feel Mr. Wickham's smirk and Mr. Darcy's cool aura of propriety.

Elizabeth chose to face Mr. Darcy's broad back. It took a long time for the other two to add warmth to her. While she shivered, she considered the two men she found herself with.

She'd once thought Mr. Wickham quite attractive. Charming, entertaining. Now, he was repugnant. His actions were those of a coward and ne'er-do-well. Shame that she'd ever been too dazzled by his outward charms to see the truth of him scalded her.

A large part of her dislike for Mr. Darcy had been founded on his treatment of Mr. Wickham. After watching the two interact, she could only surmise there was more to that story than Mr. Wickham let on, if, indeed, any of it was true. Mr. Darcy, who had seemed so aloof and rude initially, had so far evidenced exemplary behavior in their time of crisis. Why, he was quite gallant indeed. The Mr. Darcy she now knew would never have arbitrarily taken a living from Mr. Wickham.

A smile stretched her lips, the motion one exercise she hadn't been pursuing while captive. Mr. Wickham had meant to taunt but his words were apropos. Mr. Darcy was great and gallant, Mr. Wickham's sarcasm notwithstanding. Elizabeth drifted off to sleep with her forehead pressed against his broad back.

In the morning, her clothing was still damp, but only slightly so. She rose stiff, aching and bedecked in a flaking film of salt. Based on Mr. Wickham's appearance and complaints, he found himself similarly afflicted. Mr. Darcy, looking somewhat scruffy in his shirtsleeves, vest and beard, set a slow pace. Elizabeth was unsure if that was out of deference to her, Mr. Wickham's or Mr. Darcy's own tired muscles.

After a short time, during which Mr. Wickham filled what might have been a pleasant enough morning with continued complaints, they drew in sight of a cottage. Mr. Darcy halted. He turned first to Elizabeth, then Mr. Wickham.

"I believe we're in Scotland," Mr. Darcy said. "Do you both concur?"

"I did think, if we got turned about at some point, we might be in Europe, possibly Belgium or nearby," Elizabeth ventured. "In both cases, the shore faces west. Based on sunset last night and sunrise today, we've been headed west and south, all without again reaching the sea, which suggest Scotland."

Mr. Darcy shook his head with a frown. "Depending on where we wrecked, we could travel west and south across the continent for a time and not reach the sea. It's not as if the shoreline runs north and south without deviation." He turned a questioning look on Mr. Wickham. "George? Any ideas? We'll get a very different welcome in Napoleon controlled Europe than Scotland."

"How the devil should I know where we are?" Mr. Wickham muttered.

Mr. Darcy's lids dropped closed over a flash of anger. When he opened them again, he appeared calm. "We were headed north for most of our journey on the ship, but we could have gotten turned around the night before the storm. It was too cloudy to judge our direction on the day we wrecked. At least, not through that little window." He turned to Mr. Wickham once more. "You must have some idea where they were headed."

Mr. Wickham shrugged, expression annoyed. "I told you, all I know is that they eventually planned to go to Ireland."

"But Ireland makes no sense," Elizabeth protested. "We were on the eastern coast. They should have gone south if Ireland was their goal."

"They wished to avoid the channel," Mr. Wickham said.

"Because of the war?" Elizabeth asked.

"No. They'd already made the journey several times to collect brandy." Mr. Wickham scratched at his head. "They were complaining that the patrols were onto them, had a description of the boat. The channel would have been too risky. That's why they turned to kidnapping."

"You didn't feel the need to share that information earlier?" Mr. Darcy said.

Mr. Wickham shrugged. "It didn't seem important."

"That explains why we would go north to reach Ireland," Elizabeth put in, trying to head off an argument. "If this is Scotland, we're lucky they were forced to go north and that a storm came up."

Mr. Darcy frowned. "The storm accounts somewhat for wrecking the ship but why even take her so near land? Especially in precarious weather."

"They were incompetent sailors, so they liked to hug the coast," Mr. Wickham said. "I believe there used to be several competent seamen but after the boat's owner died, anyone who didn't want to turn smuggler jumped ship. They felt their skills were better served being honest."

"Not a bad lesson to take," Mr. Darcy said with a pointed look at Mr. Wickham.

"I don't have any skills. None that are profitable, at any rate," Mr. Wickham said, rather smugly. "You can blame your father for that."

Elizabeth raised her eyebrows, wondering what that meant.

"You can read and write," Mr. Darcy said. "You're an excellent horseman and can do everything to take care of horses except what a farrier does. You can--"

"Yes, I can shovel manure with the best of them," Mr. Wickham interrupted.

"You went to Cambridge, man," Mr. Darcy continued. "You can do arithmetic and keep accounts. Even if you find that work tedious, you're strong and--"

"Which might earn me a shilling a day, if I'm lucky," Mr. Wickham interrupted again. "Do you want to try living on a shilling a day?"

"I don't have to," Mr. Darcy snapped. "Neither would you if you'd invested the money you took for the living."

Elizabeth watched them glare at each other, eyebrows still raised.

What living? The living Mr. Wickham told her that Mr. Darcy had denied him? Mr. Wickham had taken money for it? That certainly wasn't how he'd told the story.

Elizabeth shook her head. Now was definitely not the time for them to argue over past wrongs. She stepped between them. "So, we're agreed that we're likely in Scotland," she stated. "With a very slight chance of the continent, which would be unfortunate to say the least."

Mr. Darcy pulled his glower from Mr. Wickham. Lines of anger smoothed from his face as he regarded her. "Correct."

Elizabeth gestured toward the cottage. "Should we hide from people until we know for sure or risk asking for help?"

"I would have had eight shillings a day," Mr. Wickham snapped, still angry and still glaring at Mr. Darcy. "You couldn't live on that much, either. What do you have? Five or six hundred shillings a day?"

"I couldn't have come up with those numbers on the spot," Mr. Darcy said, tone light. "Not in my head. Pickering would have been proud of you."

Though she'd no idea who Pickering was, Elizabeth fought down the urge to reprimand the two men. She was salt-caked, hungry, thirsty and possibly in territory loyal to Napoleon. Her companions felt now was the moment to bicker?

Mr. Wickham's hostility waned, replaced by question. "Pickering would have been? Did he die?"

Mr. Darcy nodded. "Last autumn."

"I'm sorry." Mr. Wickham actually sounded sincere.

"He spoke of you," Mr. Darcy offered.

"What did he say? That I am a good-for-nothing waste of your father's coin and goodwill?"

Mr. Darcy shook his head. "He said you could have been a brilliant scholar, if you'd worked at it."

Mr. Wickham sneered. "There you go again, harping on the fact that I don't work hard. You don't work hard."

Mr. Darcy opened his mouth to speak. He snapped it closed again and glared at Mr. Wickham.

Elizabeth rolled her eyes heavenward. "Shall we try the cottage? At least get some idea of where we are?"

"Perhaps just one of us should go." Mr. Wickham's expression grew sly. "I nominate Darcy. He speaks French. He might be better at communicating if we're in territory loyal to Napoleon."

"I speak some French," Mr. Darcy said. "Not enough for anyone to think I'm a native. If we found a priest, I might communicate pretty well in Latin."

Elizabeth frowned at the cottage for a moment. She looked Mr. Darcy and Mr. Wickham over. Mr. Wickham still had a coat and cravat, but Mr. Darcy was in shirt sleeves and a vest. They both had short beards. "I think if a woman is with you, you'll seem more innocuous." Though she was probably quite the sight herself. Anything else aside, she could tell her dark locks were one giant salt-dusted tangle.

Mr. Darcy's gaze traversed her features. Elizabeth squared her shoulders and fought down a blush. She'd assessed his appearance, after all. Turnabout was only fair. Mr. Wickham watched them both through narrowed eyes.

"You're probably right," Mr. Darcy finally said. "I think I should do the talking. As we're almost certainly in Scotland, I'll try English first. I don't know Gaelic." He gave Mr. Wickham a challenging look.

Mr. Wickham offered yet another shrug. "Feel free. When they get angry at your supercilious manner, you can let me talk next time."

A look of determination appeared on Mr. Darcy's face. "I will work hard not to offend."

Mr. Wickham snorted. "That will be hard work."

Elizabeth turned resolutely toward the cottage before another argument could break out. When she marched forward, Mr. Darcy immediately followed. A moment later, she heard Mr. Wickham's tread as he crossed the rocks behind them.

Mr. Darcy passed her, reaching the door before she could. He knocked. After a long moment, the door creaked open. A man with a surprising shock of red hair peered out. His gaze raked over Mr. Darcy and then Elizabeth, and past her. He frowned.

"I beg your pardon for intruding at this early hour," Mr. Darcy said. "We've been shipwrecked. May we enquire as to where we are?"

As soon as the man started his answer in a strong Sottish brogue, Elizabeth was sure they were in Scotland. She breathed a sigh of relief.

"May we know, then, where the nearest village or church is?" Mr. Darcy asked. "We're trying to return to England."

"Oh, aye, could tell you're English right enough," the man replied. He looked them over a second time. Again, he frowned at Mr. Wickham. His gaze returned to Elizabeth and took on a sympathetic cast. "Yea best come in and get warm by the fire, Missus. All of ya."

Elizabeth cast Mr. Darcy a quick look. Neither of them corrected the man's assumption she was married. The door opened wider and Mr. Darcy lead the way inside.

"Thank you very kindly," Elizabeth said.

There was no entryway, just a small room obviously used jointly for most every task but sleeping. From the outside, Elizabeth had already observed that the cot had but two rooms. No one else was about, no knitting, shawls or anything else to suggest the man didn't live alone.

"Always glad to help those in need," the man said. "You sit by the fire, Missus." He gestured to a lone chair.

"Your kindness does you credit, Mister…" Mr. Darcy's voice trailed off in question.

The man supplied his name.

Mr. Darcy repeated it and offered his hand, which the man shook.

Mr. Wickham looked about the small room with a slight frown. "Got anything to eat?"

"Oh, aye, been simmering gruel all morning."

Mr. Wickham wrinkled his nose.

"That would be lovely," Elizabeth asserted. She offered a warm smile. "Thank you for sharing with us."

"Oh, I don't mind, Missus." He turned to Mr. Darcy. "Prettiest lass I've seen in years. You're a lucky sort, aren't you?"

Elizabeth blushed and turned back toward the fire. She could feel Mr. Darcy's gaze on her. She resisted the urge to touch her hair, aware of just how not pretty she looked, which likely compounded the fact that Mr. Darcy didn't find her handsome.

She frowned. How odd that he'd proposed to her. For years, she's ignored suitors who were attracted only by her appearance, not knowing her at all. To think, a man had finally come along asking for her hand based on her personality and mind, and she'd refused him.

The cotter had to serve them in turns, having but one bowl and spoon. In between, he let them use his well. With no privacy, all Elizabeth could do was rinse her hands, face and hair, which she then did her best to comb out with her fingers and braid. Still, after drinking her fill, washing off at least some of the salt, and then eating her share of gruel, she felt much refreshed.

Mr. Darcy continued to ask questions, both polite and humble. He wasn't remotely supercilious. He expressed gratitude for the man's hospitality and didn't show any annoyance when the man's grasp of geography proved insufficient to pinpoint precisely how far they were from England. He simply thanked the cotter and obtained directions to the nearest village to the south. Before they left, Mr. Darcy once again asked for and repeated the man's name and location. Elizabeth had the distinct impression he planned to reward the cotter at some later date, a notion which pleased her.

It was more than an hour's walk to the next village. They approached the church, and Mr. Darcy was again the spokesman. Though the clergyman there was noticeably suspicious of them, the information they received was heartening. They were not so far north at all, where the geography would make returning to England difficult, but rather on the east coast of southern Scotland.

"May I request an additional boon?" Mr. Darcy asked the clergyman, who'd come out of his church rather than inviting them in.

The man frowned but nodded.

"If I could have but one sheet of paper and the use of ink and a pen--"

The man was shaking his head. "I've too little for myself to give out such costly items to passing vagrants," he said before Mr. Darcy could finish the request.

"I will see to it that you're repaid tenfold," Mr. Darcy said without a trace of stiffness, though Elizabeth knew it must have cut him to be called a vagrant.

Where he leaned against the outside wall of the church, Mr. Wickham smiled. Elizabeth stood with her hands clasped before her, her hair dry, once more, trying to appear refined and respectable.

The clergymen shook his head again. "Wait here." He closed the church door. Inside, a bar slid into place.

Mr. Darcy allowed a frown. Mr. Wickham chuckled. Elizabeth shot him a glare.

Moments later, the door reopened. The man held out half a loaf of bread. "Take this, so you won't go hungry." He pointed. "If it's England you're after, the road you want is that way. Follow that path. I don't expect to see you in these parts again, and I'll be telling my flock as much. We're not a wealthy parish. Nothing worth stealing here."

Mr. Darcy received the bread gravely. "Thank you for your kindness. May I ask how far it is to the next parish?"

"If you leave now and stay on the southern road, you'll be there by nightfall," the man said.

"Thank you," Mr. Darcy reiterated as the clergyman closed the church door in his face. He winced and turned to Elizabeth, bread held out. "Miss Bennet, if you would divide this, please, and hand out shares."

Elizabeth accepted the bread. While they walked, she divided it as equally as she could, keeping the smallest portion for herself. Before she could start eating, Mr. Darcy took her piece from her hand and replaced it with his. She was hungry enough not to protest.

They did reach the next church before nightfall, if just. The priest there was older. Not as trusting or helpful as the cotter, he still gave them a place to sleep in a barn and dinner but refused Mr. Darcy's request for writing supplies with the assertion they were too costly and too difficult to come by. As with the cotter, Mr. Darcy asked for the man's name and their location. As she drifted off to sleep, Elizabeth heard him repeating both, though not the name of the priest who hadn't let them into his church and had only provided half a loaf of bread.

Chapter Ten

regretted that he could not negotiate a bed for Elizabeth, only a place in a barn, but the meal they had was at least filling. In the morning, they were given gruel for breakfast and each handed a hunk of bread to carry with them. He carefully remembered the name of the church and the clergyman. Although not as generous as Darcy could have hoped, the man did ease their way. Darcy was determined to repay that charity.

Wickham's earlier prodding had only confirmed what Darcy realized as soon as he was ashore. Darcy would not be able to depend on his wealth and position. More than two week's growth of beard, combined with the absence of coat and cravat, eliminated any possibility of him looking like a gentleman. Even if he miraculously managed to wash his clothing and himself, there were tears in his pantlegs and vest. If they were in England, he might impress with his cultured accent, obviously of the upper class, but in this remote area of Scotland, the citizenry had little ear for nuances of English inflections. He'd briefly hoped the perfect fit of his clothing would demonstrate his wealth, until he realized his clothing was now loose on him.

Still, there was no point in bemoaning what he couldn't change. He had to accept reality and humbly beg for enough food to allow him to walk somewhere where he could get in touch with someone who would help him return. Who that was, and where, he hadn't decided yet. Matlock's holdings were nearest. No doubt, it would amuse his cousin to no end to have Darcy show up, George Wickham in tow, in such a complete state of disarray.

If Darcy could get off a letter, they could ask to remain at one of the churches for several days while help came to them. Unfortunately, the areas so far were too remote and poor for writing materials to be freely given to a group of what appeared to be vagabonds, no matter what assurances Darcy offered. It would amuse him, when this was over, to send stacks of paper and jars of ink, along with a note suggesting greater faith.

His greater concern by far, more than the distance to Matlock's or acquiring paper, was that he might prove unable to protect Elizabeth. She was a gently bred woman, likely unfamiliar with the dangers of the world. It was bad enough she must travel alone with two men. He couldn't spare her that, couldn't repair her reputation. Not without her accepting his proposal, which he resolved to reissue the moment they were safe.

It didn't help matters that one of the men Elizabeth must travel with was George Wickham. Wickham had tried to elope with Darcy's fifteen-year-old sister, Georgiana. Darcy couldn't quite convince himself Elizabeth was safe with a man who would do that. A man who would work to entrap a barely grown girl, all for her dowry, might attempt other unscrupulous acts.

He mulled over the idea while they walked. Casually, he stole the occasional glance at Wickham. It seemed to Darcy that George watched Elizabeth far too closely, far too often.

The next time they reached a stream and took turns freshening up, Darcy pulled Wickham aside. "You should know, I consider Miss Bennet to be under my protection."

Wickham cocked an eyebrow and grinned. "And I'm not?"

"No, you are not," Darcy snapped. "You deserve consideration as a companion on our travels but nothing more."

Wickham snorted. "I'll take that into consideration," he said and started to turn away.

Darcy stopped him with a hand on his arm. "If you harm Miss Bennet in any way, you will answer to me," he said softly.

The cockiness fled Wickham's face. He jerked his arm away. "Right. I understand."

Elizabeth reappeared, a cheerful smile turning up her perfect, bow-like lips. Darcy smoothed all harshness from his features.

"Shall we continue?" she asked, looking back and forth between them.

"Ask Darcy," Wickham muttered. "He seems to think he's in charge."

Darcy shot him a quelling look and offered Elizabeth his arm.

As they set out again, other worries crowded for Darcy's attention. It wasn't only present company that concerned him. His sister, Georgiana, was a tempting target as it was, but in his absence, fortune hunters might feel free to make a move. He hoped Richard would recognize this and look after her, but he suspected his cousin dedicated all his resources to locating Darcy. Although that thought brought some hope, Darcy knew there was no way Richard could guess he was in Scotland. In truth, as they'd been confined on a ship, even incompetently sailed as it was, their passage would have left little if any clues.

Then there were Darcy's holdings, his tenants, his estates. A hundred little details that might need his attention, might go overlooked without him there to see to them. His staff was competent and trustworthy, but for how long could they run things without him? How well would they bear up under the uncertainty of his return?

And then there was Wickham. Not as he affected Elizabeth but as a travel companion. He was having trouble keeping pace. It wasn't his leg wound, which was shallow and healing. In fact, he no longer limped, at least when he thought no one watched. His general laziness and recent inactivity while imprisoned were coming back to haunt him. It didn't help that they had inadequate food.

By midday, hours of travel remained until the next village. Darcy planned for them to reach it by nightfall. Reputedly even smaller than the town they'd sheltered in the evening before, he held little hope of writing materials but more for a warm, dry place for Elizabeth to sleep. That hope was born more of his recent practice in humbling himself than any knowledge of the village. He felt his skill in that area growing.

At bit past midday, they approached a lone building. Not, as Darcy first hoped, the next village, reached earlier than anticipated. Merely a roadside inn. A waystation for those traveling by coach or astride. As they had no money, they could hope for little more than use of the well, if the proprietor was tolerant.

"I'd like to step in," Wickham said, his pace picking up.

Darcy frowned. "Why bother?"

"Perhaps I can glean some information that might aid us."

"You mean, perhaps you can trick someone into buying you a drink," Darcy corrected.

Wickham grinned. "That as well, and it will go a sight better without you looming in the background, Darcy." He lengthened his stride further, heading toward the inn.

Darcy shrugged. He'd no need to inveigle someone to buy him ale. He would see about the well, though. Not that his opinion was the only one that mattered. He turned to Elizabeth. "Shall we try for use of the inn's well?"

She looked up at the sun, then back at the neat structure. "We may as well. It's nearly time for a rest anyhow."

While Wickham went through the front door, Darcy led Elizabeth toward the innyard. A surprisingly large and neat stable stood across the yard from the inn, a well between the two, right where Darcy had expected. A couple of blond and burly Scotsmen lounged on a low stone wall at the back of the yard. The men were similar enough in appearance to be brothers and unthreatening in demeanor, for all their height and bulk.

Darcy nodded in their direction. "May we beg the use of your well? We're simply passing by."

"Water's free," one said in a thick accent. "Help yerself."

Darcy crossed to the well, Elizabeth at his side, and drew up a bucket. He offered her use of it first, his reward a grateful smile.

"Thank you," she said. With cupped palms, she drank, then washed off her hands and face.

Darcy turned to the men. "Trough or ground?" he asked.

"Go ahead and dump it in the trough," one said. "With our thanks. One less bucket we've to draw."

After emptying the bucket in the horse trough, Darcy drew another. He mimicked Elizabeth's actions, then added the second bucket. Because the two men had been kind enough and as there was little else to do while they waited for Wickham, Darcy drew several more buckets and filled the trough. One of the Scotsmen tipped his hat in thanks. They both stood, went to the stable, and started leading horses out to drink. Darcy guessed they'd been lingering after lunch when he and Elizabeth arrived at the well.

"Do you suppose he's cajoled someone into buying him a drink yet?" Elizabeth asked in a low voice.

"Most likely," Darcy replied. He gestured to the vacated wall. "Would you care to sit while we wait?" He tamped down resentment that all he could offer her was a spot on a stone wall, when there was an inn with soft beds and food right beside them.

Elizabeth offered a quick smile. "That would be agreeable," she said and moved to the wall.

Darcy sat beside her. It was a lovely spring day, sunny and surprisingly warm for Scotland. Elizabeth had tanned slightly and now bore a smattering of freckles across her nose. He supposed most pure-blooded Englishmen, and especially genteel English women, would be appalled. Darcy felt she looked adorable. More beautiful than ever. It took daily restraint not to reissue his request for her hand.

She let out a small sigh, though her expression was pleasant. "It is nice to sit for a time."

"Are you able to continue today?" he asked. With her cheerful lack of complaint, he'd taken for granted that she didn't protest their endless walking. "I could try to negotiate a bed for you here." He looked about the yard. "Perhaps I could help in the stable, or--"

She raised a hand, cutting him off with a gentle chuckle. "I wouldn't dream of asking you to muck out a stable for my comfort, Mr. Darcy, but I'm very touched by the offer." Her gaze traversed the yard as well. "Besides, it looks as if this inn has plenty of help already. I daresay, even if we both offered to work, they wouldn't have enough for us to do that we could earn a room."

"I could inquire. I will if you're spent."

Elizabeth shook her head. Dark locks, curly and unruly, had slipped from her braid to frame her face. "Better to gain the next village. Perhaps, this time, we can get pen, ink and paper. That will serve us more than resting. Truly, I'm not that tired. I'm accustomed to walking. I enjoy the activity." She offered a slight grimace. "I will allow the salt water hasn't done my boots any favors, and that I wouldn't normally choose quite so much walking, but I'm perfectly well."

"You amaze me." The words were out of his mouth before he could stop them.

Pink rose in Elizabeth's cheeks. "To amaze you is no small feat, I warrant."

His lips twitched into a half smile. He didn't know if she could see it under his beard. "True enough, but I mean my words. We're in dire circumstance. We've been abducted, shipwrecked, and now wander Scotland, begging. Yet, you do not issue a single complaint. You cheerfully walk by my side every day. Most women would have collapsed in a fit of nerves and demanded to be left at the first church we came to while I continued on to find help." Which he would have protested, preferring Elizabeth by his side where he could look after her and, in truth, spend this time in her company.

Her cheeks still pink, she met is gaze. "And what of you? You have been similarly abused, though perhaps more so because you're accustomed to much more luxury than I, yet you bear up with fortitude and ease."

"No," he said softly. "You are in the worse strait." She looked up at him somewhat gravely. He could read the trust in her eyes. Perhaps he needn't wait until they were safe to issue his proposal. "I would muck out a hundred stables to have spared you this."

Her smile returned. "I believe I already declined your offer to make a stablehand of yourself on my behalf. Truly, the only thing I wish at this moment is for Mr. Wickham to reappear. I'm well rested and we've hours more to walk."

Darcy glanced in the direction of the sun. Wickham had been gone for an unreasonable time. "Let's see what we can do about that. I'll go in. You wait without in case he's caused any trouble."

They made their way to the front of the inn. Leaving Elizabeth on the porch, Darcy pressed the door open to a clear view of the common room. Wickham sat at a table spread with the remains of a meal and an empty flagon. There were a few other patrons as well, the general atmosphere clean and convivial, as the exterior suggested.

Darcy strode in. Aware that Elizabeth followed, despite his suggestion she wait without, the majority of Darcy's attention focused on Wickham and his nearly empty plate. A low anger simmered in Darcy's gut.

"How did you manage all that?" Anger made his whisper a growl.

Wickham looked up, grin cocky. "Would you believe through the kindness of strangers?"

"I would not."

Elizabeth came to stand beside Darcy. "You had money," she exclaimed. "All this time."

"In your boots," Darcy realized. He turned to Elizabeth. "I paid some of Mr. Wickham's debts. I saw the invoices. He had specially made boots. They contained compartments in which to hide money."

Elizabeth glared at Wickham. "How could you?"

"It wouldn't have helped before." Wickham's tone was defensive.

Darcy realized they garnered attention from others in the inn but couldn't keep the anger from his voice as he said, "We could have stayed at the first town. I could have written. My servants would have been there in a matter of days." Elizabeth could have had a bed, proper meals, a bath.

Wickham offered an infuriating shrug. "You wouldn't have paid me back enough."

"I'd have paid you double." Darcy left off the defamations crowding

100

the tip of his tongue. Wickham might still have money. Darcy didn't wish to antagonize him. Further.

Wickham's grin was sly, as if he followed Darcy's thoughts. "I'll give you the rest of my money if you pay me back a hundred-fold."

Darcy ground his teeth, considering the offer.

"No." Elizabeth's voice was firm. "I don't care if he has a shilling or twenty pounds. Better to put our fate in the hands of strangers then be indebted to him. We're not that desperate."

Wickham leaned back in his chair. He stretched his legs out under the table. "You're the one who should be desperate, Miss Bennet. Your reputation is in tatters." He looked Elizabeth over in a way that made Darcy's fists ball. "I'm willing to marry you, if Darcy gives you an appropriate dowry. I'll even accept his word on that. This is Scotland. It's easy to get married."

Elizabeth stared at him, expression stunned, but didn't speak. Darcy's fists balled tighter. He had to work to keep them at his sides.

"You know I'm attracted to you." Wickham's tone cajoled. "You're pretty, or at least you will be again when we get you cleaned up. Clever, too. You'd make me a good wife."

Enraged sputters issued from Elizabeth's mouth. She pressed her lips together, then parted them again. "I believe I already made myself clear. I wouldn't marry you if you were the last man in the world," she finally spat out.

Darcy's shoulders relaxed incrementally. A glance showed the entire patronage of the inn watched them now. The tension in his shoulders returned.

"You think you can do better? That Darcy will marry you?" Wickham gave a derisive chuckle. "At best, without me to negotiate for you, he'll give you a couple of hundred pounds and tell you to find a nice farmer to cozy up with. He'd never sully the Darcy line with a woman related to people in trade, much less one whose reputation is ruined, as yours certainly is." Wickham leaned forward, intent. "More than that, your family is totally unacceptable to any sensible man. Darcy is always sensible. Even if he was willing to accept them, his relatives never will." Wickham shrugged. "I don't have any relatives to object to them, or to you."

The back of Darcy's neck heated to hear Wickham list out the same objections he'd given Elizabeth. Had he sounded even half as pompous as Wickham made him out to be? No wonder she'd declined.

"Mr. Wickham." Elizabeth's voice was colder than the sea they'd dragged themselves from. "I have no notion what Mr. Darcy's plans are, nor expectations over them. My declaration that I would never, will never, even consider the idea of marriage to you, is founded entirely on my judgment of your character. You lie, cheat, smuggle and betray at every turn. You are indolent, feckless and unreliable. There is nothing about you, not a single miniscule detail, that recommends you to me."

A spark of elation shot through Darcy. "Miss Bennet," he said, "do you wish to continue to travel with Mr. Wickham?"

"No, I do not. Goodbye, Mr. Wickham," she said, words clipped. "Good luck on the rest of your journey." She turned on her heels and stalked out.

Darcy offered Wickham a hard smile. He followed Elizabeth without issuing a farewell, not being as generous.

Chapter Eleven

Trying to ignore how the scent of stew and bread permeating the inn made her stomach roil, Elizabeth strode from the inn, down the porch steps and back toward the road. Reaching the packed dirt they followed toward the next town, she set out at a brisker pace than they'd before employed. Mr. Darcy came alongside her and matched her stride.

Behind them, the sound of running footfalls pattered down the road. Surprised though she was that Mr. Wickham would choose to give chase, Elizabeth didn't slow or look back. He didn't relent, his huffing breath growing louder as he neared.

"Miss, Mister," a man's voice, not Mr. Wickham's and round with a Scottish accent, called out.

Elizabeth halted and turned back. Mr. Darcy, who hadn't stopped as quickly, reappeared at her shoulder. One of the two Scotsmen from the innyard was jogging up the roadway. Elizabeth quickly reordered her thoughts, realizing Mr. Wickham hadn't given chase after all.

"Miss, Mister," the man repeated as he reached them, the words a bit breathless. "My sister, the inn's cook, she overheard what you both said to that man in there." He held out a package wrapped in a greasy cloth. "She wants you to have this."

Mr. Darcy gingerly accepted the bundle. From the delicious odor, Elizabeth hoped it contained food. The man gave a quick nod and turned back away.

"Thank you," Mr. Darcy called toward the retreating form.

The Scotsman offered a wave but didn't slow his jog.

"What is it?" Elizabeth asked. Her stomach gave an audible rumble. A blush rose in her cheeks.

Giving no indication he'd heard her stomach, Mr. Darcy unwrapped the cloth. Inside were two baps, the soft rolls favored by the Scots, buttered and stuffed with their equally beloved fatty slabs of bacon. Nothing had ever looked or smelled so delicious to Elizabeth before. She reached for the one she deemed slightly smaller, though the two were near in size.

Mr. Darcy caught her hand.

Elizabeth looked up at him in surprise.

"Here," he said. He took the larger of the stuffed rolls and placed it in her hand.

"You should--" she began.

"Don't think I haven't noticed you shorting yourself," he said, interrupting her. He looked down at her, the slightest smile showing through his beard, his eyes warm. "You need to eat more."

The concern in both his eyes and tone brought a new flush to her cheeks. "Thank you," she murmured and, food in hand, turned toward the next town.

They set out at a slower pace, though Elizabeth didn't begin eating immediately, as Mr. Darcy did. A strange flutter filled her gut and stole her appetite. Mr. Darcy's hand had been warm on hers, his touch comforting. The way he looked at her, had noticed she'd been shorting herself... if she hadn't refused him so adamantly and insultingly, she could easily label him a man in love.

And that idea no longer alarmed her. Instead, it made her feel light, oddly giddy. She began to nibble on her meal, glancing at him askance as he finished his. He ate neatly and used a clean corner of the cloth to wipe his fingers. Despite some tears in his clothing, the residue of salt and rain, the dust of the road, he still stood tall. He moved with grace and assurance. His profile, impeccable, had grown so familiar during their time on the ship and their days of travel, and so dear. Elizabeth knew, should she reach for him, he would offer a strong arm on which to lean without hesitation.

It was, she realized, a singular pleasure to be there at his side, despite their circumstance. In fact, his calm and competent manner made her nearly forget they were in any straits at all. Yes, she recalled his insulting proposal, so recently reinvoked by Mr. Wickham. She also hadn't forgotten that Mr. Darcy had separated Jane from Mr. Bingley.

Now, though, neither point seemed as meaningful. Not in the face of what they'd endured, the time they'd spent together. Mr. Darcy's role in Jane's fate, especially, seemed less egregious. Certainly, he'd only done what he deemed best for his friend, Mr. Bingley. If she could make Mr. Darcy understand the depths of Jane's affections, he would change his mind about the union, despite the Bennet daughters' connection to trade and the behavior of some of her family members. Elizabeth was certain he would. After all, Mr. Bingley had connections in trade himself and was so amiable, he probably liked her family.

On top of that, how much blame could she even place on Mr. Darcy? He'd merely offered his advice to a friend, ill-conceived as that advice had been. Mr. Bingley was the one who'd acted. Fickle and faithless, he'd taken the opportunity to leave Jane. A true love wouldn't have been so easily sundered. Perhaps, inadvertently, Mr. Darcy had saved Jane a greater sorrow. Elizabeth wouldn't see her gentle, sweet sister wed to a man who didn't truly love her.

She put the last bite of bread and bacon in her mouth and chewed slowly. Once she swallowed, Mr. Darcy proffered another clean corner of the cloth, larger than the corner he'd used. Elizabeth wiped her fingers, trying to avoid the grease-soaked center. When she was done, Mr. Darcy frowned at the cloth for a moment, then headed to the edge of the road to hang it on a low shrub.

"Perhaps someone will come along to whom it's a boon," he said as he returned to her side.

Elizabeth smiled. How like him to consider the needs of others. A different man would have tossed the cloth, which could be cleaned and used again but which was too greasy to carry about, into the dust.

Unencumbered by the need to eat and free of Mr. Wickham, Elizabeth drew in a deep breath and lengthened her stride again. Although she knew she would tire soon, there was an exhilaration in walking at the speed she used when walking alone. Mr. Darcy, gait matching hers, offered his arm. She smiled at him and shook her head, swinging her arms freely.

After nearly a mile, she did slow her pace. Mr. Darcy offered his arm again. Elizabeth accepted it, more for the pleasure of his nearness than any need of support. She glanced at him askance again and found he watched her. Unaccountably, heat rose in her cheeks.

"That was odd, that man from the inn chasing us down to offer food." His tone was so casual as to be suspiciously so.

"Not so odd," she ventured, wondering what he truly wished to speak about. "If I overheard that conversation, I should have liked to help the people to whom Mr. Wickham spoke."

Mr. Darcy's lips twitched into a smile under his beard. "Yes, I daresay you would help them. You have a kind and generous nature."

"I've the luxury of that."

"It is a luxury?" He queried, tone full of genuine interest.

"Certainly." She shot him an arch look. "My family may not be well-off by some people's standards, but we've always had all we need. I've been loved, safe and provided for. That gives me a place of fortitude from which to offer aid to others. Had I very little, I may not be so generous as I am."

He shook his head. "I disagree. You would be generous regardless. The form of your assistance would simply vary based on what you might offer."

"You paint a more favorable picture of me than I can hope to deserve."

"And now I must beg to disagree with you yet again," he countered.

"Why, can this be our first disagreement?" She let out an exaggerated sigh. "And we've traveled so amiably until now."

"Yes, we have."

Elizabeth waited, sensing Mr. Darcy was near to voicing the thoughts that spurred his banter.

"Mr. Wickham is right," he said. "We must marry."

For once, she required the arm on which she leaned, for she nearly stumbled in surprise. She pressed back a thrill of pleasure at his offer and forced herself to consider the situation. "What you are really saying is that I must marry, because I am ruined. You don't have to marry me."

He shook his head. "What you say is true but not the whole story. If I don't marry you, I will be criticized for having gotten you into a situation that spoiled your reputation. You were kidnapped because of me." He shot her a quick look. "And it will be easier for both of us if people believe we were already engaged when they took us."

Elizabeth could feel the tension under her slim fingers, where they rested on his arm. Belatedly, she realized how inappropriate their circumstances rendered the simple courtesy. She wore no gloves. He, jacketless, had his shirt sleeves rolled up to his elbows. Her skin touched his, a gesture so intimate, she marveled that she'd so readily and unquestioningly placed her hand on him thus far. The act seemed so natural, she hadn't given it a second thought.

"What I mean is," he said, voice strained, "that we should act as if both my proposal and your response had gone differently." He cleared his throat. "I'm not suggesting we lie, because I will not do so, but I'm certain if we simply allow people to believe as they will, while providing certain facts, they will assume we'd already come to an understanding."

She could hear the tension in his voice, well aware of how much even the suggestion of not revealing the whole truth pained him. It amazed her that he would do that for her, though she wasn't certain there was the need. "Your proposal?" she ventured. "I believe only my response would need to change."

He grimaced. "Yes, but I would alter my proposal if I could. I was…" He trailed off, clearly at a loss.

"Pompous?" she suggested, laughter in her voice. "Rude? Condescending?" She took in his pained expression and closed her lips over more teasing.

"Yes," he finally said. "All of those things and I apologize." He covered her hand with his. "Please think over my offer and my suggestion." He squeezed her fingers and dropped his hand.

Elizabeth sobered, her pace slowing further as she mulled over his words. Mr. Darcy's offer was very generous, especially his suggestion they allow the world to think their engagement began sooner. It was true that a betrothed couple was given a great deal of leeway. The engagement wouldn't have been official when they were taken, as her father hadn't agreed, but if worse came to worst, she would be twenty-one in a few months and would not need his consent.

Mr. Wickham was correct. Her reputation was ruined. As soon as her family recovered from whatever worry and grief her disappearance inspired and their pleasure at her return dimmed, they would realize as much. She would have the choice of bringing them all down with her or consenting to be sent away to keep her shameful presence from tainting her sisters. Or, even worse, she would be married off to the as-yet-unnamed farmer Mr. Wickham had mentioned.

"You would marry me simply to keep people from decrying you?" she finally ventured. She didn't care for that idea. A part of her, perhaps even a large part, wished to accept his offer but not if he viewed it as some sort of noble sacrifice. She didn't want resentment to overshadow any life they built together.

"That would be one benefit of a union between us," Mr. Darcy replied.

"And you would have me believe you care so adamantly about what others think of you?" She cast him a quick look. "When did it come about, this concern for the opinions of others?" She bit back the observation that he certainly hadn't cared what she thought when they first met.

"I have always cared about what my family and friends think." A lately unheard stiffness entered his tone. "I also care about what I think of myself."

So, while he still didn't care what people in general thought of him, as she'd suspected, he did care what his family thought. But what of her family? Would they become his family? Would he care about what they thought, or would he keep her away from them? His offer was generous, and her family would benefit, but she was the one who must live with him and perhaps without them.

"Your behavior since we've been kidnapped has been exemplary," she said, almost to herself. Even if he behaved badly in society or, at least, in the society she moved in, his behavior in this crisis could not be criticized. "Even your behavior toward Mr. Wickham, whom I have the impression you greatly dislike."

"We were in a bad situation which would not be helped if we behaved as enemies." He looked toward her, then away. "You, in particular, had to be concerned." His tone was gruff. "A woman confined with two men? Anything could have happened. You must have been worried."

"Oddly enough, I wasn't, at least not about you." It was odd. She had never been afraid of Mr. Darcy, a man she knew many found intimidating. And she wasn't afraid of Mr. Wickham, because she was certain that he would not harm her when Mr. Darcy was there. Was it because Mr. Darcy had been considerate from the very beginning of their adventure or because she trusted him instinctively? She rather suspected the latter, for her lack of fear was a constant from long before their kidnaping.

He stopped, bringing them both to a halt, and angled to face her. Lines marked his brow. His lips, somewhat difficult to see under his beard, turned down at the edges. "You had no fear concerning my actions toward you, even though I'd professed my affection? Do you believe I don't find you attractive?"

Elizabeth nearly laughed. "Do you not recall your words the night of your first assembly in Hertfordshire? You stated, quite unequivocally, that I am not attractive enough to tempt you." She took in his wince. "When you proposed, you expounded on my personality, and my flaws, but not my beauty. Why should I suppose you find me attractive?"

"I had forgotten those ill-spoken words, until Wickham reminded me." Mr. Darcy placed a warm hand over the one she still rested on his arm. "Let me be clear, Miss Bennet. I was a fool to say your visage holds no appeal and doubly so for not making that foolishness clear when I asked for your hand. I find you exceedingly attractive. Beautiful."

He stood near enough that Elizabeth had to crane her neck to look up at him. Her heart thudded against the wall of her chest. Her pulse surged, making her lightheaded. "Even had I known that, I shouldn't have worried about you. You are a man of restraint."

His gaze slid from her eyes to her lips, then back up again. "Am I?"

Elizabeth offered a shaky nod. "Admirably so."

He released her hand to smooth curls back from her cheek. "There is a certain amount of restraint that I've exercised during our journey together, and will continue to exercise until we reach safety, that I will not employ once we are wed."

Once they were wed. Elizabeth's heart continued its erratic dance. He assumed they would marry. Maybe he was right. "In other words, our marriage would be a real marriage."

"Correct."

"I see," she said, the words coming out a whisper.

"Do you?" He cupped her cheek. "Have you any notion how you tempt me?"

She shook her head, reveling in the feel of his palm against her skin. "I can't imagine you tempted, Mr. Darcy. Especially not by a tanned, dust covered country-bred miss."

"Do you know the sun has brought out your freckles?"

Elizabeth's heart sank. Freckles? She truly must be a sight.

"There's a smattering here." His lips brushed her cheek. "And here." They moved to the other. "And I adore them."

"You do?" she breathed.

"I do." He lowered his lips to hers, his hand sliding around to cup her neck. His grip was light, as was his kiss, as if to let her know she could pull away.

Elizabeth didn't wish to pull away. She'd never kissed a man and certainly never thought she'd kiss a man with a beard, but that trifling detail didn't matter. Not when Mr. Darcy's lips pressed to hers. Not when she twined her arms about his neck to pull him closer.

After a long moment, he slid his hands up her arms and unclasped them from his neck. He gently set her away. Heat suffused Elizabeth's face as she realized she'd momentarily forgotten where they were, nearly forgotten who they were, she was so lost in his embrace.

"Was that a yes?" he asked, his hands still clasping her forearms.

It had best be, she thought, for now she truly was compromised. She studied the man before her. Tall, lean of build and handsome, he was also decent and kind. She enjoyed being beside him. His kiss, well, she couldn't possibly deny liking that. Did she love him? Did it matter when he was so good, she so in need of a husband, and their attraction so strong?

If not for her circumstance, she would be certain she loved him. As things stood, she was unsure if she could untangle her frantic need to wed from her feelings toward him. How near together in the heart and mind did desperation, gratitude and love mingle? Was it fair to accept when she wasn't sure?

Clearly, he wanted her. He must see her uncertainty. That meant he accepted it. If he could accept her lack of complete enthusiasm, she could accept his offer with a clear conscience.

"Yes. That was a yes." It wasn't that many words and she was engaged.

To her surprise, and pleasure, he pulled her back into his arms for a second kiss. This time, it was somewhat longer before he set her away. Elizabeth blushed even more deeply. He silently offered his arm, and they continued walking.

It took some time before Elizabeth could look at Mr. Darcy's face, her eyes repeatedly going to his lips, without blushing. Longer, still, before she felt she could speak in normal tones. Finally, her equilibrium somewhat restored, she sought about for a topic.

"What shall I call you in private?" She finally ventured. "I assume you wish to be called Mr. Darcy in public."

"Yes, I do, Elizabeth." He offered her a quick smile before returning his scrutiny to the roadway. "You may call me Fitzwilliam. I don't care for nicknames."

"My family calls me Lizzy," she ventured when he didn't return her line of questioning.

"I don't care for nicknames," he repeated.

Elizabeth raised her eyebrows. Was this what her life would be like? He would be so controlling, so certain his way was the best way, that she couldn't even go by the name she preferred? That would never do. She would have to keep alert to opportunities to make it clear to him that she had a mind, and will, of her own.

Chapter Twelve

Wickham enjoyed seeing the backs of his two former companions in misery. He'd had enough of Darcy's sanctimoniousness to last him ten years. Not that he would stay away that long. No, he'd make good of this whole debacle, which meant seeing Darcy again soon. Wickham would get Elizabeth Bennet to accept his proposal. She'd have to, once she returned home and found what sort of reception she got from a stodgy community like the one in Hertfordshire. Then Darcy, riddled with guilt but unwilling to shackle himself to the mouthy, poorly connected country miss, would pay Wickham well to take her.

First though, he'd make his way to London and have a little fun. Maybe look up one or two of his more willing, and friendly, companions. After all, once he wed, he'd have to play the dutiful husband for at least a few months. Just long enough to get the Bennet girl settled somewhere safe to leave her and into a properly submissive and beguiled state. He knew she didn't care for him now, but he'd charmed her once. He could do it again. Add his skills in certain marital activities, and he'd soon have her doting on him.

Wickham leaned back in his chair and stretched his legs out under the table, reveling in the pleasure of being well fed. He returned to being aware of his present surroundings when a mug thumped down on his table. He looked at the vaguely familiar woman and said, "I'm not paying for another drink." He'd already had two.

"I'm paying." She sat down next to him. She took a sip and then handed the mug to him.

Bemused, Wickham accepted her offering. Where had he seen her before? Had she been serving him but now removed her apron? He should remember such magnificent strawberry-blonde hair, which hung loose down to her waist. Certainly, he'd remember that bosom, which was nearly loose as well, what with how lowcut her gown was.

Dressed like that and buying him a drink, she must be the local lightskirt, he realized. He'd probably noticed her on the way in but dismissed her from his thoughts as not worth paying for when he was so low on funds. "I can't afford anything more than this meal," he said. Not when he could have much the same thing in London for no more than a smile.

"I'm not asking for anything." She leaned toward him. "In case you haven't noticed, we're in the middle of nowhere. It's boring here. I'm simply looking for a little entertainment."

That, Wickham could provide. Especially if she was buying. Besides which, a night in her bed would be more comfortable than sleeping under a tree. He had no schedule, and he would be better rested the next morning. His money was safely hidden in his boots. In truth, he'd nothing to lose. With any luck, she would feed him breakfast.

She reached for the mug and took another sip of ale. "What's a nice man like you doing looking like a vagrant?"

He decided to weave a tale that would give her some entertainment, since that was her goal for the evening. In his story, he was the one who'd saved the other two and they'd repaid him by giving him the smallest amount of food. He had barely enough money for a meal, which he was justified in buying to keep up his strength. She hung on every word. By the time he finished, he almost believed his own tale.

The evening went much as she had implied it would. She plied him with drink, but never so much that he lost his head. She made no effort to locate his hidden funds. She made every effort to be accommodating.

The following morning, Wickham stretched, luxuriating in the feel of a mattress and sheets. He fumbled toward the woman at his side, still half asleep. Maybe she would still be accommodating this morning.

"Not so quick, lover," she said, patting the hand he reached toward her. "There's one small detail to take care of first."

The wicked note of triumph in her voice drew his lids open. Wickham blinked, taking in a tall figure standing beside her, next to the bed. Panicked, he sat up, eyes going wide. Another large, blond Scot stood on his side of the bed and a third, a redhead, at the foot. All had arms folded, expressions hard.

Wickham whipped his head around to stare at the woman. It hit him that, even though her hair was a reddish-blonde and theirs varying from blond to red, she bore a strong resemblance to the assembled men. Sheet pulled up to her chin, she beamed at him. Her expression radiated smugness. Again, he was troubled by the notion he ought to know her from somewhere.

"Who are you?" he cried, panic only heightened by her look. "What the devil is going on? His gaze darted to his boots, but they were still heaped against the wall where he'd tossed them.

"It seems you are going to marry our sister," one man said.

"She seduced me," Wickham protested.

"You seemed willing enough," she said with a little sniff.

"I don't care if she hit you over the head with her fry pan and dragged you up here," the man beside Wickham said. "She's pregnant and needs a husband, someone who will work around the inn. We caught you with her and you're going to marry her."

"And you can settle some money on her," the one at the foot of the bed added. "That's how gentlemen do it, don't they? I saw you taking money out of your boot. Why don't I look in both boots to see if there is any left?"

"Now, let's be reasonable, friends." Wickham offered his most ingratiating smile. The expression felt flat. He wasn't accustomed to trying to charm three angry men while lying in bed beside their sister.

"If we were being unreasonable, you'd be drawn and quartered by now," the one beside him growled. "You're in bed with our sister."

Wickham stared about him at their unyielding expressions. He considered pointing out that as she was already with child, he obviously wasn't the only man who'd been in bed with their sister. They didn't seem the sort to take mention of that well, though. He swallowed hard. "I, uh, yes, I'll marry her. Now. Right here." He'd use a false name, escape the first chance he got and never come back.

The one at the end of the bed shook his head. "No. In the church. We don't need banns, but you will be in the register."

"And I'll be Mrs. George Wickham," Mary proclaimed.

Wickham turned a frown on her. How did she know his name? He hadn't used it. He couldn't recall his conversation with Darcy and the Bennet girl in perfect detail, but even had they said his name, they wouldn't have used his first name.

"You really don't recognize me?" she asked, voice touched with disgust. "Fiona Mary McClintock. I went by my middle name in England because Fiona is far too Scottish. Here, I am Fiona." She shook her head, strawberry-blonde locks cascading about her naked shoulders. "I emptied your chamber pot, but you never looked at me. I'm not surprised. You rich folk never look at your servants unless you mean to do us harm." She shrugged. "Besides, people tell me I look very different

113

with my hair under my cap. All docile and proper-like."

Wickham gaped at her. The chambermaid from the ship? Jeb's Fiona? Even knowing who she was, he couldn't recall her face from his time aboard. He had a sinking feeling in his gut, but he mustered a beseeching look. "Surely, you don't want me. You must have heard the things Miss Bennet said about me. I'm a cad. A bounder. Unreliable at best."

"But you are available and please me," she countered. "And you're handsome, with English charm, looks and connections. You'll greet the English folk who come in on their travels and get more coin from them than they'd give a Scot."

"Besides which, you're here," the brother beside her said. "Not a lot of single, foolish gentlemen come through."

"I'm not truly a gentleman," Wickham protested.

"You're gentlemanly enough to please the customers," the man who loomed beside him said.

Wickham groaned. Always, the curse of Mr. Darcy's upbringing haunted him. Better he should have been raised without a farthing than stuck between worlds, getting the worst of both. But no, he must endlessly suffer from the vaunted Darcy generosity.

He shot her a reproachful look. "I wish you'd been quicker getting the bar off that door," he muttered.

"How's that?" she asked, expression curious.

"If you'd set Darcy free, unwed and with child or no, he would have seen you were taken care of for the rest of your life."

She snorted. "I wasn't coming to remove the bar. I came to see what the pounding was." She arched a brow at him, mocking. "What about you? You should have made your move on Miss Bennet before she caught you stuffing your face in my inn. Maybe she would have preferred you then, and Mr. Darcy would be paying you to marry her even now."

"If I'd made any move toward Miss Bennet, Darcy would have killed me." Despite Darcy's endless calm, his nearly unshakable self-control, Wickham knew that fact to the pit of his soul. If he'd taken advantage of the Bennet girl, his life would have been forfeit, no matter how much Darcy claimed he couldn't kill anyone.

It was sad Darcy cared for the girl so much yet would be too proud to wed her. So sad, in fact, that it lightened Wickham's mood. Darcy's suffering always made him smile. "He's very protective of those for whom he considers himself responsible."

"Too bad he doesn't consider himself responsible for you," Fiona said, smug once more.

Wickham looked around at the bedroom at her three burly, frowning brothers. "Yes, it is."

Fiona looked about as well. She flipped a hand at the looming men. "Give us a moment."

"He's going to marry you," the brother beside her said, scowl aimed at Wickham.

"Yes, he is. We need to speak alone, though," Fiona said.

"Seems to me you were alone enough last night," the one at the foot of the bed observed.

Fiona rolled her eyes ceilingward before casting a hard stare about the room. "I said out."

The three exchanged looks. The one beside Wickham shrugged. They turned and marched toward the door. The first two went out. The final one stopped in the doorway.

"This is the only way out," Fiona's brother said. "You jump out that window, you'll break something, and then we'll break something more." His gaze narrowed. "And one of us will be down there, waiting, never doubt it. The other two will be right here outside this door."

"Yes, you will be," Fiona snapped. "Now."

Her brother scowled but vacated the room. The door slammed closed in his wake. In case he doubted them, Wickham heard the heavy tread as one of them headed down the hall and then the staircase.

Wickham drew in a deep breath and plastered on his most reasonable expression. Now that he had Fiona alone, maybe he could convince her that he wasn't the right man. For once, he'd be honest. He simply wouldn't make a good husband for her, or for any woman.

"You'll own this inn," she said before he could open his mouth.

"I beg your pardon?" he asked.

"This was my mama's inn," Fiona said. "When she married, it became my father's, but he willed it back to her. When she died, she willed it to me. It's mine until I marry. Then it will be yours."

"Your brothers don't own the inn?"

She shook her head. "They work for me."

"Why did you leave?"

She sighed. "I was real sad after my mama died. It felt like all I did was work, all the time. My jobs, her jobs. I couldn't see an end to the work and the sadness, but I couldn't give up this inn she loves." She

115

shook her head, eyes shimmering slightly. "I think I went a little mad. Then Jeb came along and offered to take me away with him. I jumped at the chance." She grimaced. "Only, it wasn't so much an opportunity as the single biggest mistake of my life."

"So, you own this inn?" Wickham reiterated.

"That's what I'm telling you."

Wickham stared at her. That certainly made the prospect of wedding Fiona Mary more appealing. Why, once they married, he could sell the inn. There'd be nothing she could do about it. Suddenly, his morning was looking up. "Can you prove that?"

"I have the deed."

"Show me the deed and we have a deal."

She offered a bright smile, then angled her face toward the door. She cupped her hand around her mouth. "Send over to the church, boys, we're having a wedding."

Chapter Thirteen

Elizabeth hadn't eaten so well in weeks as she did at the remote rural church they found the evening they left Mr. Wickham behind. It amused her that he'd abandoned his subterfuge only miles before he would have received a hearty meal for free. The fates had certainly smiled on her and Mr. Darcy when Mr. Wickham made the choice to indulge.

All the priest at the little church asked in return was that Mr. Darcy read to him while Elizabeth do a bit of mending. As she stitched, she realized she could listen to Mr. Darcy's pleasing baritone reading the Bible for all her days without tiring of the sound. She wondered if, once they were wed, he could be persuaded to read to her.

In exchange for their services, the aged priest let them wash up, eat their fill of dinner and breakfast, and sleep inside on the floor before the fire. It still wasn't a bed, but the rug was thick, and he lent them each a blanket. He also sent them on their way with a sack that contained sausage and cheese stuffed rolls, more cheese, bread and a few dried apples. Still, Mr. Darcy didn't appear cheerful as they set out in the bright morning sunshine.

"It looks as if today will be lovely," she ventured. As she couldn't imagine what troubled him, doubt began to gnaw at her. Was his glumness born of remorse? Did he regret his offer for her hand now that he'd spent the night thinking on what being wed to her would be like?

He squinted up at the sky. "It's difficult to say. The weather in Scotland is mercurial."

As were his desires, she worried. She squared her shoulders. "If I may make the observation, you seem unduly glum for a man who's had his first real meal and first night in a proper home in weeks."

"That's the crux of it," he replied. "Our host was more than generous. He stinted us nothing he had to offer. Yet, when I asked for a pen, ink and paper, he refused me. Does the world conspire to keep us wandering about like homeless drifters?"

Elizabeth cast him an amused look askance. They would need to work on this underlying current of believing all things to be directly related to him and not, at times, the product of someone else's existence. She supposed, as wealthy and sought after as Mr. Darcy was, he was accustomed to being at the center of things. "I suspect he didn't have anything to write on or with, and that his ink has long ago dried up."

He angled his frown at her. "The food he gave us says he wasn't poor."

"Wealth is not the only factor in how a person lives and behaves."

Mr. Darcy narrowed his gaze. "Why do I feel you have an explanation already?"

"Because you've come to know me during our travel together?" she suggested, tone teasing.

"Well enough to know when you're trying to make a point," he countered, his dour look wavering in the face of her glibness.

Elizabeth smiled, pleased he would permit her to tease him, and relented. "There was a large magnifying glass on the desk but it, and everything else there, was covered in dust. His books were worn, as if well read, but they too bore that tell-tale film. Even the mending he asked of me wasn't out of the realm of average capability and many a remote priest has the skill to mend."

Mr. Darcy nodded his understanding. "You think his vision has failed to the point where he cannot read and write any longer, or mend."

Elizabeth suppressed a thrill of pleasure that he took her observations seriously and willingly applied them. "I suspect so, yes."

Finally, Mr. Darcy's expression fully cleared of disquiet. "That's good to know. Perhaps I will be able to make arrangements for someone to read to him regularly. He was very kind to us."

Elizabeth smiled at that but as she watched Mr. Darcy's features, fine despite his beard, she saw them tense. She followed his gaze up the roadway. Two men, both in patched trousers, shirt sleeves, caps and vests, strode toward them and where nearly upon them. One walked with a staff and the other looked old enough to be the first man's father. While they looked no less disreputable than Elizabeth knew she and Mr. Darcy did, the way their eyes roved, sizing them up, made her wary as well.

Mr. Darcy angled so he would be in the center of the road as the men passed. The one with the limp, farther from Mr. Darcy, tipped his cap. The one with the staff nodded. Elizabeth nodded back. She relaxed as the men passed by.

There was a grinding sound behind them, like a boot heel spinning in the stray gravel and dirt. Mr. Darcy shoved her. She stumbled toward the heather-cloaked verge, a cry of surprise flying from her. She caught her balance and whirled.

Mr. Darcy grappled with the man carrying the staff. They each had two hands locked on the heavy wood. The sack of food lay in the roadways nearby. The older man started to circle around behind Mr. Darcy.

"Run, Elizabeth," Mr. Darcy called but didn't take his gaze from the staff wielding man.

Elizabeth whirled back to the verge. The dirt road boasted only small smatterings of gravel but no rocks small enough to throw. She grabbed a handful of gravel and ran back toward the men.

The older man lunged at Mr. Darcy. Elizabeth threw the gravel. At least one piece hit Mr. Darcy in the back, but some hit the face of the older man, who flinched.

Mr. Darcy lunged forward. His tall form collided with the staff-wielder. The older man missed his mark and stumbled a few feet down the road, cursing and rubbing at his face. Not convinced he was yet out of the fight, she ducked down for another handful of gravel.

Broad shoulders bunching, Mr. Darcy twisted the staff and turned his back to his attacker. Somehow, he ended up between the staff and its owner. The older man turned back and made to launch himself again.

Elizabeth flung more gravel at the man's face. This time, she missed her mark. He turned to her with a scowl.

Behind the older one, Mr. Darcy ducked low and flung out his arms. To Elizabeth's surprise, the man with the staff sailed over Mr. Darcy's head to land in the dirt with a loud grunt and an audible whoosh of breath.

Scowling, the older man charged Elizabeth. The staff, now in Mr. Darcy's hands, swung out and knocked her attacker's legs from beneath him. He hit the ground with a softer thud but a louder yelp than his companion. Both men lay on their backs looking dazed.

"Your boots," Mr. Darcy ordered. He prodded the nearest man with the staff.

Elizabeth stared at him. His boots had been in salt water and the leather was cracked but these men's boots looked too small for Mr. Darcy. Besides which, she hadn't pegged him for a thief.

"Boots. Now." Mr. Darcy punctuated the command by prodding

each in the side.

Both groaning and blinking, the two began to fumble with their boots. Elizabeth made a wide circle around them. She picked up another handful of gravel. They didn't even look at her as she reached Mr. Darcy's side.

"What are you doing?" she whispered.

"I don't feel like looking over my shoulder."

One of the men pulled off a boot. Mr. Darcy prodded the other. Any time either faltered, or even looked up at them, Mr. Darcy poked them or hefted the staff, expression hard. Soon, he stood over two bootless men.

"You have a fair throwing arm," he said to Elizabeth. "Take two of their boots and toss them as far from the roadway as you can."

"But them's my only pair," the older of the two cried.

"I suppose you'll be very diligent in searching for them, then," Mr. Darcy said flatly.

Elizabeth took both right boots, though she supposed it didn't matter which she threw. She walked to the edge of the roadway and, with a strength born of her shock, outrage and fear at being set upon, she threw one at a time. In satisfaction, she watched them sail high in the air and come down among the rocks. She turned back to see Mr. Darcy holding the other two boots.

"What's the next habitation we'll come to?" he asked the men.

Expression suspicious, the staff-wielder named a village.

"We'll give these boots to the first person we meet there." Mr. Darcy turned to Elizabeth. "Shall we?"

"My staff," the younger man cried.

"Is mine now," Mr. Darcy stated without turning back. "And I thank you for the use of it, which almost makes up for being attacked."

Elizabeth grabbed the bag of food, which Mr. Darcy had dropped, and hurried to his side. They set out at a fair pace. Behind them, Scottish patois echoed down the roadway as the two men uttered some unflattering observations about Englishmen in general and Mr. Darcy in particular.

They kept the quick pace for nearly a mile, with no sign of pursuit. Elizabeth, flushed from more than their rapid stride, found her gaze continually drawn to Mr. Darcy. She knew he fenced and shot, having learned as much on the ship. She'd supposed he hunted and had observed him riding on occasion in Hertfordshire, and so knew he kept a good seat. Who would have thought, though, that the upright, somewhat stiff and withdrawn Mr. Darcy knew how to brawl?

Elizabeth would never have imagined the ability to fight as a recommendation in a husband. If anyone had suggested the qualification to her, she would have laughed. Now, the idea thrilled her. So much so, she was surprised by her own rush of feelings.

Raised as she'd been, she'd never had need of the sort of protection Mr. Darcy had proved capable of only a mile past. A month ago, she would have been taken aback. Perhaps even scandalized. She could imagine the quips she would have made at Mr. Darcy's expense, likely along the lines of him solving a problem with brute force rather than reason, as a gentleman ought. Now, reason seemed far removed from their current trial.

Had Mr. Wickham known of Mr. Darcy's skill? Was that part of Mr. Wickham's grudging but unwavering respect? As far as she could ascertain, they'd grown up quite close, a large part of their present animosity.

After another mile, they reached a small cluster of houses. Mr. Darcy looked around, then led her toward a man working in his garden. The man halted his work as they approached, frown suspicious.

Mr. Darcy stopped outside the man's fence. "We were set upon on the road. We relieved our attackers of their boots, which I told them I would leave here. You can keep them or ransom them, as you wish."

The man stood. He dusted of his hands and moved nearer. Mr. Darcy dropped the boots over the fence. The man's gaze, suspicious, followed them.

"You don't want to sell them?"

"Two left boots?" Mr. Darcy raised his eyebrows. "No."

"Why'd you take them, then?" The man inched closer.

"I didn't want to be followed or ambushed."

"I know those boots." He squinted at Mr. Darcy. "And that staff."

Mr. Darcy waited. Beside him, Elizabeth held her breath. The cluster of houses, churchless, couldn't be called a village. There were enough people about, though, to give them trouble if the community decided to side with their assailants.

"Them two should know better, at least the father should," the man finally said. "I'll let them tell their tale, and I'll ask how they were bested by one man and a small woman. Perhaps I'll let them complain they were attacked and expose their lie. They deserve to be shamed."

121

"As you see fit," Mr. Darcy said.

Elizabeth relaxed marginally.

The man nodded toward the staff Mr. Darcy held. "Garth'll want his staff back. He put a lot of evenings into carving it up nice."

Mr. Darcy examined the staff with a frown. Finally, he held it out to Elizabeth to show her a barely recognizable carving of a bull. A touch of amusement shone in his eyes when she lifted her gaze to meet them.

"If that took him a lot of evenings," she said, "he needs the practice of carving another."

Mr. Darcy nodded and turned back to the man behind the fence. "I'll keep the staff. It might frighten off other attackers."

The man shrugged. "Suit yourself, but his mama praised that staff and he's her youngest. She'll get all his older brothers stirred up about it. If they get riled, won't matter that you're just one man and a little slip of a thing. Just that you're English and robbed their kin."

Elizabeth gave the man a startled look. How anyone could take that view of what had happened on the roadway was beyond her. She stepped forward, intent on defending their actions.

Mr. Darcy placed a hand on her arm. "I think it's time we moved on."

She pursed her lips but nodded. He offered his arm. Elizabeth placed her hand on his warm skin. Staff in his free hand, bag of food in Elizabeth's, Mr. Darcy set a strident pace through the almost-village. He didn't slow as the final home dropped from sight behind them.

"Let's try to make good time," he said, attention on the road ahead. "Perhaps even skip the next habitation. We have enough food for a while. I'm worried our attackers might rally reinforcements and come after us."

"You could have left the staff."

He shook his head. "I earned the right to keep it." He shot her a quick grimace. "And I've let my anger get the better of me. I want them to pay for their attack in some small way."

Elizabeth hadn't realized he was angry. She would have to better recognize the signs in the future. Still, she could understand his reasons for keeping the weapon. She let the matter drop.

They walked through lunch, eating their stuffed rolls, and passed another small cluster of buildings. Late in the afternoon, they reached a washed-out section of roadway. After Mr. Darcy helped her across, they headed off the road, upstream, by mutual consent. Once they'd moved far enough from the road to be shielded by a tall, nature-crafted cairn of boulders, they sat down to drink from the stream and rest. After a moment, Mr. Darcy selected a sharp-edged rock from the scattering on the ground and began to scrape at the poorly-carved bull on the staff.

Elizabeth cast him a questioning look.

His answering expression was pained. "Perhaps I am technically a thief. I must be, as I don't want there to be evidence of my thievery. I want to keep the staff to deter future attackers."

At peace with his reasons for taking the weapon, and sure their attackers deserved more punishment than simply a lost stick, however nice, Elizabeth took no issue with Mr. Darcy's scraping. "We weren't attacked before."

"I was more vigilant before." He paused in his work to level a look on her that made her pulse flutter. "I'm afraid I permitted myself to become distracted by my beguiling new betrothed. I'm sure my lack of proper mindfulness made us appear an easy target. I should have looked more menacing, as if I wanted a fight." He dropped his gaze to the staff, his expression morphing into a grimace, and returned to work.

"Surely, it's not just a question of staring down passersby." She hadn't even realized he had been. She'd thought he simply preferred to appear unfriendly most of the time.

"We were also carrying something, which they had no way to know wasn't aught but a meal. In addition, there were also three of us before, two of us men."

Elizabeth frowned. "Should we have waited for Mr. Wickham to finish his meal and accepted him back into our party?"

"In theory, yes." Mr. Darcy skimmed the rock over the now nearly smooth wood. "In practice, I'm not certain I could have stayed on good terms with him. On board the ship, we had a balance of sorts. Even though I received less food than he did, I controlled it. I could have insisted he take a turn on the floor but there was no point in fighting each other. I'm sure you noticed he obeyed me once we got ashore."

"In gratitude?" Elizabeth asked, thinking of Mr. Darcy's saving Mr. Wickham's life.

"He is never grateful, especially to me. I've paid his debts many times. He always accepts it as his due."

This was not the picture of the relationship between them that Mr. Wickham had conveyed to her when first they met. Now, with all she knew of both men, it seemed ludicrous to have ever believed Mr.

Wickham's side of the tale. When the two had argued about Wickham's finances, Mr. Darcy had mentioned paying Mr. Wickham for the living he'd claimed was taken. Elizabeth didn't even need additional information to know who stood in the right. The more she learned of both men, the more she could see that Mr. Darcy was everything Mr. Wickham had pretended to be, and so much more.

Chapter Fourteen

Once he was satisfied with his alteration to the staff, Darcy climbed onto some of the lower boulders to peer over the top of the pile toward the road. He scanned the line of dirt that wove among the heather-clad hills in both directions. He saw no one.

"Do you think it's safe to return to the roadway?" Elizabeth asked from where she still sat beside the stream.

The worry in her tone pained him. He had more resources at his disposal than most any other man in England, yet those resources weren't here. All that stood between the woman he loved and terror were his wits, his fists and now a stolen staff. He scanned the roadway again. They'd been walking quickly but anyone with access to a horse could expect to overtake them. Two horses and a wagon, and they could be overrun by angry Scots.

He molded his face into a look of easy assurance as he climbed back down. "It looks clear." He offered a hand and helped her to her feet. He didn't relinquish her fingers as they wound their way back toward the road.

Aware Elizabeth's sentiments toward him didn't match his ardor, Darcy treasured her every touch. When she turned a smile on him or teased him, a harsh mixture of pleasure, sorrow and pain churned in his gut. He knew he would suffer if her love never grew to match his, but he would also dwell in misery if she wasn't a part of his life.

And he had reason to hope, a hope he didn't believe imagined. Yes, she'd agreed to wed him out of necessity, but he was certain she looked on him more favorably now than when she'd refused him. Sometimes, her expression was even warm.

When they reached the roadway, he settled her hand on his arm. Even when the air was cool, he kept his shirt sleeves rolled up so he could revel in the feel of her soft palm against his skin. Besides, he was never cold with Elizabeth beside him. Not walking down the roadway, not drinking water from a stream, and certainly not when she pressed her slim form to his for warmth and security as they fell asleep at night.

"I'm so sorry, Bessie girl. So, so sorry."

The voice, a man's and marked by anguish and an English accent, came from the road ahead, somewhere beyond the turn they approached. Darcy strained to maintain an unfaltering stride and even expression, but inwardly he cursed. He'd been doing it again. Woolgathering when he should be applying his attention to the world about them. How great a fool was he, to keep letting daydreams of Elizabeth threaten her reality? There would be more than enough nights spent by her side once she was safe and they were wed.

The Englishman's voice continued in the same distraught, agitated vein, growing clearer as they neared the bend in the trail. Elizabeth's hand tightened on Darcy's arm. She cast him a worried look. He did his best to appear in control and reassuring.

They rounded the bend to the sight of an overturned, smashed gig. The vehicle was half on the road and half scattered among the ever-present boulders. A young man, clothing torn but appearing generally unharmed, stood over a horse. She lay on her heaving side, legs at all angles, blood-flecked foam about her mouth.

As they watched, the man raised a pistol, hand shaking. "Oh Bessie. What have I done? I'm sorry," he rambled, profile a mask of grief.

His hand shook so much, it seemed unlikely he'd hit the poor suffering beast at his feet. He clasped both hands on the gun. They both shook. He lowered the weapon to his side and drew in several too-quick breaths. As they drew nearer, he started his mumbled apology again and once again attempted to aim the pistol.

"Broken leg?" Darcy asked, tone pitched low and gentle, the same as he'd use to sooth the poor doomed horse.

The man whirled. To Darcy's relief, he kept the pistol angled toward the ground. He blinked in their direction, owlish. Now that he could see the man's face more fully, Darcy marked a wound to his forehead.

"At least two," the man said. "Maybe all four. I don't know. And blood. Blood in her mouth. Must be her lungs."

Darcy nodded, leading Elizabeth closer. He'd already assessed as much. "There's nothing to do for her."

"I know." The young man agreed, tone grief stricken.

"You're doing the right thing," Elizabeth said her voice brimming with compassion.

The young man looked at her. His surprise, the way he started

126

blinking again, made it clear he hadn't even noticed her. Blood from the wound reached his eyebrow. He wiped his forehead with his sleeve, smearing it. "I've only one ball. I don't want her to suffer. I...I can't seem to get off the shot."

At his feet, the horse rolled her eyes. A thin whine of pain pressed from her. Darcy didn't think she would last much longer but she was undoubtedly suffering. "Do you want me to do it?" he offered gently.

The man hurried forward, pistol hilt extended toward Darcy. Darcy hid a grimace, for the man had the gun aimed right at his own gut. He accepted the weapon with care. The last thing Darcy wanted was to accidentally shoot the young Englishman in the stomach.

"Thank you," the young man whispered as he relinquished the gun.

Passing the staff to Elizabeth, Darcy went to the horse. He crouched and smoothed a hand along her sweat-soaked neck, then murmured a few soothing words. The beast's eyes closed. She let out a long sigh and stilled, save for slow, shallow breaths.

Not wanting the blood spatter to reach him, Darcy stepped back a bit. He took careful aim and squeezed the trigger. The horse went rigid for a fraction of a second, then limp. Air seeped from it in a final sigh.

When Darcy turned to return the pistol, he found the young man beside Elizabeth, hands over his face. She rubbed his back and murmured something Darcy couldn't hear. Though the scene was more that of a mother comforting a child, jealousy stabbed at Darcy. He cleared his throat.

The man dropped his hands. He swiped his shirt sleeves over his face, mopping up tears, then stepped forward. To Darcy's relief, Elizabeth let him, her hand falling to her side.

"Thank you," the man said. "My name is Everett."

"Darcy, and this is my betrothed, Miss Bennet."

Elizabeth curtsied. Darcy realized he had temporarily forgotten the formality of society. It was too late to bow. He handed the pistol back to Everett.

Expression still dazed, Everett looked about at the dead horse and the remains of his gig. "I'm not certain how I'm going to get home."

"Where do you live?" Darcy asked.

Everett named a town which was perhaps fifteen miles south of Pemberley. Darcy nearly laughed. Not only were the fates conspiring to keep him and Elizabeth from Derbyshire, they apparently wanted to keep all residents of that general area stranded in Scotland if they found themselves there.

He surveyed Everett for a moment. He appeared an upright, if overly sensitive, young man, already regaining calm now that his horse no longer suffered. Darcy looked to Elizabeth for her opinion. She nodded and offered a slight smile.

"We have a similar problem," Darcy allowed. "We're trying to reach Derbyshire as well. We were kidnapped, imprisoned on a ship and shipwrecked. We've been walking south ever since we escaped."

Everett stared at him. "Kidnapped? Shipwrecked?"

Darcy could read disbelief in the young man's open features and regretted his bluntness. As he'd been living their story, he hadn't stopped to consider how fantastical it might sound. Especially given his appearance. He doubted he looked worth kidnapping.

Where she stood slightly behind Everett, Darcy could read the amusement on Elizabeth's face. Did she find humor in his casual summary of their plight or his usual lack of tact? Knowing her, both. Somehow, when the mockery of any other would have found Darcy either looking down his nose or grinding his teeth, Elizabeth's amusement at his expense lightened his mood. Through her eyes, he could see why his words held humor.

Darcy spread his hands wide. "I suppose that since you do not know me it's not much, but I can offer you my word that what I've said is true."

It was Everett's turn to look Darcy over. "You said your name is Darcy. Are you related to the Darcys of Pemberley?"

Elizabeth's mirth was palpable.

Darcy kept his expression bland as he said, "I am." It was not, after all, a lie and he felt offering the whole truth would only convince Everett that Darcy was either insane or a swindler.

"Is that why you're going to Derbyshire, to seek Mr. Darcy's charity?" Everett asked. "You may receive it, if you can prove your tale to him. They say the current Mr. Darcy of Pemberley is stern but fair. He fixed the roadway through our town, although we're outside his district. People consider him generous."

Still standing behind Everett, Elizabeth pressed her hands to her lips. Her eyes danced.

Darcy cleared his throat. He sought about for a reply that wasn't a lie yet wouldn't scare Everett off. Headed to Derbyshire, he could be a good travel companion. Even if they still had to walk, they'd be three once more. "Yes. It is my expectation that we shall receive aid once we reach Pemberley, especially since I'm known there."

Everett nodded. "I wish you luck with that hope." He turned and went to the remains of his gig. He began lifting splintered boards.

Darcy tried to formulate a way to request Everett's company on their journey that wouldn't be refused. What would Wickham say? For all he loathed his childhood companion, Wickham did have a way of charming people.

Before Darcy could speak, hooves sounded farther down the roadway, from the direction they were headed. They grew in volume, one set, until a man astride appeared around the next bend. He slowed when he sighted them, his expression cautious yet touched with avarice.

"I heard a shot," the man called as he drew near.

Everett looked up. "My horse," he replied, a slight catch in his voice. "She had to be put down."

More hooves sounded down the road behind them, along with the creak of a wagon. Darcy tensed. A load of Scotsmen coming to settle with them? He didn't take his attention from the crafty looking rider, drawing every nearer, but he did step closer to Elizabeth.

The rider nodded as he came abreast them. "My farm's just over that stand of pines." He looked Everett up and down with growing greed. "If you pay me, I'll clear the horse and this wreck off the road for you."

"That would be--" Everett started to say.

"Unacceptable," Darcy cut in forcefully. He aimed a look of reprimand at the farmer and said, "If you pay him, he'll give you the right to the horsemeat, hide, harness, and the remains of the gig. One wheel looks in pretty good shape and I bet there are other parts you can salvage."

"How's this?" a voice called from behind.

They all turned to see a man in a wagon approaching. He did not, to Darcy's relief, have a load of angry Scotsmen in the bed. Rather, he had a few sacks of what were likely root vegetables dug up after the winter.

The crafty farmer frowned. "Overturned gig. I'm handling it, McFarlin."

"I'm sure you are, Mather." He turned to Darcy. "What'd he offer you for the horse? I might bid more."

Darcy gestured to Everett. "The horse and gig belong to this young man."

"But Mr. Darcy speaks for me." Everett accompanied his words with a hopeful look Darcy's way.

McFarlin turned back to Darcy. "So, what'd Mather offer?"

"His first offer was to remove the horse and gig as a kindness," Darcy said, tone dry. "I deemed that offer unacceptable."

McFarlin surveyed the wreck from his wagon seat. He snorted. "I can do better than free."

"And I can do better than McFarlin," Mather cut in.

With two bidders, Darcy was able to negotiate a decent price. He ended up going with McFarlin both because he seemed more honest and had a wagon. Everett received less coin than Mather offered but got a ride to the nearest town with a stage as part of the bargain. Although Darcy didn't presume, Everett insisted he and Elizabeth be taken to town as well.

When the negotiations were through, Mather turned his head and spat in the dirt. "I came along first. You should have taken my coin." He glared at Darcy through narrowed eyes. "Let's hope you don't ever regret siding with McFarlin."

"Do you know," Darcy said, smile easy. "If we're to ride, I don't need this staff any longer." He reached for the staff, which Elizabeth still held.

She handed it over, brows raised.

Darcy turned back to Mather and held out the staff. "How about you take this, with my thanks."

Mather huffed but he took the staff, that avaricious gleam back. "I suppose it's something, and it's free." He cast McFarlin a smirk and turned his horse. Staff clutched in one hand, he rode away.

McFarlin cast Darcy a suspicious look. "That staff seemed familiar, now you drew my attention to it," he said, voice pitched low.

"We came by it on the roadway," Darcy said blandly, tone equally soft.

Still seated in his wagon, McFarlin shrugged. He surveyed the ruined gig, dead horse and three of them. "Well, best get your luggage and climb up" he finally said. "I'll have a time getting you to the coach and be back before Mather can steal half of what I paid for," he added in a near yell.

Mather heard him and turned around. "What will you pay me to guard what you bought?"

While the two negotiated, Darcy and Everett dug the young man's somewhat excessive seeming pile of cases from the wreck and put them in the back of the wagon. Just enough room remained for Darcy and Elizabeth. Everett, as their benefactor, would ride up front with McFarlin. Darcy suspected he could press the young man into letting Elizabeth ride in front but, selfishly, he preferred to keep her by him. He took comfort in the thought that the seat wasn't cushioned, anyhow, so she wouldn't be much more comfortable in front.

"About ready?" McFarlin said, still in his wagon.

In the road beyond, Mather dismounted and moved to sit on a crumbled bit of wall. "I rarely make money just sitting," he said, expression smug.

"Just make sure you earn it," McFarlin warned, then snapped the reins to set his team moving.

McFarlin set a fair clip and their ride was very jostling. Darcy kept an eye on Elizabeth, but she showed no outward misery. He loved that about her, her unflagging spirit. He could imagine the fuss a woman like Miss Bingley would be making in similar circumstances.

When they reached town, the largest they'd yet seen on their journey, McFarlin set out the moment Darcy and Everett had his luggage out of the bed. Darcy watched the farmer go with mild amusement. Obviously, he expected to make more from the poor horse and broken gig than selling his scant few sacks of what, when Darcy had peeked inside, turned out to be onions.

Darcy turned from watching the departing wagon to offer Everett his hand. "Thank you for the ride to town. I believe I got you enough money for the stage." Should he ask the young man to go out of his way and stop at Pemberley with word of where he and Elizabeth could be found? Would his staff believe the conscientious Mr. Everett if he arrived with their tale?

Everett shook Darcy's hand. "Oh, I had money. I just didn't have enough to pay for your and Miss Bennet's journey."

"Our journey?" Elizabeth prompted, tone hopeful.

Everett nodded. "The stage doesn't go right to Pemberley but there's a mail coach that goes somewhat close. Certainly, the two together will save you many days. It's the least I can do."

"Thank you, Mr. Everett," Elizabeth exclaimed.

Darcy's face broke into a smile under his beard. "I'll pay you back."

Everett shrugged. "Don't worry about it. It's money I wouldn't have if not for you."

Feeling as if things were looking up for the first time in many days, Darcy offered Elizabeth his arm. His mind filled with dreams of clean clothes, a beardless face and offering up the amenities of Pemberley to Elizabeth. If all went well, he and Elizabeth were nearly done with walking about the countryside half-starved and sleeping in stables.

Chapter Fifteen

Both the stage and the mail were a trial to Elizabeth. As the stage was nearly booked, they were forced to ride in outside seats. Air that seemed pleasant for walking in the day was bitterly cold riding on the outside of the coach as afternoon faded toward night. As a kindness to her, the two gentlemen put her in the middle, where she could be warmer. She was also uncomfortably squeezed, a state that moved from unpleasant to somewhat painful as the evening wore on.

When they reached the town where they were to switch from stage to mail coach, they were lucky enough to acquire two inside seats, at least. She found herself crammed in next to Mr. Everett because Mr. Darcy insisted he ride outside. Half of Mr. Everett's luggage was on her lap.

She could hardly begrudge him the lap space since he paid her fare, but she couldn't help but dwell on how much more pleasant the journey would be if Mr. Darcy sat beside her. More than his physical attractions, she missed him. It seemed silly as he was only riding without, mere feet from her, but she'd grown accustomed to his presence. His absence left disquiet in his wake, as if something important had gone missing from her life.

She had plenty of time to dwell on her feelings, for the mail went all night, and dwell she did, in earnest. Unaccountable as it may seem, she thought she may have fallen in love with Mr. Darcy. While convenient, her fickleness dismayed and surprised her. She'd despised him on the afternoon of his proposal, not even a month ago. Of course, she knew him so much better now.

He was upright. Noble. Generous. Caring. Knowing him, she could reinterpret many of his actions, understand them through his sense of right and wrong. For she was certain Mr. Darcy rarely, if ever, conducted himself in a manner he deemed wrong.

The coach hit a larger than usual bump. Elizabeth gritted her teeth as luggage clattered about her. Beside her, Mr. Everett let out a snore.

Elizabeth sighed and willed sleep to take her as well.

By morning, she'd only managed a smattering of naps. Her whole person felt stiff and somewhat bruised. She was half sure she would have preferred to walk the journey they'd made by stage and mail.

The door opened, and Mr. Darcy stood without, bearded and tired looking, but with a warm smile when his gaze met hers. Elizabeth responded with a smile of her own. As quickly as he was able, he divested her of luggage, which he piled outside while the horses were changed.

Once he'd unearthed her, Mr. Darcy offered his hand. Elizabeth clasped it, aware of tension leaving her at his touch, and permitted him to help her down from the coach. He then helped Mr. Everett unload the remaining luggage. Two other passengers disembarked. Both were well on their way by the time the luggage was unloaded. The coach, the driver appearing somewhat annoyed by the delay Mr. Everett's luggage caused, pulled away.

"I'll go inquire about the Lambton stage," Mr. Darcy said. His words must be meant for her and Everett, but he aimed his smile at Elizabeth. "From there, it's only a five mile walk to Pemberley. Nothing, really, after what we've done."

Elizabeth answered his smile with one of her own and offered a nod of agreement. A tremor of worry went through her as he turned toward the nearby inn. Would Mr. Darcy still look at her the way he had just now once they were in his home?

Mr. Everett patted his pockets, the frantic nature of the motion drawing Elizabeth's attention. Horror stole over his features. He met her gaze with wide eyes.

"Whatever is it?" she asked, brow knitting.

"My wallet is missing," he cried.

Mr. Darcy turned back, obviously overhearing Everett. He quickly reached Elizabeth's side. "Are you certain?"

"Very," Mr. Everett said.

Elizabeth turned her head to look about. "Where is that man who was seated beside you, Mr. Everett?"

"I don't know. He might be on the coach. He might have gotten off. I was too sleepy to notice."

"I don't see either of the men who disembarked," Mr. Darcy said, gaze scanning those visible on the street. "Not that we have any proof either of them took your wallet."

"Of all the rotten luck," Everett moaned.

"I'm sorry," Elizabeth said, thinking that if she hadn't slept, Mr. Everett would still have his money. "Was it very much?"

He grimaced. "Enough for the stage, for all three of us."

"There's nothing we can do about it now," Mr. Darcy said in a voice laden with suppressed irritation. He frowned at Mr. Everett's heap of possessions. "We're still twenty miles from Pemberley. We'll never be able to carry all that so far."

Mr. Everett looked back and forth between them. "Don't let me hold you up. Maybe I can find something in one of my cases to sell, so I can catch the next stage."

"I said I would repay you," Mr. Darcy said. "Part of that repayment should be that you don't have to sell your possessions to get home."

"Even with your help, we can't carry all of it," Mr. Everett pointed out. "I'm going to lose something either way. I may as well pick what to sell and get transport for the rest."

"I think I have another way." Mr. Darcy's tone lightened as he spoke. "I have an acquaintance in this village. The uncle of a school friend. I met him once, years ago, when I invited said friend to spend the winter holiday with us." Doubt clouded Mr. Darcy's features. "I'm not certain he'll remember me, or recognize me with this beard, but I may be able to persuade him to send a message to Pemberley. Will you be able to watch your luggage while Miss Bennet and I go beg the favor?"

Elizabeth wondered if Mr. Darcy was remembering their earlier discussion about being less threatening with a woman in the party or if he simply didn't wish to leave her with only Mr. Everett as a guard. Or, and the thought pleased her, perhaps he enjoyed having her by his side. Beside her, Mr. Everett nodded, though he didn't look hopeful. Elizabeth suspected he would begin searching through his things while they were gone.

"We shouldn't be more than an hour or two," Mr. Darcy said. He offered Elizabeth his arm.

She accepted, pleased to walk again. It felt good to loosen her stiff limbs and move, but if she hadn't wished to remain with Mr. Darcy and take some exercise, she would rather have remained with Mr. Everett and the luggage. She didn't relish the thought of meeting anyone, even the uncle of a school friend, in her state. Her hair was a dirty, tangled mess. Her gown bedraggled and torn. Her skin tanned and freckled. She knew she must look thoroughly disreputable.

Mr. Darcy led them away from the coaching inn and into a

respectable looking part of town. Neat homes and gardens lined the street. Passersby looked at them askance, confirming her suspicion of how terrible she looked. For his part, Mr. Darcy stood tall and exuded command, even if he had a thick beard and no jacket or cravat.

He slowed and took in the homes for a long moment. Elizabeth realized he was trying to recall which one he sought. She held her breath until he nodded sharply and turned them up a well-swept walk. They climbed the three steps to the small porch and Mr. Darcy knocked.

The door opened to a smartly dressed butler. He took one look and raised his eyebrows. "Can I help you?" he asked, his tone implying he knew he could not.

"We're here to see Mr. Robinson," Mr. Darcy said in a voice Elizabeth recognized as his most authoritative.

The butler blinked. Elizabeth could see him struggle with what to do. On the one hand, they appeared to be vagabonds. On the other, Mr. Darcy's accent was cultured, his bearing impeccable. Not to mention, he'd obviously found the correct house and used the correct name.

"I can see you're unsure if you should announce us," Mr. Darcy said. "My name is Fitzwilliam Darcy. I visited this house with Mr. Robinson's nephew, Nathan, about ten years ago. As I recall, you were the butler at that time and your cook served excellent raspberry tortes from a recipe she brought with her from Austria."

The butler appeared even more surprised. "You could have heard about the tortes," he finally said.

"I could have," Mr. Darcy allowed. "However, I suggest you permit Mr. Robinson to decide."

Finally, the butler nodded. "I shall inquire if Mr. Robinson is at home."

"Thank you." Mr. Darcy said.

The butler closed the door, not inviting them to wait inside. Elizabeth didn't begrudge him the precaution. She wouldn't have let them in, either. They looked as if they would steal something.

After a wait that seemed long but likely was not, the door reopened. Elizabeth couldn't help the surge of hope she felt. A feeling near giddiness washed through her when the man bowed and gestured them into the foyer. Though his expression was dubious, he turned and led them down a hall and to an open parlor door.

An older gentleman sat within. Keen eyes studied them from beneath thinning gray hair. He didn't stand and didn't ask them to sit.

Elizabeth was aware the butler remained, hovering in the doorway behind them. Mr. Darcy bowed. Elizabeth added a hasty curtsy.

Mr. Robinson, as Elizabeth assumed the man to be, asked Mr. Darcy something in a language she didn't know but guessed was Greek.

Mr. Darcy replied haltingly, his answer including his name and hers, at which point he gestured to her.

Eyes narrow, Mr. Robinson asked another question, this time in a language Elizabeth recognized as Latin, though she didn't speak or read it.

Mr. Darcy's reply was somewhat smoother and lengthier.

Mr. Robinson smiled and stood. He crossed the room to offer his hand, which Mr. Darcy shook. "Mr. Darcy, it's a pleasure to see you again after all these years." He turned to Elizabeth. "And to meet your lovely betrothed."

Elizabeth flushed, unsure if he mocked her, though he seemed sincere. "Thank you, sir," she murmured.

"Fetch paper, ink and pen," Mr. Robinson said to the butler. He cast them a questioning look. "Tea as well?"

"Thank you, but we left our companion, Mr. Everett, waiting outside the coaching inn," Mr. Darcy said. "We ought not remain for tea."

Elizabeth suppressed a sigh. She agreed with Mr. Darcy, but she hadn't eaten since a hastily obtained meal Mr. Everett bought the three of them at one of the stops the day before.

"Perhaps this Mr. Everett could join us?" Mr. Robinson suggested. "How will my men recognize him?"

"He's young, nervous, slight of build and overly sensitive of nature, with a small but fresh cut above his left eyes. He'll be standing beside an almost comical heap of cases," Mr. Darcy supplied.

"He likely has a somewhat lost expression and may be rummaging through one of the cases, all with total disregard to the fact that someone might run off with his possessions while he's occupied," Elizabeth added.

Amusement sparked in Mr. Robinson's eyes at their description. He looked past them to his butler. "Did you get all that?"

"Yes, sir."

"Go bring the young man in, then, and send for tea for four, and the writing materials. Oh, and why don't you bring John to help you with the luggage?"

"Yes, sir," the butler said and disappeared.

"Now, Mr. Darcy, while we wait, please tell me your tale again," Mr. Robinson said. "Your Latin isn't what it could be. I'm not certain I understood aright. Did you say you were stolen from a church?"

Mr. Robinson gestured for them to take the sofa opposite him as he reseated himself. Elizabeth felt terrible letting her filthy skirt touch his upholstery, but Mr. Darcy sat without hesitation. She followed, realizing the moment she did how pleasant it was to sit in a nice parlor again and wait for tea. She supposed, if they ruined Mr. Robinson's sofa, Mr. Darcy would simply pay to have it repaired.

Mr. Darcy repeated their tale of abduction and shipwreck in his usual succinct way, though with more detail than he'd given Mr. Everett. Mr. Robinson listened with great attention and asked many questions. These, Elizabeth noted, were mostly attempts to catch them out, which led her to guess he didn't completely believe Mr. Darcy to be who he claimed.

The writing materials arrived while they spoke and were placed on a side table, but Mr. Robinson asked another question rather than invite Mr. Darcy to use them. Tea came next, which Elizabeth served, though the state of her hands embarrassed her. As Mr. Darcy's recounting drew to a close, Mr. Everett appeared. He looked suitably impressed to find himself in a pleasant parlor.

Mr. Robinson turned to their travel companion. "Now, Mr. Everett, please sit. Tell me about yourself."

Mr. Everett looked to Mr. Darcy, who shrugged. Elizabeth agreed. She could see no harm in telling Mr. Robinson anything he wished to know. Also, she was curious to hear Mr. Everett's tale. As they'd ridden in the back of the wagon and he in the front, then in cramped misery surrounded by strangers, and Mr. Everett had somehow managed to sleep the last leg of their journey thus far, Elizabeth and Mr. Darcy hadn't had the chance to hear how their companion had ended up stranded in Scotland.

"I went to visit my cousins, you see," Mr. Everett began as he sat. He accepted the cup of tea Elizabeth offered him with a grateful look.

"How did that land you traveling with more luggage than you can manage?" Mr. Robinson asked.

"I started with my gig and horse." Mr. Everett swallowed, sorrow sliding across his features. "I crashed the gig on my way home. My horse had to be put down."

Mr. Robinson frowned. "Then how is it that a young man who can afford a horse, gig, and whatever all is in your excessive luggage, didn't have a servant with him? Or more funds?" He looked to Mr. Darcy. "That is, I assume none of you have funds or you wouldn't be begging pen and ink from me."

Mr. Darcy offered a nod of confirmation.

Mr. Robinson turned his keen gaze back on Mr. Everett.

Mr. Everett tugged at his cravat. "My mother, she still controls the funds of our estate, though my father has been gone some time and, really, the estate is mine. That is, I'll be of age in less than a year, so it's nearly mine. She wouldn't give me the funds to take a servant or travel by coach, and she'd ordered our coachman not to take me."

Mr. Robinson thought on that for a moment, nibbling on a tea cake. "In the past, you've let people take advantage of you when she's given you funds?" he suggested.

Mr. Everett shook his head. "Oh no." He grimaced. "Well, on occasion, but not often and not much. No, the truth is, my father died while traveling to visit his kin in Scotland and Mother worries she'll lose me the same way." He sat up straighter. "But I can't be kept in cotton wool all the time."

"Very well," Mr. Robinson said. To Elizabeth's surprise, he turned to her. "Miss Bennet, can you favor me with a song? The pianoforte is in tune, although I don't have any music."

Can you, not will you, Elizabeth thought. She cast him an amused look as she stood, wondering what he'd do if she said she couldn't play. Ask her to sketch? Quiz her in French? Fortunately, he'd hit on the one talent she did possess.

She walked over to the instrument and sat. Staring down at the keys, her amusement left her. For some reason, her mind couldn't call up a song. She took a deep breath and launched into a simple piece, usually practiced by beginners. She was nervous enough that she stumbled over part of it.

When she finished, face hot, she turned toward the three gentlemen. "I'm out of practice," she apologized. "It would help if you had some sheet music."

Mr. Everett hopped to his feet. "I have some sheet music in my luggage," he said with surprising enthusiasm. "Perhaps you can play that?" He didn't wait for a reply but hurried from the room.

"Sheet music?" she murmured. "That's one reason for all the

cases?"

"May I have use of those writing materials now?" Mr. Darcy asked with a slight frown. He glanced toward the clock on the mantlepiece.

Elizabeth followed his gaze to see that the day was ticking by. Hadn't he said Pemberley was twenty miles away still? How quickly could a messenger reach there, and a carriage return for them?

Before Mr. Robinson could reply, Mr. Everett returned. "Here it is," he proclaimed and rushed toward the pianoforte.

"Perhaps after Miss Bennet's performance, Mr. Darcy," Mr. Robinson said. "It's been years since I've heard that pianoforte play."

Elizabeth could read the annoyance in Mr. Darcy's features, even with his face half hidden by a beard. She understood why the delay chaffed him. He must hate being so near home, where he was lord and master, and yet still beholden to charity from this near-stranger.

"Play this, Miss Bennet," Mr. Everett said and placed the sheets in the stand.

As it seemed her playing was required to see them on their way, Elizabeth applied herself to the tune. Mr. Everett's hovering didn't help her learn, but she soon got caught up in the music. After mastering enough of the keys, which took several passes, she attempted the verses.

The lyrics gave voice to a young woman who was dying. She was engaged to be married but knew she wouldn't live to wed. She sang about all the things she would miss. The love of her husband. The children she'd expected to bear and watch grow. As well as little things like the change of the seasons and the first flowers of spring. She even spoke of the sorrows she anticipated and how she regretted missing them as well. It nearly broke Elizabeth's heart to sing the tune.

After a fairly reasonable rendition, Mr. Robinson raised a stilling hand. "I would love to hear you sing it once you master it but if I keep you any longer, you wouldn't get to Pemberley by dark."

"We won't reach it by dark now, even though you offered a rider to carry my letter," Mr. Darcy said, his tone betraying annoyance.

Elizabeth, who could only assume the offer of a rider had come while they conversed in Latin earlier, suspected the irritation that touched Mr. Darcy's tone was only a sampling of what he felt.

Mr. Robinson cast him an amused look but turned his attention back to Elizbeth. "Even if you aren't who you say you are, your music made it worth my while to help you. I've never heard that piece before."

"It's a beautiful song," Elizabeth agreed, aware the quality of the piece shown more brightly than her renditions.

"Thank you," Mr. Everett said, face flushed. "I wrote it. I didn't have anyone to sing it. I'm glad I heard you do so."

Elizabeth turned to him with no small amount of surprise, and with newfound respect. "It's a beautiful piece," she reiterated. She frowned. "But very sad."

"I know." His face folded into lines of sorrow. "It's about my betrothed. She died almost a year ago. We were going to marry when we were of age. I was mourning her and bemoaning my loss, and my mother said that I should think of what Lucy had lost."

"You should be proud of it," Elizabeth said. "It is a fitting memorial."

Mr. Darcy stood, garnering everyone's attention. "Even if we aren't who we say we are," he said to Mr. Robinson, a touch of sarcasm in his tone, "you offered us your assistance in the form of writing materials and a rider to take my words to Pemberley. May I avail myself of those writing materials now?"

Chapter Sixteen

Seated at the pianoforte in Mr. Robinson's parlor, Elizabeth held her breath. Thus far on their journey, Mr. Darcy had reined in the more commanding side of his nature and sought aid humbly. She knew this final delay tormented him. She sympathized but hoped he hadn't allowed that torment to rob them of an opportunity.

Mr. Robinson turned an amused look on Mr. Darcy. "I recall you being authoritative even as a young man."

Elizabeth let out her breath in relief.

Mr. Darcy frowned.

Mr. Robinson's smile widened. "I will do better than writing materials and a rider. My carriage has a broken axel, but I can loan you some horses." He nodded toward Mr. Everett. "My carriage should be ready the day after tomorrow. I can send your luggage on then or Mr. Darcy can send back for it."

"I don't ride," Elizabeth said with sudden dismay. Mr. Robinson had obviously kept them late knowing he would make the offer. He hadn't worried over a rider getting to Pemberley and the carriage coming back because he'd expected to send them on his horses, but Elizabeth couldn't ride twenty miles. She'd never even ridden two.

"I have a seventeen-hand horse who can easily carry two," Mr. Robinson said with a look between Mr. Darcy and Elizabeth.

Elizabeth looked to Mr. Darcy as well. He nodded, face a mask but a gleam deep in his eyes. She shrugged. If Mr. Darcy thought she could make the journey with him, she believed him.

Mr. Robinson sent for the horses. While they waited, he pressed more food on them. Elizabeth was happy for the offer, especially for tea as her throat was tired from multiple renditions of Mr. Everett's song, but Mr. Everett declined. Instead, he went to the hall to reorder his luggage, having one case small enough to secure to a saddle. Elizabeth couldn't help but wonder how much of Mr. Everett's precious luggage brimmed with sheet music.

In short order, she sat before Mr. Darcy in the saddle. Elizabeth hadn't fully appreciated how tall seventeen hands was before. The ground seemed very far below, but Mr. Darcy's arms were about her and he guided the animal with such confidence that his actions seemed almost unconscious, the horse an extension of his will.

If being atop the horse made her nervous, her place essentially in Mr. Darcy's lap, his arms about her, made her doubly so. Not in a fearful way, like the horse, but in a strange, jittering sort of way. As they rode, all she could think about were Mr. Darcy's kisses the day of his second proposal.

Mr. Everett seemed nervous as well, a state that grew during the ride, seeming to swell as they got closer to their destination. Finally, he drew abreast them. He kept casting questioning, worried looks their way. At one point, he nearly guided his horse off the road.

"Are you well, Mr. Everett?" Mr. Darcy finally asked.

"Yes, it's only, and I don't mean offense as you've been truly valuable travel companions, but I must still make my way fifteen miles south of Mr. Darcy's estate." He tugged at his cravat. "You've made quite the journey to reach your relation. You seem certain of his aid. What if, that is, what if Mr. Darcy turns you out and me with you? What if he invites you in but not me? Do you suppose Mr. Robinson would take it amiss if I ride on into the night to reach home? I'll send his horse back, I swear."

Much of Elizabeth's nervousness fled in amusement. She'd all but forgotten they'd let Mr. Everett assume Mr. Darcy was a relation of himself, rather than further test his faith in two strangers he'd met on the road, no matter how helpful.

Mr. Darcy was silent for a long moment.

"Uh, Darcy?" Mr. Everett prompted.

When Mr. Darcy still didn't reply, Elizabeth elbowed him.

"If, when we reach Pemberley, you aren't made extremely welcome, I am sure Mr. Robinson won't mind your further use of his horse," was all Darcy said.

Elizabeth shook her head but held her peace. If Mr. Darcy would rather wait a few more miles and show Mr. Everett who he was instead of arguing the point now, she would abide by his wish. She didn't half wonder, though, if Mr. Darcy didn't derive some hint of amusement from his plan.

Just about the time Elizabeth began to wonder if riding a horse was just a new way to make her uncomfortable, they turned from the lane onto a well-kept drive. Trees lined the way, then opened to a lawn. Situated atop a low hill stood a large, elegant manor. The neat green lawn, manicured garden and backdrop of forest combined with the stateliness of the structure to create what Elizabeth deemed the most picturesque vista she'd ever beheld.

She was to be mistress of this? Something akin to shock reverberated through her, followed hard by worry. She'd known of Mr. Darcy's wealth. She hadn't fully understood the implications, however. The grandness before her made Elizabeth feel small and quite, quite grimy. Why, they should dunk her in a trough before allowing her into the place.

"Stunning, isn't it?" Mr. Everett said. "I toured it once, last autumn. A truly magnificent place. It's the inspiration behind one of my compositions." He let out a sigh.

Elizabeth craned her neck to look at Mr. Darcy. He offered a reassuring smile as he urged their mount up the drive. By the time they reached the mounting block, several liveried footmen and groomsmen waited. All bore perfectly composed expressions but, somehow, Elizabeth could still feel their doubt that the approaching party had any right to be on Mr. Darcy's grounds.

"Marcus," Mr. Darcy said to the one who stepped out in front of the others to speak with them.

The footman cocked his head to the side. He frowned, confusion clear on his face. "Do I know you... sir?"

Elizabeth could all but feel Mr. Darcy's amusement.

"Please send for Mrs. Reynolds. She knows me."

"Mr. Darcy's housekeeper?" The footman, Marcus, appeared dubious. "Are you expected?"

"In a way," Mr. Darcy said dryly.

Elizabeth caught the general nervousness of the gathered footmen and Mr. Everett. The latter's borrowed horse sidestepped uneasily. She noted Mr. Darcy's horse evidenced complete calm.

She also noted that, while the footman obviously didn't recognize his employer under the beard and grime, Mr. Darcy knew the man. That both surprised and pleased her. Obviously, Mr. Darcy didn't associate with the footman much, for the beard wasn't that great a disguise, but he'd still taken the time to learn the man's name.

She would have assumed he wasn't the type to pay attention to his lower staff, especially after he hadn't recognized Fiona and Jeb. Had he ignored them because they were Mr. Collins' staff, or had he been too distracted on his visits to the parsonage to note much of anything? The latter idea was flattering.

"Please, it is important," Elizabeth put in, when Mr. Darcy didn't speak again, and no one moved. "I can assure you, Mrs. Reynolds will be pleased to see the man I'm riding with."

"He's a relation of the house," Mr. Everett added.

Behind Elizabeth, Mr. Darcy coughed. Elizabeth was certain the sound hid a bark of laughter. So, he was enjoying his anonymity after all. She resisted the urge to again poke him in the ribs with her elbow.

The footman studied them a moment longer. Finally, he nodded and hurried off. A groomsman came forward to take hold of the bridal. With strong hands, Mr. Darcy lifted Elizabeth from the horse and set her on the mounting block. Fortunately, he didn't let go immediately. Her legs could hardly hold her. She took a breath, marshaled her flagging resources, and stepped away from his steadying hands and down from the mounting block.

Mr. Darcy swung free of the saddle with practiced ease. So much so, she doubted he required, or often used, a mounting block at all. With a nod to the groomsman, he headed toward the broad front steps. To her relief, he stopped at the base. It would be cruel to test his staff by trying to stroll inside. Elizabeth came forward to stand at his shoulder. Mr. Everett stayed by his mount. She noted neither horse was escorted away.

After what seemed ages to Elizabeth, the large front door opened. A tall, pleasant looking middle-aged woman came out, Colonel Fitzwilliam behind her. Mr. Darcy stepped forward and bowed. Even through his beard, Elizabeth could see the grin on his face.

"Darcy," Colonel Fitzwilliam exclaimed. He rushed down the steps to pull Mr. Darcy into a quick, back-pounding embrace. "By God, Darcy, it's you." His eyes went even wider as they settled on Elizabeth. "And Miss Bennet."

"Mr. Darcy." The woman, whom Elizabeth assumed was Mrs. Reynolds, had followed the colonel down the steps. "Oh, Mr. Darcy, you're a happy sight. We've been beside ourselves with worry. Miss Darcy will be so pleased. She's cried every night."

Elizabeth was aware of the footmen and groomsmen gaping at Mr. Darcy.

"I say, Darcy, you look terrible," Colonel Fitzwilliam added. "What under heaven happened to you?"

"I was at the parsonage proposing to Miss Bennet," Mr. Darcy began.

Although she'd accepted his offer and knew his plan, shock still reverberated through Elizabeth to hear him state as much to his cousin and before his staff. She could see like shock echoed on Colonel Fitzwilliam's face. Mrs. Reynolds turned curious eyes on her.

"About the time I finished making my case," Mr. Darcy continued, ignoring their surprise and with a dry note in his voice, "we were kidnapped at gunpoint, thrown into the bottom of a smugglers' wagon, driven to the coast and put on a ship, which subsequently wrecked, allowing us to escape."

Now, everyone appeared surprised. Even, Elizabeth realized, Mr. Everett. His surprise, undoubtedly, stemmed from a growing realization of Mr. Darcy's identity as master of Pemberley.

"I say," Colonel Fitzwilliam murmured, appearing flabbergasted. He shook his head. "I've never seen Lady Catherine so right and so wrong."

"How do you mean?" Mr. Darcy asked.

"Aunt Catherine said you must have been kidnapped and that Miss Bennet's disappearance was unrelated." Colonel Fitzwilliam glanced toward Elizabeth, eyes bright. "Some people said you'd run off to Scotland to wed Miss Bennet and took along the Collins' servants. That didn't make sense with one horse between the four of you. So, when there was neither a ransom note nor an explanation from you, I thought you'd been killed. Despite that, your man Edwards and I have more than a dozen men scouring Kent for some sign of you. I never dreamed you'd reappear on your own, having been to Scotland and wed after all."

Elizabeth's face heated. "We did end up in Scotland," she allowed. "We aren't yet wed." Her blush intensified as everyone looked at her. She was acutely conscious of her thoroughly disheveled, grimy appearance. She'd never imagined meeting Mr. Darcy's staff and being announced as the new mistress of the manor. Had she, she would not have wished to do so while in so disreputable a state as she was now.

"But he did ask, and you accepted." Colonel Fitzwilliam offered Elizabeth a bow. "If I'm being honest, even though I had no thought the two of you had eloped, I suspected that's why he rode over that day and deliberately didn't accompany him. Congratulations to both of you."

"Thank you," Elizabeth murmured, still blushing.

"But if you were kidnapped, why didn't a ransom letter come?" the colonel asked, turning back to Mr. Darcy. "Your missing horse, Miss Bennet's joint disappearance and the lack of a ransom letter were all details that didn't make sense." He shook his head, expression rueful. "I'm sorry I didn't stay in Kent to conduct the search. If I'd been there, I could possibly have discovered something which would have led me to find you."

"I'm glad you didn't stay" Mr. Darcy assured his cousin. "There was nothing in Kent that would have let you know what happened. Anyone could have looked for me. Few could guard Georgiana."

Mr. Darcy's sister, Elizabeth realized. Why would she need guarding? Were fortune hunting gentlemen truly that persistent? Elizabeth's eyes went to the glorious manor before her. Perhaps, in Miss Darcy's case, they were.

"As to the lack of a ransom letter," Mr. Darcy continued. "I've no idea why they didn't send one. They took Edwards' address and my ring, as proof they had me. All I can say is, they seemed incompetent in most every way. That's how we wrecked. They'd no real notion how to sail the ship, which they'd come by in some sort of accidental way, and so ran it onto rocks off the coast of Scotland. We were lucky enough to make it to shore. I don't believe most of those onboard did."

"Most of those onboard?" Colonel Fitzwilliam repeated. "How many of them were there?"

Mrs. Reynolds stepped forward. "I don't mean to intrude sir, Colonel, but it seems to me the details of the story may be lengthy, and Miss Bennet and Mr. Darcy will need time to clean up before dinner. It might be preferable to permit Miss Bennet to rest as well. Do you want me to delay dinner?" The last statement was aimed at Mr. Darcy.

Mr. Darcy turned to Elizabeth. He had the good grace to offer a look of apology. "Of course. Please put Miss Bennet in the gold room, Mrs. Reynolds. She'll likely wish to bathe, and she'll require clothing for dinner, which probably should be delayed." He turned to Mr. Everett, who stood slightly to the side, expression still dumbfounded. "This is Mr. Everett, who's been gracious enough to aid us on our journey home. He will require a room as well. He may also wish to bathe. I know I do."

Mrs. Reynolds nodded. "I'll see to it." She extended a hand to Elizabeth. "Come with me, you poor thing. What a trial you've had."

Elizabeth took the housekeeper's hand, although she cringed at how dirty hers was. Mrs. Reynolds led her toward the broad steps. Behind them, she could hear Mr. Darcy issuing orders regarding Mr. Everett's luggage and the horses, interspersed with Colonel Fitzwilliam's questions.

"You poor dear," Mrs. Reynolds repeated as she took Elizabeth through a daunting, two story foyer and up a broad set of elegantly curved steps.

Elizabeth craned her neck, worried she must be leaving muddy footprints in her wake. She felt horrendously dirty. Mr. Darcy's home gleamed from floor to ceiling and here she was, hair in a sloppy braid tied with a bit of lace she'd tore off the tattered hem of her dress. Smelling unsavory, even to her own nose. She'd washed her hands and face in streams but doubted she looked as if she had. To make matters worse, she knew she was brown and freckled.

The gold room proved to be so luxurious, Elizabeth stopped just inside the doorway, afraid to ruin anything. Gold was the accent color, most of the plush claddings and furnishing done in a warm cream. Elizabeth's eyes were drawn to the open bathing room door, though she didn't know how she could even undress without creating a horrifying ring of dirt.

"You'll feel more yourself once you bathe, I'm sure," Mrs. Reynolds said. "And I'll go ask Miss Darcy if she's anything you can wear. Delicate little thing, aren't you?" She pursed her lips, looking Elizabeth over. "Maybe something from when she was younger." A smile bloomed on her face. "And I'll tell her that her brother is home safe. She'll be overjoyed."

This was said in such a tone of true happiness as to recall Mr. Wickham's long-ago description of the young woman. He'd called her proud and aloof, like her brother. Not that Elizabeth credited a word Mr. Wickham said but if she had, Mrs. Reynolds obvious affection for the young woman would go a long way toward discrediting the standoffish image.

"Don't you worry, Miss Bennet, we'll have you right in no time," Mrs. Reynolds continued as she turned back toward the room's door. "Your bath will be ready soon. I'll send some maids to assist you and when you're done bathing, you just lie down and rest. I'll send for you when it's time for dinner, but you're only to come down if you feel up to it. You need a respite, after such an ordeal."

The door closed softly behind her. After surveying the lovely room again, Elizabeth gathered her tattered skirt, so no strands could drag on the cream carpet, and tiptoed to the bathing room. There, she began to gingerly strip away her grimy clothes.

Chapter Seventeen

Elizabeth bathed, reveling in the luxury. The staff changed the water and she bathed again. Her clothing was whisked away, and she was given what she recognized to be an old dress suitable for a girl who not only wasn't out but was perhaps not even grown up. Several sets of slippers in various sizes were also brought. After helping Elizabeth dress, two maids set to work on her hair. Somehow, between them, they managed to untangle her locks with very little pain to her scalp.

Once everything was cleared up and the final maid left, Elizabeth lay down atop the soft coverlet. She truly did want to go to dinner and so didn't dare get beneath the sheets. Simply to lie atop the bed was luxury enough. She couldn't recall ever feeling anything so soft and plush. Her eyes drifted closed.

They opened to a knock. She was in a very fine room atop a bed that was too soft to be real. Her hand stole out, seeking the reassurance of Mr. Darcy by her side, and found nothing. Elizabeth sat up, panic surging through her.

She blinked, coming fully awake. The door cracked open. Mrs. Reynolds' kind visage peeked in.

"Would you care to come down to dinner, dear, or would you prefer to sleep?" the housekeeper asked. "I've a maid to assist you with either."

"Dinner, please," Elizabeth said. She was terribly tired, but she couldn't quite divest herself of lingering panic. She needed to see Mr. Darcy. This was the longest she'd been absent from his presence in weeks.

Mrs. Reynolds smiled, nodded and disappeared, to be replaced by a maid. The maid helped Elizabeth with her hair, which was still wet from being washed. At Elizabeth's suggestion, the locks were pinned up in a simple knot. Elizabeth studied the effect in a tall mirror as the maid slipped from the room.

As she'd feared, her face and neck were marked by the sun, and there was a smattering of freckles splashed across her cheeks and nose.

Her mother would be absolutely horrified. She'd be at Elizabeth with a jar of powder the moment she set eyes on her.

Elizabeth started. She hadn't thought on her mother, any member of her family, in days. Mortification swept through her. Why, they'd no idea she was safe. She looked about the room again. Or engaged.

She must write to them. Immediately. She should have thought of as much, insisted on it, at Mr. Robinson's or before her bath.

Elizabeth went to the bedroom door but hesitated to open it. She had the overwhelming sensation she'd be trespassing were she to move about Mr. Darcy's magnificent home unescorted. That, of course, was silly. She squared her shoulders and pulled the door open.

Arms crossed, one shoulder propped against the wall and looking impeccable in a dark suit, Mr. Darcy waited. Elizabeth went still in the open doorway. She hadn't minded the beard as much as she would have thought but she'd somehow forgotten just how incredibly handsome he was. The feeling that she was an interloper intensified. Any moment, he would come to his senses and realize he didn't wish to marry a ruined, poorly connected country miss with atrocious relations and a dowry he might spend in a week in London.

Yes, she would write to her family to tell them she was safe, but she wouldn't say ought of her engagement until Mr. Darcy spoke to her father. Elizabeth required that assurance, for she would never hold Mr. Darcy to a proposal made during the trials of their journey. Her reputation was in shambles, but the scandal would be doubled if Mrs. Bennet told all of Hertfordshire that Elizabeth was engaged, and it turned out she wasn't.

Part of her mind knew this was illogical. By announcing their betrothal to his cousin, his servants, and Mr. Everett, Mr. Darcy had committed himself to the marriage. But after seeing Pemberley, she still didn't quite believe she could actually marry someone so much above her.

Whereas in the past, such uncertainty and her list of shortcomings would have had Elizabeth stand tall and defiant before Mr. Darcy, now, her heart stuttered. Somewhere along the road from Scotland, living without Mr. Darcy beside her had become unfathomable. Yet, she wouldn't change who she was and, deep down, she knew she would still resent him if he couldn't accept her.

A smile spread across his face to chase her dour thoughts away. "You look beautiful."

Elizabeth flushed. "I'm freckled."

"I love your freckles."

Her breath caught. Not I love you, but nearly. "I'm wearing your sister's childhood dress. She must be much taller than I am."

He peeled himself away from the wall and moved toward her. "She is, and I don't recall the dress." He stopped in front of Elizabeth and looked her up and down. "Nothing about you is childish."

Perhaps her insecurities were, but she wouldn't admit that to him. Instead, she offered a smile, even as her face heated under his gaze. "And nothing about you bespeaks of a vagabond."

"Are you saying I clean up well?" He rubbed his chin. "You don't miss the beard?"

She shook her head. She hadn't seen his jaw since the start of their journey. What would it be like to kiss him now? Better, she imagined, though she didn't know if that was possible.

His thoughts must have echoed hers, for he moved nearer still. His face lowered toward hers. Elizabeth's heart took up an erratic beat.

Someone was whistling, she realized. The sound of footfalls on the staircase penetrated her mind. Annoyance flickered across Mr. Darcy's features. He stepped back and offered her his arm. Elizabeth accepted, mildly begrudging his jacket and shirt the right to encase his arm, to actually touch him. Colonel Fitzwilliam, dressed for dinner, appeared at the top of the steps. He stopped when he saw them.

"Darcy, Miss Bennet," he said, nodding. "Darcy, I thought you'd like to know your man reached the mail in time. The express you sent should be well on its way, the other letters as well."

"Thank you," Mr. Darcy said and started them walking toward the colonel.

"I missed the mail?" Dismay filled Elizabeth. Not that the few moments would have mattered, from the sound of things, but she couldn't believe that the instant Mr. Darcy had smiled at her, she'd again forgotten about writing. "I need to write my father. He must be so terribly worried."

"I took the liberty of sending an express to your father, telling him you are here and that, after resting here for two weeks, you will return to Longbourn," Mr. Darcy said.

Gratitude and annoyance sparked in equal measure, but she kept walking and endeavored to keep her expression bland, as the colonel waited for them at the end of the hall, eyes on them. His action was kind, considerate, but also highhanded. What if she wished to leave tomorrow? Did he mean he wouldn't permit her? "Thank you. There are others I would like to write but the letters need not be sent by express."

He must have heard something in her tone, for he cast her a quick glance. "I chose two weeks as the outside, not wishing to wake you. I felt it would be easier to surprise your family with an earlier arrival than disappoint them with a later one."

"How very thoughtful of you," Elizabeth said, chastened.

"Met your father," Colonel Fitzwilliam said to her as they reached him. "Exemplary fellow, even if he was quite distressed."

"You met my father?"

The colonel nodded. "He came to Rosings to search for clues as to your whereabouts." He grimaced. "I'm afraid Aunt Catherine was her usual self, but I did my best by him, as did your friend, Mrs. Collins. Anne made an effort as well," he added as he turned and headed back down the steps.

Elizabeth couldn't be certain, but she thought she heard him mutter, 'though that cousin of yours was an ass,' as they followed.

They rounded the curved staircase to find Mr. Everett and two women Elizabeth didn't know waiting in the foyer below. The younger of the two women, who hovered behind the elder like a displaced stork, was tall, light haired and possessed of a reserve to rival Mr. Darcy's, could only be Miss Darcy. She stared at them as they descended, wide blue eyes set unwaveringly toward Elizabeth. As soon as they left the bottom step, she hurried forward, her mien one of nervous excitement.

"Georgiana," Mr. Darcy said. "This is my betrothed, Miss Elizabeth Bennet. Elizabeth, my sister, Georgiana."

Elizabeth noted the general surprise at Mr. Darcy's use of her Christian name. She wasn't certain he realized his breach. His calm countenance didn't alter as she dropped into a curtsy, mirrored by Miss Darcy who dropped her gaze now that they all stood together.

Miss Darcy cast Elizabeth a quick, shy look. "Miss Bennet, I am so very pleased to meet you."

"And I you," Elizabeth supplied. She offered a warm smile, but Miss Darcy had already focused on the inlaid floor again. Not wishing to press the girl, Elizabeth turned toward the only person with whom she was not yet acquainted and soon discovered her to be Mrs. Annesley, Miss Darcy's companion.

Mr. Darcy escorted Elizabeth into the dining room. Colonel

Fitzwilliam, with his usual affability, insisted Mr. Everett escort Miss Darcy in, while he escorted Mrs. Annesley. Dinner had only one course but there was plenty of food. That was fortunate, for Elizabeth hadn't realized how hungry she was. Aside from a celebratory toast to her and Mr. Darcy's engagement, conversation mainly centered on Colonel Fitzwilliam and Mr. Darcy talking about everyone's reactions to Mr. Darcy's disappearance. Miss Darcy only spoke when spoken to and even then, very briefly. Mrs. Annesley remained silent as well. Mr. Everett spent most of the dinner looking about him as if he wanted to store up the atmosphere for future use.

After dinner, Elizabeth and the other two women retired to a stunning, yet also comfortable, parlor of dark wood and hunter green fabrics. The three of them settled into a small semicircle on an armchair and sofa, with Mrs. Annesley occupying the center position. Silence descended. Elizabeth didn't truly mind. She knew she ought to strike up conversation, Miss Darcy obviously too shy to do so, but now that she'd eaten, she was exceedingly tired.

"Miss Bennet, we know some of the tale," Mrs. Annesley said. "We know Mr. Darcy asked for your hand and then the two of you were immediately abducted and put on a ship, which subsequently wrecked, and then you had to walk from Scotland back to Derbyshire, but that's all the detail we've heard."

Realizing what they had heard was likely all gossip from servants, passed along from Mr. Darcy's explanation to Colonel Fitzwilliam on the steps, Elizabeth mustered energy for the tale. Not only did it behoove her to ensure her future sister by marriage knew the truth, insomuch as she and Mr. Darcy had discussed revealing it, Elizabeth was a guest and obligated to provide entertainment.

"Yes, we were at the parsonage and Mr. Darcy had only recently finished his proposal," she began. From there, she told of the men with pistols, the horrible wagon ride and the even more terrible ride on the little rowboat, hands bound and unable to swim, even had she been free. Her audience listened with rapt interest. Elizabeth was aware, as well, of several servants, both those stationed in the room and those clustered in doorways.

She detailed how they'd freed her hands and made her climb a ladder onto a ship, then locked her in a small room. "It wasn't until Mr. Darcy arrived that I realized I hadn't been alone at all. Mr. Wickham was in the room with me."

Miss Darcy gasped. "No. They'd taken him, too?"

Belatedly, Elizabeth realized that if Mr. Darcy had grown up with Mr. Wickham, Miss Darcy must have as well. That she could hold any affection for the man surprised Elizabeth. By her estimation, no one who knew him well could. Still, she bore Miss Darcy's concerned tone in mind as she continued with the tale, downplaying Mr. Wickham's egregious behavior by not mentioning how he always took the most food and leaving out his continued antagonism. She also, when she reached the point, tried to skim over the reason she and Mr. Darcy parted ways with him.

"But I don't understand," Miss Darcy cut in. "Why would you and Fitzwilliam abandon George that way? He was imprisoned for longer than either of you and injured. He had even less hope of making his way home. Oh, only think, he's stranded somewhere in Scotland right now." Her gaze went to the door. "I shall ask my brother to put out a search for him."

That, Elizabeth couldn't countenance. She would defend Mr. Darcy's treatment of Mr. Wickham to anyone as more than laudable. Furthermore, for all he'd born up well, Mr. Darcy had suffered the trials of their journey as much as she had. He deserved better than being railed against for leaving Mr. Wickham behind, especially by his own sister.

Elizabeth drew in a steadying breath. "We left him because he'd hidden the fact that he had funds on him the entire time," she said, tone gentle. "We could have used those funds to send word to you here and saved us all a lot of struggle and you considerable worry."

Miss Darcy stared at her. "I can't believe that. If he had money, he would have sent word. Why would you possibly think he had funds? He was a prisoner, like you."

Elizabeth could read strain in Miss Darcy's face. Seated between them, Mrs. Annesley gave her head a little shake, as if urging caution. Was that the sort of coddling that had left Miss Darcy fond of her childhood acquaintance? Elizabeth wouldn't put it past Mr. Darcy to protect his sister from the truth. Didn't he see how dangerous naivete could be? Not only could Miss Darcy trust Mr. Wickham too much, she might come to resent a brother she should rely on.

"He said he went into the inn to gather information," Elizabeth said. "When we looked for him, he was finishing a lavash meal."

"Someone bought it for him," Miss Darcy said with absolute conviction.

Elizabeth's head throbbed slightly. She realized she was likely much too worn for the conversation she'd allowed. "He admitted he'd bought it himself and had deliberately hoarded his funds."

Mrs. Annesley winced.

A frown marred Miss Darcy's face. "George wouldn't do that. He's a good man. He's noble and honest. He wouldn't behave that way." Her expression lightened. "Maybe you mean a different Mr. Wickham."

Elizabeth caught Mrs. Annesley's hopeful look. Should she take that avenue of escape? She hardly knew Mr. Darcy's sister. She wasn't his wife yet. Was it her place to set the young woman straight?

She rubbed at her forehead. She was definitely too exhausted from their journey to undertake what was obviously a serious conversation. Also, she should seek Mr. Darcy's thoughts before moving forward.

"The Mr. Wickham I'm speaking of is about my height with blond curls and very handsome," Miss Darcy pressed. "He's charming and kind. He listens well and tells wonderful stories. He and my brother grew up as dear friends. So, you see, the man you speak of can't be the same Mr. Wickham. George would never behave so dishonorably. Or, if he did, it would be Fitzwilliam's fault."

Stung on Mr. Darcy's behalf, Elizabeth dropped her hand. "Your brother's fault? The man who was there, whom I knew from Hertfordshire as Mr. George Wickham and who claimed to be a favorite of your father, is precisely the man of whom we both speak," Elizabeth snapped. "Furthermore, I can assure you he is in no way honorable. Why, he even tried to argue me into marrying him for the purpose of getting your brother to pay him for the act."

Miss Darcy shot to her feet, fists balled at her sides. "You are lying to me. George would never do any of the things you said." Her face went from red to white, to red again. "Especially not that last thing." Tears appeared in her eyes. "He is kind and good and giving."

"He is petty and selfish," Elizabeth said. "And he admitted smuggling and running from debts he couldn't pay."

Miss Darcy glared down at her, face a vivid red. Elizabeth stared back, features set in lines of surety. Miss Darcy looked so livid, Elizabeth half worried the tall young woman would attempt to strike her.

Chapter Eighteen

Having spent days in the company of Mr. Everett and already conversed with his cousin for most of dinner, Darcy didn't see any reason to linger over port. Aside from which, Elizabeth looked particularly alluring that evening. Her beauty hadn't dimmed in his eyes while they traveled. Far from it. He'd been impressed with how lovely she looked despite their circumstance. He doubted most women he knew, dependent on wardrobe and primping, would have looked anywhere close to as good.

Tonight, though, divested of the stress of their journey and in a different gown, her long tresses pinned up in an elegant coif, yet still with that smattering of freckles to set her apart from the usual, stiff, superficial women he socialized with, she looked amazing. Why sit in a room with two gentlemen, no matter how pleasant, when he could be looking at Elizabeth? In as little time as he deemed socially acceptable, he suggested they rejoin the ladies.

Darcy led the way toward the green parlor, pointing out various portraits and other details to Mr. Everett, who walked beside him. Richard, already well acquainted with every facet of Pemberley, trailed behind. They turned a corner and Darcy gestured Mr. Everett to proceed him into the green parlor.

"I hate you," Georgiana shouted.

She flew through the parlor door and slammed into Mr. Everett. She let out a shriek, Mr. Everett an exclamation. Arms flailed as both struggled for balance. Mr. Everett caught her by the shoulders and steadied both of them, then abruptly released her.

Darcy stared at his sister as Richard came to stand beside him. "Georgiana, what is the meaning of this? Why did you attack Mr. Everett? What reason could you possibly have for hating him?"

Had something untoward happened while Darcy bathed, wrote Mr. Bennet and sent Edwards, his London agent, a list of those people he wished to compensate for helping him? Would Darcy be required to duel the young man? The thought saddened him. Where he stood at Darcy's side, Richard eyed Everett curiously.

Georgiana, face red and streaked with tears, whirled to face Darcy. "I don't hate Mr. Everett. I hate that woman you brought home."

Darcy's confusion redoubled. "Elizabeth?"

"Don't call her that," Georgiana cried. "You can't mean to marry her. She's horrible."

Darcy looked past his sister to see Elizabeth seated in a plush armchair. She looked nearly as tired as after they swam from the shipwreck. She offered him an apologetic shrug. Seated on the sofa next to her, Mrs. Annesley appeared troubled.

"What reason do you have, then, for hating Miss Bennet?" Darcy asked. He couldn't fathom one. There must be a misunderstanding.

"She said the most horrible things about George," Georgiana wailed. "I know they aren't true. She's a liar. You can't marry a liar."

Darcy looked past his sister again.

Elizabeth let out a slow breath. "I was merely recounting the details of our journey. Frankly, I left most of Mr. Wickham's behavior out. Only when Miss Darcy decried you for leaving him behind did I feel compelled to speak plainly." She spoke in a reasonable tone but her eyes glittered.

Darcy bit back an expletive. This was somewhat his fault. He hadn't prepared Elizabeth for the affection in which Georgiana held Wickham. Nor, in truth, had he realized her regard remained so high. He turned to his sister in question. "I thought you'd…"

He trailed off as he looked about, taking in Elizabeth, Richard, Mrs. Annesley and Mr. Everett. There ought to be servants but, somehow, they'd all vanished. The pained look on Mrs. Annesley's face told Darcy she knew some, possibly all, of what had transpired. Georgiana had likely confessed, what with Mrs. Annesley being her constant companion. Richard knew everything and Mr. Everett, of course, knew nothing. Nor did Elizabeth, though Darcy suspected she'd now guessed much.

"I thought you'd grown apart from our childhood companion," Darcy settled for.

"No," Georgiana said in a low voice. "I simply got scared." She dashed at her cheeks with one hand.

Mr. Everett pulled free a kerchief and proffered it.

Georgiana accepted the unadorned square without looking, her gaze locked with Darcy's. "You sent him away and you made certain I couldn't see him again. Those were your decisions and, I suppose, what I get for going running to you when--"

"I thought you wanted my intervention," Darcy broke in to prevent her from admitting anything worse than her behavior already implied.

"I wanted your advice and your understanding, not your decisions," Georgiana snapped.

Darcy rocked back on his heels. He'd never seen his sister so angry. He didn't realize she could muster so much emotion.

"And now not only can I not see him, I must listen to this woman spread lies about him?" Georgiana's anger faltered. "I don't even know why. Miss Bennet seemed so kind. Why should she…" A hand flew to Georgiana's mouth as she watched Darcy with wide eyes. "Did she want to marry George and he turned her down?" she whispered.

That was more than Darcy could endure, even for his sister. "Most certainly not. He tried to persuade her to marry him so that I would provide him with even more funds than he's already received. She refused him, in no uncertain terms. Twice." Both memories still filled Darcy with smug satisfaction.

Fresh tears spilled from Georgiana's eyes. She blinked them back, Mr. Everett's kerchief clutched tight in her fingers. "But, only because he's in such dire straits. Only because you turned your back on him. You drove him to ask her. He doesn't love her."

Darcy stared at his sister, aware everyone else watched him. In a way, what Georgiana said was true. If he'd been more generous with Wickham, the man would never have asked for Elizabeth's hand. He wouldn't wed for less than ten thousand pounds, or until he was forced to. "No, he doesn't love her."

Beside Darcy, Richard shifted.

"And the other things Miss Bennet said?" Georgiana pressed. "About how George behaved?"

What could Darcy say? His sister was so fragile, so young. There was much she didn't know about the world, and he would keep it that way for as long as he could protect her.

Inside the parlor, Elizabeth tipped up her chin. "I believe it would be best if you recounted to Miss Darcy what you observed of Mr. Wickham's behavior."

Darcy shook his head. His gaze flicked over their overly large audience again. "I don't think it is appropriate to tell her the details of our journey at this moment," he said, voice tight. Elizabeth didn't understand the depth of Georgiana's affections, as he hadn't until that moment. The truth would hurt her.

Georgiana looked from Elizabeth to Darcy with wide, watery eyes.

"If you don't confirm what I said, she and I will never have a chance of getting along." Elizabeth's tone was eminently calm but underscored with unmistakable firmness. "I only ask that you tell her the truth. Nothing more, nothing less."

Annoyance flickered in Darcy. He didn't appreciate Elizabeth pressing him before so many witnesses. "And I told you, I don't believe this is the time."

Elizabeth's expression remained tranquil, but he could read the surge of will in her eyes. "I've given my opinion. I'll content myself with your assessment of its value."

Darcy's gaze narrowed. Her words seemed reasonable but, somehow, he sensed he stood on dangerous ground.

"She's trying to get you to lie to me," Georgiana accused, turning a glare on Elizabeth.

Elizabeth raised an eyebrow. "During the time I've spent with your brother, I've found him to be eminently honorable. I suspect you know that. When he does choose to speak to you about the events of our journey, I believe you should trust what he says."

Elizabeth's praise elicited a strange mixture of pride and shame. Shame because he endeavored to avoid confronting Georgiana with the truth. Pride because Elizabeth's words sounded sincere. On top of the compliment, she'd relented and given him a way out by conceding that there would be a when, instead of now.

But she hadn't implied never. What was the point of delaying telling the truth to Georgiana? Was maintaining her innocence for longer worth keeping her from accepting Elizabeth? Wouldn't Elizabeth's innate goodness and grace win Georgiana over despite this disagreement about Wickham?

"I know George behaved honorably," Georgiana declared. "And Miss Bennet is correct on one thing. We must settle this now."

Darcy looked to Richard, who nodded. Ignoring their audience of Mrs. Annesley and Mr. Everett, Darcy studied first his sister's tear-streaked face and then Elizabeth's calm one. The two people he loved most in the world were in front of him, both wanting him to describe things differently. The difference was, what one of them asked of him was the truth.

He drew in a deep breath and took his sister's hands. He would not lie. He wouldn't even attempt to soften what he said. Georgiana obviously held an idealistic view of Mr. Wickham. There, framed in the doorway of the green parlor, Darcy told her the truth. He stripped that image away.

As he spoke, Georgiana pulled her hands free of his. Her expression moved from disbelief to horror. She brought her hands up to cover her eyes. Mr. Everett's kerchief, forgotten, sailed to the floor. He dipped down to reclaim it. Stuffing the kerchief into one pocket, he pulled a fresh one from another. As Darcy's tale concluded, Georgiana lowered her hands to stare at him with haunted eyes. Mr. Everett proffered the fresh kerchief. She snatched it from him and wiped her cheeks.

"George did all of that?" she whispered.

Darcy nodded.

"What of the living you withheld from him?"

Darcy grimaced. Had Wickham told everyone his false version of the event? "He asked me to buy it from him, so I did. For three thousand pounds."

"I witnessed the documents," Richard added.

Georgiana looked back and forth between them, dazed.

Behind her, Mr. Everett looked a bit shocked as well. Three thousand pounds was arguably less than the living had been worth, but it was still a large sum.

Taking in his sister's stricken countenance, Darcy sought about for some reassurance. "For what it's worth, I believe Wickham was telling the truth when he said he did not want me kidnapped." Perhaps it would be more accurate to say that he didn't want to participate in the kidnapping, but Darcy would give Wickham the benefit of the doubt. "He paid for that reluctance by being held captive."

Mrs. Annesley appeared beside Georgiana. "Miss Darcy, perhaps you should retire?"

Georgiana shook her head. "No. No, I need to think. I couldn't possibly sleep."

Mrs. Annesley cast Darcy an apologetic shrug. Georgiana stood blinking, her face still damp where she'd missed with her borrowed kerchief. Awkward silence descended on the party. Only Elizabeth remained seated in the parlor. Darcy, Richard, Georgiana, Mrs. Annesley and Mr. Everett all stood in the hall, some of them half in the doorway.

Mr. Everett cleared his throat. "I hear you have an exquisite pianoforte, Miss Darcy."

She turned to him with a slight frown. "I beg your pardon?"

"I play," he elaborated. "I should be honored to see the instrument. Even more so to be permitted to play for you."

"Yes, of course," she said.

Without another glance at any of them, Georgiana turned and headed down the hall. Mr. Everett offered a hurried bow, angled halfway between Darcy and the parlor door, and turned to follow, Mrs. Annesley on his heels. Richard raised his eyebrows. Darcy shook his head, bemused. His gaze sought Elizabeth.

Inside the parlor, she came to her feet. As she crossed the room toward them, Darcy could read her fatigue in the stoop to her shoulders and the dimness of her usually bright eyes. He realized it had pained her nearly as much as him to visit such unhappiness on Georgiana.

"I, however, should like to retire," she said with a small smile.

"I'm sorry it took me a moment to understand," Darcy told her.

"You wish to keep your sister safe. No one will ever condemn you for that."

Darcy wished he could hold her, offer comfort and strength, but Richard stood beside him. "Sleep well, Miss Bennet."

"Thank you, Mr. Darcy." Her smile widened slightly. "In the morning, if I may, I should like to beg some writing materials from you. Paper, ink and pen."

He answered her smile with one of his own. "I'll see if I can spare some."

Richard looked back and forth between them, eyebrows once more raised. He turned to Elizabeth and bowed. "Good evening, Miss Bennet."

"Thank you, Colonel Fitzwilliam," Elizabeth said.

Her shoulder brushed Darcy's as she passed between him and Richard. He didn't know if the touch was deliberate. He did know it wasn't enough. Tonight, when he slept alone in his oversized bed in Pemberley's largest suite, he would mourn that Elizabeth wasn't beside him.

Richard gestured toward the parlor. "Shall we?"

Darcy nodded. He strode in and took the chair Elizabeth had occupied, his favorite. Perhaps he'd commission a second, identical chair to place beside it. His gaze drifted to the sofa. Or take to sitting on the sofa, where they could be together.

Richard settled onto the sofa, shattering Darcy's daydream. He stretched out his legs before him. "You didn't tell Miss Bennet about Georgiana and Mr. Wickham."

"I'm not in the habit of revealing my sister's secrets," Darcy said, then grimaced. That was the sort of pompous declaration Elizabeth would tease him for and rightly so. "More to the point, it never came up."

Richard nodded. "You believe Wickham's tale that they imprisoned him because he wouldn't participate in your kidnapping?"

"Oddly, yes," Darcy said. "Wickham has many faults, but he wouldn't go that far."

"From the sound of it, you had quite the adventure." Richard favored him with a somber stare. "You're lucky you and Miss Bennet survived."

Darcy waved that off, not of a fatalistic bent. "We were lucky they were very incompetent. They couldn't even sail the ship properly."

Richard nodded. "Wouldn't they have killed Wickham in the end?" he asked after a time. "You never knew who they were, but Wickham surely had names."

"All Wickham got were names like Smith and Jones," Darcy said. "We'd the first names Jeb and Mary, from the parsonage. I have little faith any were real. Wickham felt Mary also went by Fiona, but we didn't have any way to confirm that. She may have had a few other names."

Richard shook his head. "You're sure most of them died?" he said, visage cold. "I take exception with the danger in which they put you and Miss Bennet."

"I know the woman swam to shore, whatever her name." Darcy could still picture the churning waves and hear the final, tearing, cracking sounds as the ship shattered. He frowned. "I'm uncertain if the one they meant to send to Edwards was on the ship when we wrecked or not, but the last we saw of the other three men, they were arguing over the rowboat. At least one body bobbed in the ocean after the ship sank."

The grim look of satisfaction on Richard's face was almost frightening. "Good. He, and likely at least two of the others, got what they deserve, then." He shook his head. "All that risk. What did they even hope to gain?"

"I believe they had plans to move to Ireland or some such to live in luxury," Darcy said. "They undoubtedly didn't realize how little of my funds Edwards can lay his hands on without my person, or at least my witnessed signature."

"How much could he give them?"

"About four thousand pounds."

"Shared between five people at least?" Richard said. "That wouldn't last all that long."

Darcy smiled slightly. "No, not really. Even three thousand doesn't last long, if you ask George Wickham."

Richard chuckled. They returned to talk of their relatives. Lengthy as his journey had been, it wasn't long before Darcy retired as well. Not that he found sleep easily, alone in his bed, Elizabeth several rooms away.

Chapter Nineteen

After a restless night, Darcy rose early, but readied for his day in a leisurely fashion. He reveled in the ability to bathe. The selection of clothing. A clean-shaven face. His valet's assistance. He especially enjoyed the anticipation of descending to his own parlor, selecting from his favorite foods and eating his fill, seated at a linen bedecked table and accompanied by the paper and coffee.

And, hopefully, Elizabeth. He assumed she was an early riser. During their travels, they arose early. He could only guess what she would do otherwise, but he suspected she wasn't the type to lie about until noon.

In delightful accordance with his wish, Elizabeth entered the breakfast parlor mere moments after his arrival. She wore a different, equally borrowed looking gown. He was pleased Mrs. Reynolds had taken the initiative. He gestured to the seat at his side. Elizabeth glided across the room toward him, smile warm.

Darcy rose and pulled out her chair, waving off a footman. Her hair was up again, emphasizing her long, graceful neck. As she sat, he couldn't help but lean over the back of the chair to take in the scent of soap and lavender.

Mouth near her ear, he whispered, "I missed you last night." He suppressed a satisfied smile as a blush colored her cheeks.

She tipped her chin toward him, giving him a tantalizing near profile of her lips. "I missed you, too."

Darcy's hands tightened on the chairback. He forced his fingers to open and back to straighten. He would not kiss her in the breakfast parlor, in front of the staff, before they were even wed. Instead, he returned to his seat and tried to remember how pleased he was for the taste of coffee.

Footsteps sounded in the hall. Richard strode in, dressed for travel. "Morning Darcy, Miss Bennet."

"Good morning, Colonel," Elizabeth said brightly, though a trace of pink still stained her cheeks.

Richard looked back and forth between them with a faint smile and headed for the sideboard. "I won't play chaperone for long. I'm here for an early breakfast and then I'm off."

"So soon?" Darcy asked, ignoring his cousin's teasing.

"You can write all you like but my brother and our aunt won't be satisfied until they've heard the tale from one of us." He paused in loading his plate to cast a twinkling glance over his shoulder. "I thought better me than you, especially as I'm not needed to watch over Georgiana any longer."

Darcy maintained a bland expression, aware Richard was enjoying the opportunity to tease him and that the teasing was exceedingly good natured. "Thank you for that, by the way. I was worried about her."

Richard turned toward the table, plate full. Chagrin suffused his features. "If I'd believed the rumors that you'd eloped I might have found you faster, but I couldn't imagine the both of you would throw propriety to the wind or, even if you did, leave without at least a note to assuage our worries. Neither of you are reckless."

Elizabeth's smile was mischievous. "Even I couldn't inspire so anomalous a course in Mr. Darcy, making you right in not believing the rumors."

Darcy turned to her, surprised. "But I was overcome by 'an uncharacteristic fit of passion.'"

"Yet, you didn't consider whisking me off to Scotland."

Darcy couldn't deny that, but he didn't wish any doubt as to the depths of his affection. "I did not consider marrying in Scotland. Had I thought of it, I may have attempted some whisking."

Elizabeth offered a raised eyebrow, eyes dancing. "If you demand it, we shall return to Scotland this minute and wed, although I would prefer a more conventional wedding."

Richard laughed. "I believe Darcy has enough of a backlog of estate business that Scotland is not his choice." He came to sit on Darcy's other side. "But you haven't eaten yet. Try the ham. Not that everything isn't superb. I daresay Darcy's cook has outdone himself, everyone is so overjoyed to have him home, and to meet you."

Elizabeth offered Richard a smile. She made to stand.

Darcy covered her hand with one of his, staying her. "What is your pleasure? I'll fetch it." He could feel Richard's surprise.

"How can I know, when I haven't seen what is offered?" she

replied.

"You make a fair point, Miss Bennet," Darcy said. "Why don't we go together? That way, I shall know your preferences, for the future."

Expression somewhat bemused, Elizabeth nodded.

Darcy stood to help her with her chair.

The rest of breakfast passed quite amiably, despite Richard's continued teasing. Elizabeth was more than up to the challenge of bantering with Darcy's cousin and he didn't even permit himself to feel jealous of their easy repartee, so reminiscent of their time at Rosings. At least, not very jealous. Any time he did succumb, Elizabeth seemed to sense as much. She would turn to him with a warm smile, or brush his hand with hers, or any number of small intimacies which assured him that she preferred him over all others.

After they bid farewell to Richard, Darcy took Elizabeth around Pemberley, proudly showing her what would soon be her home. He introduced her again to Mrs. Reynolds and to the rest of the household. He soaked up her looks of admiration both for the home he loved and for when he knew the name of every member of his household they encountered. He thought, as well, she appreciated his easy manner with his staff.

Darcy ended his tour on his favorite porch, overlooking the grounds. He led Elizabeth to the broad stone balustrade. They stood shoulder to shoulder, looking out over the skillfully manicured grounds. Darcy considered them the perfect balance between cultivated and wild.

"Your home is absolutely beautiful, Mr. Darcy," Elizabeth said. She made a sweeping gesture to take in the view. "And this... glorious. I hope we soon may explore the garden?"

Darcy studied the sweep of her neck, the few loose curls that fluttered in a light breeze. Her shell-like ear. "Our home," he corrected. "And I hope to share every facet of it with you."

She turned to look up at him. Her eyes held an emotion akin to wonder as she studied his face. "If I'd known you then as I do now, I should never have refused you."

Warmth unfurled in him, but he couldn't let the misconception stand. "I'm not quite the same now as I was then. I changed."

"So quickly?"

"Some would say not quickly enough."

A shadow flickered in her gaze.

"What is it?" he asked.

"If you can change so quickly, mightn't you change back?"

Darcy opened his mouth to speak, then closed it again. Might he? Could he? In what ways had he truly changed?

"Answer me this," she said. "If your friend, Mr. Bingley, wished to wed my sister Jane right now, today, would you advise him against doing so?"

He considered his reply carefully, aware of the question's importance to her. "That depends. In your hypothetical, does he love her? Does she love him?"

"I thought he loved her. I know she loved him."

That surprised him. "She did?"

Elizabeth tipped her head to the side. "Of a certainty." Anger sparked in her eyes. She closed them over it, took a deep breath, and opened them again to take in his face. "You did not believe she loved him."

"I believed she found him amiable, as all do, and would certainly agree to marry him." At Mrs. Bennet's insistence, he added, but only to himself. "Furthermore, I was uncertain if he loved her. Bingley has a habit of falling in love for a month, even two, but then someone new catches his eye."

"I see." A slight frown shadowed her features. "Well, then, if you felt them both truly in love, would you attempt to stand between the union?"

"If I felt them both sufficiently invested, I would be happy for the union," Darcy stated. "Your sister is lovely, kind and well mannered. She would make any man a good wife."

"Even without a dowry?"

"Bingley can afford to pass up a dowry for happiness."

"And even with my family's connections to trade?" Elizabeth pressed.

"Bingley's family is already connected to trade."

Elizabeth's frown didn't vanish, as he'd hoped. Her fingers drummed an agitated rhythm on the balustrade. Darcy anticipated her next question. Could he accept the crasser members of her family? He could all but hear Elizabeth thinking the words. He couldn't let her ask until he knew how to reply. He had enough sense of the depth and strength of her convictions to know she wouldn't wed him if his answer didn't satisfy her.

He couldn't lose her. Not now, after all they'd been through. He couldn't let her go. "Elizabeth," he said, voice low. "I love you."

Her eyes flew wide. Her lips parted in a small gasp. She stared up at him, her expression suffused with happiness.

And Darcy berated himself as a lowly cad, hardly worthy of her. He hadn't meant to speak the words aloud and shouldn't have. Fear of losing her had driven them from his lips. His profession of love, however heartfelt, served as a delay, a decoy. Shame filled him for employing so desperate a tactic, however inadvertently.

"There you are, Mr. Darcy, Miss Bennet." Mrs. Reynolds' voice broke into the stillness that engulfed them. "I've been searching high and low. I've a selection of gowns and other necessities for Miss Bennet to look through."

Elizabeth whirled toward the manor. "Thank you, Mrs. Reynolds. That's very kind of you."

Darcy turned to the garden, taking a moment to compose himself. "Yes, thank you, Mrs. Reynolds," he said, pleased his voice came out even. "Your timing is perfect," he added as he faced her. "I've some matters to attend to."

Elizabeth cast him a surprised look, likely for the sincerity in his voice. It must seem to her they'd been interrupted at a terrible moment. Still, she gave him a smile he didn't deserve and headed off with Mrs. Reynolds.

Darcy retreated to his office. He needed time to grapple with his thoughts. Elizabeth would ask her question again. As much as he wished otherwise, before they wed, she deserved an answer.

He ended up throwing himself into work, unable to resolve his feelings about certain members of Elizabeth's family. He'd many letters to read and write, and estate business to see to. In truth, the sheer volume of items requiring his attention was somewhat daunting, and heartily distracting.

After a time, he missed Elizabeth too much to remain hidden in his office. He closed his inkwell and put his pen aside. Knowing he was a coward, he resolved not to bring up her mother and younger sisters if she didn't. In that way, hopefully he could buy himself the time he needed to resolve his feelings.

He checked the green parlor first but found it empty. That set him wandering the halls, which also felt empty. Every room did, without Elizabeth by his side, as she'd been for so many days, nights and miles.

It was her singing that drew him. The thrum of sorrow in her voice birthed an ache in his chest. He followed that sound, soon realizing she played as well. Long strides brought him quickly to the music room.

Elizabeth sat at Georgiana's pianoforte, performing Mr. Everett's composition to his lost love. Apparently competent with the music now, her eyes were half closed as she gave voice to the lost young woman's sorrow. Darcy leaned against the doorframe, entranced.

"No, that's not right."

Georgiana's voice halted Elizabeth's performance and snapped Darcy from her spell. He realized his sister sat on a settee near the pianoforte, listening. Georgiana stood. The look she gave Elizabeth was one of dislike. She strode toward the instrument.

"It should be faster," his sister said.

"I know," Elizabeth agreed. "I'm playing it slowly to ensure I have it right. Poor Mr. Everett has already endured too many missed notes from me. I hope to give him a clean performance when next he listens."

Darcy didn't know what the tempo should be. He'd enjoyed Elizabeth's slow rendition. The sorrow of the piece seemed, to his ear, to demand a stately pace.

Georgiana made an imperious gesture. "Let me do it. I'm sure I can play it correctly."

Darcy winced. He half expected Elizabeth to rebuff his sister, but her expression was bland as she stood and moved from the bench. With another hostile look for Elizabeth, Georgiana took her place. From his spot in the doorway, Darcy couldn't see his sister's face once she turned to the instrument, but he could see the compassionate, understanding one Elizabeth angled at Georgiana.

Elizabeth must have guessed much, he realized. Not that it wasn't obvious, to anyone, that his sister held Wickham in great affection. He hoped no one realized how great. He should tell Elizabeth. She had the right to know, especially as she'd obviously become a target for Georgiana's misery.

His sister struck up the song. Elizabeth went to the settee, expression neutral.

Darcy had to concede that Georgiana played the piece better, which didn't surprise him. She'd had the finest tutors and practiced daily. But Elizabeth sang better. Her rich alto reverberated with emotion, captured more of the sadness of the song.

Georgiana was perhaps two thirds of the way through when Mr. Everett came striding down the hall. He brushed past Darcy in the doorway, giving no appearance of noting him, and rushed toward the pianoforte. Sheets of music fluttered in his hand. His hair was disheveled, his suit as well. Dark rings stood out under his eyes.

"I've composed a new piece," he declared. He thrust the music at Georgiana.

She took the pages with a frown. "It's similar."

"Yes, yes, but not the same," Mr. Everett said. "I changed the tune. You see, here and here?" He jabbed his finger at the pages. "And I've written new lyrics. It's a new song. Would you do me the honor of playing it, Miss Darcy?" he asked, voice almost desperate.

"Me? Not Miss Bennet?"

Mr. Everett didn't so much as glance Elizabeth's way. Darcy wasn't certain the younger man had noticed her, or him. "No, not Miss Bennet. It must be you."

Georgiana cast Elizabeth a smug look. She arranged the pages on the stand, perused them briefly, and began to play. Mr. Everett hovered beside her, turning pages. To Darcy's ear, she had no difficulty with the change in the notes. When she was finished, she turned the pages back to the beginning.

She started again, adding in the words, the notes better suited to her higher voice now than Elizabeth's sweet alto. As Georgiana sang, it quickly became clear that the new lyrics were about a young woman who loved a man she later discovered wasn't what she thought he was. It ended with her claiming his death would have been be easier to bear than learning the truth. At least then she would have had her time with him to cherish. Now, possessed of the truth, she had nothing. The man she thought she knew, the man she'd loved, had never existed.

Though he couldn't see his sister's face, Darcy could hear the tears that suffused her voice. Near the end, her fingers faltered but she squared her shoulders and finished the song. Silence filled the chamber. Not looking at Mr. Everett, Georgiana slammed the fallboard closed over the keys and ran from the room.

Chapter Twenty

As soon as the coach stopped, Wickham jumped out. He strode quickly across the square, half an eye behind him. He took several sharp turns, ducked through a narrow alley choked with hanging wash, and spilled out onto one of London's busiest streets. There, stride hurried, he wove through the crowd, into a building, out the back, and down another alley.

Finally, he felt sure that even if his wife's brothers had somehow followed him or beaten him to London and been watching the main coach stops, no one followed him anymore. Whistling, he made his way toward the house of one of his usual lady friends. He had several goals now that he'd escaped his Scottish bride, but first and foremost was a little fun.

He strolled down several quaint, cobbled streets and across a square, then turned onto his lover's road. As he neared, his elation dimmed. She had the curtains tied back with red ribbons. That meant her husband was at home.

Of all the bad luck, Wickham thought as he strode by with a glare for the ribbon color. Green for come on by, red for stay away. Not only for her sake but for his. Her husband was reputedly quite the brawler.

Wickham's forehead creased in thought as he continued down the street. Fiona was already with child when he married her. Did that mean her favors were easy to come by? The night after he snuck away, and every subsequent night, was she in the inn's common room plying men with ale, as she'd done to him?

He scowled, not caring for the idea. One of the most pleasant things about his forced marriage had been the marriage bed. Fiona was his wife and he shouldn't have to share her, even if their union was nothing more than a backwoods Scottish wedding he'd deny till the day he died.

No matter, as well, that he'd left as soon as he could manage, because his plans required no one in England hear any rumor of the union. Not that he worried overmuch about that. There was little chance of word spreading so far so quickly, if ever. Besides, Scottish weddings didn't really count.

Feeling ill-used by both his usual lady friend and his wife, Wickham altered his course. Fiona had mended his clothing, quite well in fact, but his garments still looked second hand after the wear they'd taken. Wickham preferred to look much smarter. Even smarter than he would once he reclaimed the possessions he'd left with another friend last time he was in London. Only something new would suffice.

He also required someone to repair his boots, for no cobbler existed within miles of the inn. At least, Wickham hoped they could be repaired. They would be expensive to replace, not to mention that new boots took time and Fiona's brothers were sure to be on his trail.

Wickham grinned, wondering if they'd noticed the inn's deed was missing. They were more likely to be concerned about the money that was gone. He felt little guilt about either. The inn was his. So was the money. Besides, he'd taken only what he needed to get to London. Not that he was sure why he'd left the rest. What did he care if they weren't able to buy the food they needed for travelers? He never expected to see the inn or any of its inhabitants again.

Deprived of the fun he'd planned for the morning, he went first to reclaim his old possessions, at the bargain price of a kiss for leaving them longer than he'd planned, and then on to the bank to extract his funds. First, a new wardrobe. Looking respectable would help him sell the inn, his second task. Third, he'd make his way to Darcy's man, Edwards, for step two of his plan to gain enough wealth to embark on a new, lavish life.

After taking out the money he'd put in after his gambling spree in Hertfordshire, Wickham spent considerable time at the haberdashery and cobblery. He enjoyed himself thoroughly. Once they realized he had money to spend, they fawned over him as much as he could wish. The only downside was that he had to pay the full price, which grated. They wouldn't give credit to an unknown man with no fixed address.

He spent the evening in one of London's better inns. The fare wasn't as good as Fiona's. She was, he would readily allow, quite an excellent cook. The woman he spent the night with wasn't as lively or pleasing as Fiona either, leaving him with a sense of disquiet. He didn't care to pay for what he could have for free, especially when what he got for free was preferable.

The accommodations were superior, though. He caught himself

considering what might be brought to Fiona's inn to improve it, so they could charge more, ranking amenities by expense versus potential return. Once he realized what he was doing, he stopped. He was, after all, selling the inn out from under her to fund his new life, so why worry about how to make the place better?

The following day he went to a man who was reputed to arrange for the sale of remote property.

"What can I do for you, Mr...." the man behind the desk let his voice trail off in question.

"Wickham," he supplied and took the seat across from the man, uninvited.

"What can I do for you, Mr. Wickham?" The man offered an ingratiating smile.

"I'm interested in selling a property. An inn in Scotland. I have the deed."

The man blinked. It was easy to see the wheels in his mind turning. "Near the border?"

"Not really but it's a fine establishment. Three stories. Clean. Large stable and innyard. Excellent cook."

The man nodded along with Wickham's points. "Can you guarantee the cook will stay on if you sell?"

"I believe so." After answering, Wickham thought that over. Would Fiona stay? She would be very angry, but she'd be alone and with a babe. She wouldn't have any choice but to remain.

"Excellent. Wonderful." The man pulled out a ledger and flipped through the pages. "I've sold a property in Scotland before, and I have information on several others, carried by various firms. Let me see the deed, if you don't mind."

Wickham showed it to him.

"The inn is the property of Fiona Mary McClintock, spinster."

"She recently married."

"Are you her husband? If so, you need documentation to prove it. The deed should be reissued in her husband's name."

Wickham hesitated. If he admitted being her husband and proved it, the information would eventually be public knowledge in London. He had no faith in the man's desire or ability to keep that secret. He had a great deal of faith in Fiona's brothers' persistence in finding him and punishing him if he sold the inn. Suddenly, he realized that selling the inn was not a good idea. He could not do it without revealing he was married, and he could get more from marrying well than he could for the inn.

"No. I'm acting for him, and I realize I can't prove it. I'll return when he gives me the proper paperwork."

Wickham stood and walked out. In a foul mood, he made his way to one of the most prestigious streets in London, to see Darcy's man. It was time to implement his second plan for acquiring the funds he needed for his new life.

Edwards' office was five times the size of the little land agent's. Even the office his clerk used was twice as large. Both boasted richly upholstered sofas, fireplaces, plush carpets and expensive accent pieces. Normally, being treated with respect in such a lavish setting would please Wickham, but his mood was in no way improved as the clerk showed him in and then bowed his way from Edward's office.

"Mr. Wickham," Edwards greeted with a nod. "What an unexpected surprise. Please, sit. Can I get you anything?"

"A brandy," Wickham said, happy to take advantage of the man's liquor cabinet, paid for by his exclusive clients.

Edwards rang a bell. The clerk reappeared and was sent for a brandy. Edwards returned his attention to Wickham. "What can I do for you?"

"I don't know if Darcy has reached Pemberley yet, but when he does, I have a message for him." A pang stirred in Wickham at the idea that Darcy might not have made it home. Who, then, would inherit his fortunes? Colonel Fitzwilliam? Wickham would never get a farthing from the colonel.

Edwards nodded. "I can certainly get word to him. You'll be pleased to know he arrived safely home some days ago."

Relieved, Wickham asked, "Was Miss Elizabeth Bennet with him?" He accepted a glass of brandy from the returned clerk, who then bowed and left.

"I can't say, Mr. Wickham," Edwards said.

Wickham sipped his brandy and narrowed his eyes. He wondered if Edwards didn't know or simply wouldn't tell. Not that it mattered. Wickham's threat was two-fold. It would be best if both prongs struck home, but either one would be enough.

"What information would you like me to pass along to Mr. Darcy, Mr. Wickham?"

"A letter. I'm sure you have ways to get it to him promptly."

"I do."

Wickham took another sip of brandy.

"Ah, may I have the letter, sir?" Edwards asked after a moment.

"I haven't written it yet. I'll need writing supplies," Wickham said, inwardly amused he could enter the most prestigious firm in London and be assured to readily receive what Darcy had spent days begging for, to no avail.

Edwards rang the bell again and sent the same clerk into a side room to organize the items Wickham required. "Would you care to compose your letter in there? There is a desk in that room, for the convenience of my clients."

Wickham drank down the remainder of his brandy. "Yeah, I'll write it in there. And I'll have another brandy."

"Of course, sir."

When the clerk returned, Edwards issued his instructions. Soon, Wickham was ensconced in a smaller, equally plush office. He closed the door and sat at the desk, pleased to see the clerk had brought sealing wax. Wickham sat to write and took another mouthful of Edwards' superior brandy.

Dear Fitz,

Wickham smiled at his overly-familiar salutation, sure to make Darcy grind his teeth. Calling Darcy by his first name was bad enough, but Darcy hated that nickname.

I hear you're safely returned. Congratulations. I thought for certain your arrogance would offend someone into shooting you somewhere along the way.

Wickham snickered at his joke.

But enough banter. I'm sure, being overly responsible, you have numerous correspondences to catch up on, so I'll get straight to the point. I wish to begin anew in Ireland.

Or should he start the letter again and say Canada, which was his real goal? Would Darcy guess Ireland was a lie? Would the truth, in this case, be the best lie? Throw Darcy off the scent should he ever launch a pursuit?

Wickham shrugged and moved on. Darcy wouldn't come after him. He'd simply be happy to see Wickham gone.

I wish to offer again to alleviate your conscience in the case of Miss Elizabeth Bennet. Before you decline, keep in mind that I know much which would ruin her reputation beyond repair, so not even a lowly farmer would take her. Nor would even a distant relation permit her to grow into an old maid in their household, she'll be so sullied if I talk. Sleeping in the same place with you and me, night after night? In the eyes of the world, she's no better than a common whore. I'll share all I know unless you pay me to marry her.

I know she declined my earlier offer, but I'm sure you sent her home with alacrity. By now, she's realized how lacking her options are, how ostracized she undoubtedly is. How much her four sisters and mother resent her.

For six thousand pounds, I'll marry her and alleviate your conscience in this matter. I'll move us to Ireland, where none know her shame, and you'll never have to think on her again. As an added incentive, if you also acquiesce to my next demand, you have my word you will never have to think on me again, either. I will never return to England.

Wickham leaned back and studied his words. He was torn between the desire to aggravate Darcy and the need not to alienate him to the point where he would decline out of hand. Perhaps he should rewrite the letter and leave out the word whore? That was a bit harsh.

He wanted harsh, though. Darcy must be angry enough not to consider Wickham's real plan to take the funds and run. A vision of Elizabeth Bennet, before she became all freckled and bedraggled on their journey, came to mind and he grinned. Maybe he wouldn't run immediately. He could enjoy a second marriage bed before he left.

Even as I write this, I can feel your elation at the idea of me in Ireland, for good. So, on to my second demand. It's also occurred to me that I can defame someone far more important to you than Miss Elizabeth Bennet. So important, in fact, that I won't name her. I do not need to. For an additional four thousand pounds, I shall forget she ever loved me and agreed to run away with me.

It's up to you. I could have asked for more. Ten thousand pounds is nothing to you. Consider it as making up for how little I thought to request for that living, if it makes you feel any better. However you want to see it, that's my price. Pay and you'll be rid of me forever. I'm staying in London. I'll tell your man, Edwards, where to find me.

Sincerely,

George

Wickham reread the letter several times. Finally, smile wide as he imagined Darcy's impotent anger, he folded the pages and sealed them.

He drank down the last of his brandy, stood, stretched, and left the little room, handing the letter to the clerk on his way out.

As he left, he had an epiphany. He might take Elizabeth Bennet to Canada with him. She would make him a good wife. He was angry with her because she preferred Darcy to him, but what choice did she have? Darcy was the one who would be most likely to take care of her during the journey and afterward. Did he really want a wife who was too stupid to know that?

She was attracted to him and disliked Darcy. That wouldn't have changed. Once she understood the situation, she would be happy to follow her heart. Necessity and love would make her retract her vehement rejection with a humble apology and explanation. Perhaps the two of them would laugh over the letters she would write to Darcy bemoaning her fate and asking for more money. She would be an asset both for being a loving, faithful wife and as a means of squeezing more money from Darcy.

He whistled as he walked back to his lodging.

Chapter Twenty-One

Despite Georgiana's inauspicious first performance of Mr. Everett's newest work, the two took to spending a great deal of time together. This was generally in the music room, either at the pianoforte or bent low over a table, working on lyrics. Darcy worried briefly about permitting his sister to spend so much time with a young gentleman, but Mrs. Annesley was in constant attendance of the two. Moreover, Georgiana's preoccupation with Mr. Everett and his music gave Darcy more time alone with Elizabeth.

Darcy also had a reply from Mr. Bennet, thanking him profusely and wishing them good speed on their journey to Longbourn. Mr. Bennet also made it abundantly clear that he considered Elizabeth's health more important than her speedy return. Darcy felt only a little bit of guilt in not taking Elizabeth to Longbourn immediately. They really did need time to rest and recover from their ordeal. He also needed more time to sort out his feelings regarding Elizabeth's mother and younger sisters before he asked Mr. Bennet's permission to wed her, something he wished to do in person.

Darcy consulted with Elizabeth about the list of people who had helped them. Although Edward's agent was already on his way to retrace their steps, Darcy was concerned he might forget someone. Elizabeth checked his notes and suggested that the clergyman who gave them half a loaf of bread to share between the three of them and threatened them if they stayed in his parish deserved at least the price of the bread. After a little discussion, they agreed he was to be given the price of five loaves and then forgotten, while others would be given repeat gifts next year. Mr. Robinson, when consulted, asked that Darcy make a donation to his favorite charity. Mr. Everett reluctantly accepted the price of Elizabeth's and Darcy's fare on the stage and mail but refused any additional compensation.

To Darcy, the first of the two weeks he'd given them to rest passed in a blink, though he knew the time chaffed more on Elizabeth. Though happy and pleasant, seeming more relaxed in Pemberley every day, he also caught her often pensive looks. When he asked, she confessed to missing her home.

Darcy planned the journey to Longbourn in much greater detail than the short trip, with a pause to drop off Mr. Everett, required. After all their trials, he wanted to show Elizabeth how smooth a journey could be. More than that, he wished to show her the ease with which she would be able to travel between both her new and old homes. Unfortunately, the weather refused to cooperate. A heavy rain started before dawn the day they were going to leave. By their planned departure time, it was clear the roads would be unreasonable, and his servants would get soaked. The rain continued for several days.

"We should wait until the roads are passable," Elizabeth said. "I'll write my family."

"I'm sorry. If I had known, I would have left a day earlier." Darcy endeavored to sound sincere as he was sorry. For her sorrow, not for the delay. Every day he had Elizabeth so nearly to himself was a boon.

Elizabeth offered an only slightly sad smile. "Then we might have been stuck in an inn instead of Pemberley. I know you are planning to take me to an inn with better accommodations than usual, but I doubt it would be an improvement to where we are staying now."

They waited an extra day after the heavy rain stopped, to give the roads a chance to dry, and then departed. When his carriage finally rolled to a halt outside Longbourn, Darcy had his pocket watch out. It pleased him they'd reached Elizabeth's family home a full seventeen minutes ahead of schedule. The only thing that didn't please him about their journey was that he still hadn't reconciled his sensibilities with certain members of Elizabeth's family.

Longbourn's front door flew open and people spilled out. Elizabeth cast Darcy a quick, joyous smile, then flung the carriage door open. Not waiting for him or a footman, she jumped out and ran to her father. He opened his arms, tears in his eyes, and Elizabeth flung herself into them.

Darcy alighted more slowly. A bit daunted by the chaos before him, he remained off to the side, near the carriage. People pulled Elizabeth from embrace to embrace. A cacophony of voices rose. It seemed to him at first that half of Hertfordshire must have been hidden within Mr. Bennet's humble home. As he sorted out the faces, he realized most of the assemblage was Elizabeth's family, augmented by members of the staff.

184

The last to embrace her, including those members of the staff who seemed to feel they'd a right to, was her mother. Unlike the other welcoming hugs, Mrs. Bennet's appeared less loving and more perfunctory. Almost the moment she touched Elizabeth, she was already setting her away.

"Lizzy, I can't believe you did this to me," Mrs. Bennet cried, her screech easily discernable above the babble of voices. "You frightened me so much that I've had such fluttering and heartache since you disappeared without so much as writing us a note. No one cares about my poor nerves. Now you've come back ruined. Mr. Darcy must marry you."

Darcy couldn't keep the scowl from his face. Did Mrs. Bennet not realize he stood right there, mere feet away and well within earshot?

As if in answer to that unasked question, Mrs. Bennet cast a quick, smug look over Elizabeth's shoulder, aimed at him, before turning back to her daughter. "It's either that or we're sending you away. We can't have your disgrace sully your sisters. I don't know what will become of you if Mr. Darcy won't do the right thing."

Darcy's jaws clenched. Did she think he didn't realize his duty, his culpability in this? He recognized that he had to marry Elizabeth. He wanted to marry her. Under the most trying of circumstances, she'd behaved beautifully. He had loved her before and his love had only grown upon spending more time with her.

"This all might turn out to be a good thing," Mrs. Bennet continued in her half-shout. "Even though we all know you can't stand Mr. Darcy, you'll marry him, and he will introduce your sisters to rich men. I bet Lydia will catch a duke. She only needs Mr. Darcy to introduce her to one, which he will, once you wed, which he'll do because it's only right."

Elizabeth leaned toward her mother, speaking too low for Darcy to hear, but Darcy had heard enough. Both obligation and choice bid him wed Elizabeth. To that, he agreed. He was not going to put up with introducing her wild, crass younger sisters to his friends, though.

"Thank you for taking care of my daughter and bringing her home," Mr. Bennet said quietly. Darcy hadn't noticed Elizabeth's father was at his side. "Mr. Bingley is at Netherfield Park and has extended an invitation for you to stay with him. You are, of course, welcome to stay here, but it isn't what you are used to."

Darcy grimaced and bowed slightly to Mr. Bennet. "Then I will go there now and call on you tomorrow."

Mr. Bennet offered a return nod.

Trying not to listen to Mrs. Bennet's reiteration of her rant, Darcy strode to the front of the carriage to speak to his driver, who well knew the way to Netherfield. The man passed down Elizabeth's one small case, full of borrowed goods. Darcy set it on the ground beside Mr. Bennet and climbed back into his carriage.

"Mrs. Bennet," Mr. Bennet said, without.

Darcy glanced out the window as his driver clicked to the team. Mr. Bennet had spoken his wife's name in a firmer voice than Darcy had ever heard him use. The carriage started moving.

"There will be no more talk of Elizabeth being ruined," Mr. Bennet continued in that same tone.

"But she—"

"No," Mr. Bennet snapped. "None. Nothing. She is home and I, for one, am very grateful. Have I made myself clear?"

Darcy didn't hear a response from Mrs. Bennet, though he was uncertain if that was because his carriage had rolled too far down the drive or she hadn't issued one. Belatedly, he sought a glimpse of Elizabeth, but he couldn't see the gathering before the door any longer. Perhaps if he stuck his head out the window... but no. A Darcy didn't do such things. He pressed his shoulders back against the seat instead.

It took him most of the journey to Netherfield Park to reorder his thoughts and shake his anger at Mrs. Bennet's words. By the time his carriage rolled to a halt and he disembarked into the blessed civility of Bingley's liveried and quiet footmen and groomsmen, Darcy had managed to compose his features into a neutral expression. He strode, delightfully verbally unaccosted, up Netherfield's steps to be greeted by an equally civilized and deferential butler, who went to see if Bingley was at home. The butler returned a moment later to escort Darcy to one of Netherfield's well-appointed parlors. There, he raised his voice ever so slightly and announced Darcy to the room.

"Darcy," Bingley exclaimed, looking up from his paper.

He came to his feet as Darcy strode into the parlor. Behind him, the butler disappeared. Miss Bingley, whom Darcy was unsurprised to see, also stood. Brother and sister came forward to converge on him just inside the doorway. Bingley extended a hand in greeting, which Darcy clasped warmly. Miss Bingley curtsied.

"You're a welcome sight, let me tell you," Bingley said. He gestured toward the collection of chairs and sofas. "Come, sit." He turned to his sister. "Caroline, send for tea," Bingley said before returning his attention to Darcy. "We hoped you'd come. Caroline set aside the same room you occupied last time we were here."

"It's good to see you, as well." Darcy angled the words at Bingley as they all sat. It was never a good idea to encourage Miss Bingley's hopes, especially now that Darcy was engaged. "For a time, I worried I might never again see anyone but my kidnappers and my fellow prisoners."

"Fellow prisoners?" Miss Bingley asked. "We'd heard about Miss Elizabeth, but who else was there?"

Bingley leaned forward, expression eager. "Yes, tell us all about it."

Bingley showed all the enthusiasm of someone waiting to hear about a particularly fine hunt. This, Darcy realized, was how most of his peers would take the incident. An adventure. They wouldn't think about or comprehend the danger or hardship. Briefly, he considered trying to convey the true nature of his and Elizabeth's journey, especially how much she must have suffered. He gave his head a slight shake. No, better the ton devour the tale with their usual fleeting interest.

"I called on Miss Elizabeth at the parsonage," he said, seeking a light tone for what had been a singularly aggravating and humiliating interaction with the woman he loved. "Some men with pistols came in and kidnapped us." He'd leave out the joint intimacy and horror of being locked, bound, under the false floor of a smuggler's wagon. "We were taken to a ship and locked in a room where we found, to our surprise, that Mr. Wickham was already being held." He ignored Bingley's look of surprise and Miss Bingley's gasp. "We escaped when we were shipwrecked."

"Shipwrecked?" Bingley repeated, expression avid. "Fantastic."

"Yes, shipwrecked." So few words to describe another harrowing experience. Fear still stabbed through Darcy whenever he thought on how near he'd come to losing Elizabeth. He could only thank heaven he'd proved a strong enough swimmer to save them both. "We made it to shore, though I believe most of the others on the ship did not." Except for the woman, Mary.

Should he try to track her down? She'd claimed to be on her way to help them. He didn't believe her enough to want to help her, though. Should he take the opposite tack, actively harming her? Did he hold enough rancor to wish her brought to justice?

"Then what happened?" Miss Bingley prompted, expression as

eager as her brother's.

"After we made it to shore, we realized we were in Scotland and headed south," Darcy continued. "A few days later, we parted company with Mr. Wickham. Not long after that, we finally made it to Pemberley." No mention of the dirt, cold, begging or hunger. Nor of Wickham's betrayal, being attacked or the endless looks of suspicion.

Maids bustled in with the tea service. Conversation halted while they set out pots, cups, plates, finger sandwiches and a selection of delectables. Miss Bingley began fixing tea when they departed. She handed Darcy his, prepared to his liking, with a smile.

"So, Mr. Wickham was with you most of the way," she said, tone thoughtful.

Darcy nodded. "Much of it."

"But that's perfect." Miss Bingley's smile was radiant. "Miss Elizabeth can marry Mr. Wickham. She's always fancied him." She handed Bingley a saucer and cup.

Darcy set his tea down, untouched. "No."

Miss Bingley made a sweeping gesture, as if brushing aside his denial. "Oh, I realize he won't want to. She's much too poor, even for him." She offered Darcy an ingratiating expression. "But I know you. You have an over-developed sense of obligation, especially for those who are beneath you. You'll want to see her wed now that she's ruined and he's the perfect choice."

"No," Darcy repeated, tone even harder than the first time.

Bingley must have caught the anger in that syllable, for he shot Darcy a quick, questioning look.

Miss Bingley took a sip of tea. "Of course, you'll need to settle a generous purse on her to persuade Wickham to marry her, but he's the sort who will be happy to do so, with a little money." Her expression turned thoughtful. "It would probably be cheaper than buying her off, and neater, if I may say so. No loose ends. No criticism from people who think you should have married her. And in the long run, it will save you money, because you can certainly marry someone with more money than you will have to spend to get even Mr. Wickham to take Miss Elizabeth. She is, after all, impertinent, and her family is impossible."

"Now, Caroline, they aren't that--"

"Hush, Charles. We aren't speaking of your ill-advised infatuation, though we will." She turned back to Darcy with a bile-evoking look of conspiratorial suffering. "As I'm sure you've guessed, Mr. Darcy, the only reason we've returned to Netherfield is Charles' unsavory attachment to Miss Jane Bennet. Not that there's anything wrong with her, aside from being a bit long in the tooth, all but penniless, of poor lineage and possessed of a disgraceful, vulgar family. None of that is her fault, sweet as she is."

Bingley glared at his sister.

Darcy was a touch surprised to hear Bingley hadn't gotten over his attraction to Miss Bennet. Perhaps, then, it wasn't mere infatuation. If Miss Bennet did truly care for Bingley, as Elizabeth believed, Darcy could soon have one of his better friends as a brother. The thought pleased him.

What didn't please him was Miss Bingley's tirade against Elizabeth and her continued pairing of the woman he loved with George Wickham. "Do you mean me to believe, Miss Bingley, that you have not one good thing to say about Miss Elizabeth?" Darcy asked, voice quiet.

Bingley left off glaring at his sister to turn surprised eyes on Darcy. Again, he must have read into Darcy's tone. Bingley shot his sister a warning look, but her attention remained focused on Darcy.

"Something good about Miss Elizabeth?" Miss Bingley repeated. She gave a little laugh, as if Darcy played a parlor game. "I daresay her only virtue is she is an excellent walker, but I suppose you found that out when walking across Scotland."

"I see," Darcy said. "So, that is the only commendation you can muster for the woman who will be my wife?"

Miss Bingley's eyes flew wide, emphasizing the narrowness of her face. "Mr. Darcy, I beseech you, don't destroy your life over something of which you had no control."

"You are correct that I had no control over our predicament," he agreed. "But I do have control over my actions now. I shall wed Miss Elizabeth Bennet."

Desperation flickered across Miss Bingley's face. She leaned toward him. "Miss Elizabeth is irrevocably ruined. I realize that. It does you credit that you would rectify her disgrace, but please don't let her ruin lead to yours." To his utter shock, she placed a hand on his knee. "Only, think how terrible it will be to be tied to someone by an accident of fate. Especially someone as low as she. Surely, your journey only served to emphasize how unworthy she is of you."

Darcy stood, relieved when Miss Bingley's hand slid free of his person. She stared up at him, expression pleading. On her other side,

Bingley appeared thoroughly embarrassed and a touch angry.

"The time I spent with Miss Elizabeth has only amplified my good opinion of her," Darcy said. He permitted a slight, grim smile as he looked down at Miss Bingley. "And my opinion must have already been quite good, because I proposed to her before we were kidnapped."

Chapter Twenty-Two

Over her mother's shoulder, Elizabeth saw Mr. Darcy's carriage head down the drive. Despair snaked through her. She was so accustomed to being near Mr. Darcy, his departure evoked something akin to physical pain. He hadn't even said good bye. Or when he would return.

Or if he would return. She looked about at her family, took in her mother and younger sisters squabbling in the yard like hens. Had Mr. Darcy been forcibly reminded of one of his main objections to her? Even when he'd proposed in Kent, he'd done so away from her family, perhaps with their behavior no longer fresh in his memory, for all he'd decried it. Now, he'd been handed a fresh, unfettered example of how ill-mannered they could be.

She pressed her lips into a tight line. No, Mr. Darcy was a man of his word. He wouldn't back out of his offer of marriage. He wouldn't change his mind about wedding her.

But he might, she realized, change his mind about wishing to wed her. Worse, if he planned to behave in so highhanded a manner, would she change her mind about wishing to wed him? Elizabeth watched the dust from his carriage settle in the drive, worry spiraling in her gut.

"Lizzy, come in," Jane said softly, appearing at her side. She took Elizabeth by the arm and turned her toward the front door of Longbourn.

Elizabeth permitted Jane to guide her into the house. They stepped into the foyer, dark after daylight.

Jane leaned near. "Do you know, Mr. Bingley is back?"

Elizabeth turned a surprised look on her sister. Jane's eyes glowed. She looked radiant. Happy. Much happier than last time Elizabeth had seen her, and she didn't think it was only Jane's joy at her return.

"No, I didn't know." Elizabeth could still hear the other's squawking without. "Have you any notion what drew him back to Hertfordshire?"

Jane blushed. "The fishing?" she suggested.

"Hm." Elizabeth nodded. "Or perhaps the hunting. Maybe there's something he's particularly hoping to catch."

Jane's blush deepened. She turned and led the way into the front parlor.

Everything inside Longbourn was as blessedly familiar as the approach and exterior. Elizabeth let out a deep breath. There was something so very right about coming home. Every scuff on the floorboards, every garish knickknack on her mother's shelves, they were all as familiar as her own face. Even the sofa she and Jane settled onto, the one on which they always sat, provided an overwhelming sense of rightness and comfort.

Voices and footsteps signaled the others had followed them. Soon, Elizabeth's mother and younger sisters settled into their usual spots as well. Even her father came in. Elizabeth had expected him to disappear into his library, even though she'd only now returned home. She offered a smile as he took his favorite armchair.

"You must tell us everything that happened to you," Lydia declared, expression eager.

Elizabeth took in six pairs of eyes, ranging in degrees of eagerness and concern. She was aware, as well, that several of the staff clustered in the hall. Indeed, she did have to tell them, for rumor would spread soon enough. Her family, at least, should hear some of the truth from her. She drew in a deep breath and marshaled her thoughts.

"Mr. Darcy had called at the Hunsford parsonage. Three men came in with pistols. They tied us up, put us in a wagon and took us to the coast. We were taken to a ship and imprisoned in a small room with Mr. Wickham."

"Mr. Wickham," Mrs. Bennet and Lydia both exclaimed. Both, as well, appeared happy with this twist to the tale.

"Yes. He was also a prisoner." Elizabeth hurried onward, not wishing to delve into why. "There was a shipwreck. Mr. Darcy got both of us to shore." She shuddered to recall the dark, icy water. "Mr. Wickham never did thank him," she added, mostly to herself.

"But he was always so polite," Lydia said. "He must have done so."

"You just didn't hear him do it," Kitty added.

"We were all soaked through, and it was cold," Elizabeth continued, sorry she'd let the words out. She didn't wish to argue the merits of Mr. Wickham with her besotted little sisters, which wasn't, she assured

192

herself, the same as Mr. Darcy not wishing to argue the same point with his sister. It was obvious Miss Darcy's affection for Mr. Wickham was much more deeply rooted than Kitty's or Lydia's. Both as a diversion from Mr. Wickham and because the truth must be told, she said, "The first night, we slept on the ground, side by side for warmth."

"But, that means you are ruined," Mrs. Bennet cried, her tone almost triumphant.

"One more word on that, Mrs. Bennet, and you will go upstairs to your room," Elizabeth's father said. His quiet voice reverberated with a firmness Elizabeth had never heard before. He nodded toward her. "Elizabeth, continue."

"We started walking," she said, picking back up the tale. "We spent the second night in a barn, which was better." She shook her head, deciding to hurry her rendition of events. They didn't need every detail. "Eventually, we came to an inn. Mr. Wickham had money he hadn't told us about, which he used to buy himself a meal. Mr. Darcy and I decided to part from him."

"He didn't share?" Jane asked, clearly shocked.

"He did not." Certainly, she wouldn't mention Mr. Wickham's horrible proposal or being set upon by would-be-robbers. Those things, she would tell Jane later.

"After that, Mr. Darcy helped a man who'd crashed his gig," Elizabeth continued. "That man paid for all three of us to go by stage and mail to near where Mr. Darcy lives. Mr. Darcy knew someone there who lent us horses to ride to Pemberley." She might also tell Jane about the ride. She glanced at her gentle sister. Or not. Perhaps that was a memory Elizabeth would keep for herself.

"You rode?" Mary asked.

"I was on the same horse as Mr. Darcy." Elizabeth fought down a blush. "We then went to Pemberley."

"You rode on a horse with Mr. Darcy?" Lydia cried.

"But you hate him," Mary said.

Jane touched Elizabeth's arm, her expression sympathetic.

"Oh, my poor girls, all ruined," Mrs. Bennet wailed.

"Mrs. Bennet," Elizabeth's father snapped.

"Now I can't talk of any of my daughters?" Mrs. Bennet cried. "My hearts and soul and you forbid me to speak of them? Oh, my nerves, my head. Why am I cursed with so callous and unfeeling a husband?"

"So you don't know what happened to Mr. Wickham?" Kitty asked.

Elizabeth looked about the room as the questions, reprimands and wailing escalated. No one seemed to mind that she wasn't replying. They simply spoke for the sound of their own voices. Lydia and Mary fell into an argument about where Mr. Wickham could be. Kitty took Lydia's side. Jane sat in stoic silence. Mrs. Bennet berated Mr. Bennet, whose replies grew terser by the moment.

Elizabeth let out a sigh. She couldn't really begrudge Mr. Darcy for fleeing. She sought for a unifying topic, to bring some semblance of order. Not more details of her journey, though. Much of it she didn't wish to relive, and much else she deemed private.

"I wrote to Charlotte, to let her know I'm well," Elizabeth said into the din. "Her reply said she was here, with her parents. Is she still here?"

"Yes," Jane said.

"She and that horrible Mr. Collins brought over your things," Lydia said.

"He claimed your being kidnapped was an afront to Lady Catherine," Mary said.

Elizabeth's father swiveled his head toward the front window. "In fact, they appear to be here now." He stood. "I've had enough of Mr. Collins," he said. With a nod to Elizabeth, he left the room.

A moment later, a knock sounded, followed by a brief commotion in the foyer. Charlotte and Mr. Collins were shown in.

Elizabeth stood, arms open to greet Charlotte, who rushed into them. Tears pressed against Elizabeth's closed lids. She hadn't permitted thoughts of Charlotte while on her journey and had, to her mild shame, been too wrapped up in her time with Mr. Darcy to do more than write Charlotte one letter from Pemberley. Elizabeth couldn't help but imagine how terrible her friend must have felt, how worried she would have been. Perhaps even, and Elizabeth didn't relish the thought, guilt ridden.

"Oh, Lizzy," Charlotte whispered. "I've been so worried. My only solace was that Mr. Darcy disappeared as well and two of our staff. I so hoped, but didn't believe, you'd both gone mad and run off together."

"Cousin Elizabeth, we're very pleased to find you returned," Mr. Collins said. He sounded as if he might even mean his words. "Mrs. Collins and I were terribly upset when we returned from Lady Catherine's to find the parsonage empty of everyone but Sally. She couldn't tell us a thing. She'd fallen asleep. Without even baking the bread. Imagine that? I nearly let her go on the spot."

"Who is Sally?" Mrs. Bennet asked.

"One of the maids," Elizabeth supplied.

"Harrumph," Mrs. Bennet muttered as she eyed the cakes. "You ought to have let her go, if you ask me."

Elizabeth reflected that no one had asked but kept her peace.

"We couldn't let her go," Mr. Collins said. "Lady Catherine hand selected all of our staff. I wouldn't dream of questioning..." He trailed off and cast an apologetic glance Charlotte's way.

Elizabeth followed that look to find her friend watching Mr. Collins with raised eyebrows and a hard expression.

Charlotte caught Elizabeth watching and smoothed her features into a smile. "At first, we didn't think much of your absence," she said, taking up the tale. "It was a bit late for a walk, but I've known you to enjoy the air at a variety of hours. One of our other maids, Rose, if you recall her, Lizzy?"

Elizabeth nodded.

"She returned somewhat later," Charlotte continued. "She'd been visiting her sick mother."

"Without permission, no less." Mr. Collins added a scowl to his words. "I don't mind saying, I was quite put out and near to letting her go as well, especially when all there was to eat was cold roast. No cabbage had been prepared at all. If we hadn't had a nice tea at Rosings, I would have been very hungry. Lady Catherine always serves a nice tea."

"Our third maid, Mary, did most of the cooking," Charlotte said to the room at large.

"Where was she?" Lydia asked.

Charlotte cast Elizabeth a questioning look.

Elizabeth shook her head. She'd rather hear the remainder of Charlotte's side of the tale than launch into more of her own.

"Likely off with some gent," Mrs. Bennet predicted. "It's impossible to find good staff. They all whine about wages and time off for sick mothers and the like. Nonsense."

"Yes, well, Rose's mother really is sick," Charlotte said firmly. "When Mary didn't return, we looked for our manservant, Jeb." Charlotte cast a quick look about the room. "They were on good terms. That's when we realized he was absent as well. By then, it was quite late, and we were beginning to worry for you, Lizzy."

"Mrs. Collins urged me to send up to Rosings and ask if they'd any news." Mr. Collins snorted. "As if I would trouble Lady Catherine over something as trivial as my relations."

Charlotte leveled another hard stare on her husband. "So, we didn't alert anyone at Rosings that evening." She turned to Elizabeth. "I don't mind admitting, it was a sleepless night. I was so worried for you."

"I slept perfectly well," Mr. Collins said. "Lady Catherine always advises a good night's sleep."

Across from him, Lydia rolled her eyes at Kitty, who snickered. Mr. Collins didn't seem to notice but Mary elbowed Kitty in the ribs. Kitty turned a glare on her.

"When did you realize I was truly gone?" Elizabeth asked, more to cut off an argument between her younger sisters than out of any need for a reply. Charlotte would already have realized something was amiss. The real question was how long it took her to convince Mr. Collins.

"The next morning," Charlotte said. "Colonel Fitzwilliam appeared quite early, asking if we'd seen Mr. Darcy, who was also missing and who, the colonel said, had come to the parsonage the previous afternoon. Some people suggested that the two of you eloped." Charlotte shook her head. "None of us truly believed that. If the two of you wanted to get married, there would be no need to elope. Also, only Mr. Darcy's horse was missing, the one he takes riding. His carriage remained."

"Oh, but Lizzy loves riding on horses with Mr. Darcy," Lydia snickered.

This set Elizabeth's mother and younger sisters off again. Elizabeth closed her eyes, seeking her own council rather than listen to them. Should she tell them about her engagement to Mr. Darcy or wait until he elected to speak with her father? A small part of her was despairingly uncertain Mr. Darcy still wanted her.

Even as she knew he'd keep his word, she knew she wouldn't force him to do so. After the way he'd raced away, without even a look of goodbye... She resisted the urge to wrap her arms about herself. She missed him already. Even there, surrounded by friends and family, she felt oddly bereft and alone without Mr. Darcy beside her, like something terribly important was missing.

Jane placed a light hand on Elizabeth's arm, as if sensing her disquiet. Elizabeth opened her eyes to her older sister's concerned look.

"I knew they didn't elope," Mr. Collins stated, speaking over Elizabeth's mother and younger sisters. "Everyone knows Mr. Darcy is going to marry Miss de Bourgh, as Lady Catherine wishes. I tried to stop

Mrs. Collins from even telling Colonel Fitzwilliam about Cousin Elizabeth's disappearance." He turned in his seat, angling toward Elizabeth. "With the shock of her nephew disappearing, Lady Catherine should not have been bothered by the absence of a nobody like you, Cousin Elizabeth."

"Whatever the reason for your disappearance," Charlotte said over the squeals of indignation Mr. Collins' words elicited from Mrs. Bennet, "Colonel Fitzwilliam and I agreed that it was likely that your disappearance was connected to Darcy's."

"What I want to know," Mr. Collins said, "is what became of my staff if they weren't traveling to Scotland with you?"

Once more, everyone turned to look at Elizabeth. Elizabeth stared around the parlor, trying to decide how much to tell. The more information she gave, the more her family would pry. Much of her journey she wished to spare them. Other parts were too private to share, treasured interactions with Mr. Darcy. Still, she must give them some details. Obviously, they would never be content with her brief explanation of earlier. The truth about the servants, certainly, wasn't something she need keep secret.

"Mary and Jeb?" She shrugged. "They were among our kidnappers. They were smugglers, I believe, but failing at that, so they took jobs at the parsonage in the hope of robbing from Mr. Collins."

Mr. Collins stared at her, eyes wide. "But, Lady Catherine selected them herself," he reiterated. "You must be mistaken, Cousin."

Elizabeth shook her head. "I am most definitely not mistaken. They brought several cohorts to the parsonage, with pistols, and kidnapped us. They also stole Mr. Darcy's horse," she added. "You may ask him for confirmation if you like."

"But...but..." Mr. Collins sputtered, face wreathed in confusion.

Charlotte lightly touched his sleeve. He fell silent.

"But what happened to them?" Mary pressed. "And the others? Shouldn't they be arrested?"

"They're all dead," Elizabeth said flatly.

Everyone stared at her again, though Charlotte and Jane wore like looks of sympathy.

"Dead?" Mrs. Bennet squawked.

"How?" Lydia asked, sounding a touch too eager to Elizabeth's ear.

"Did Mr. Darcy kill them?" Kitty added.

"Certainly not." Elizabeth took a calming breath. She'd felt well-recovered from her ordeal after days in the luxury of Pemberley, but her family was testing her reserves. "Mr. Darcy is a gentleman. He doesn't kill people." He did best those two would-be ruffians on the road, though.

"Then what did happen to them?" Mary asked.

"I believe they all drowned in the shipwreck." Elizabeth decided going into details over Mary's escape would be too troublesome. It wasn't as if that mattered. Not now. Not even at the time of the wreck.

"Was it very terrible?" Jane asked, eyes brimming.

Elizabeth took another breath, Jane's sympathy harder to bear than her other relations' thoughtlessness. "Sometimes. Certainly, when the ship crashed, and we had to swim to shore through cold water, rain and waves, it was quite awful. Especially since I can't swim." Frightened as she'd been at the time, looking back she realized she would have been much more afraid had Mr. Darcy not projected such unwavering confidence. His calmness, as much as his strength, had saved her. "If not for Mr. Darcy, I would have joined our kidnappers at the bottom of the ocean."

The room dropped into silence again. Even Lydia appeared subdued.

Mrs. Bennet turned to Charlotte. "Do you have more servants now?"

Charlotte, who'd been staring at Elizabeth, looked at Mrs. Bennet and blinked.

"Yes, we do," Mr. Collins said before his wife could speak. "Mrs. Collins said that under the circumstances, we should not bother Lady Catherine about hiring servants. As I said, Lady Catherine did us the great kindness of selecting the servants we had, and I would have liked to take advantage of her wise advice, but Mrs. Collins made it clear that Lady Catherine's comfort should come before ours. She hired the new servants, so we wouldn't need to trouble her ladyship." He frowned. "She insisted we keep Rose on, though I don't know why."

Elizabeth exchanged an amused look with her friend, though it took effort to muster one.

Charlotte, as well, looked a bit strained. She touched Mr. Collins lightly on the arm again. "Do you know, Mr. Collins, I believe Elizabeth only recently returned." She turned back to Elizabeth. "I was so eager to see for myself you're well, and to express my happiness in your return, that I insisted we visit immediately. Now I see we should give you more time with your family."

"I was eager to see you, as well," Elizabeth said, standing as Charlotte did.

With brief farewells and another hug from Charlotte, the Collins departed. As soon as the foyer door closed behind them and before Mrs. Bennet could launch into a post-visit dissection, Mr. Bennet appeared in the parlor doorway. Such was his alacrity, Elizabeth half-wondered if he'd been waiting nearby. Ignoring the others, he gestured to her.

"Lizzy, I wish to speak with you alone in my library," he said firmly. "Now."

Too relieved to escape her mother and younger sisters to care what her father wished to speak about, Elizabeth hurried across the room, then followed him down the hall to his sanctuary. Mr. Bennet closed the door firmly behind them. Instead of sitting at his usual place behind his desk, he pulled two chairs together and gestured for her to sit in one. Once they were seated next to each other, he took her hand.

"I thought I'd lost you," he said, squeezing her hand.

"Oh, Papa." His choked tones a floodgate, Elizabeth burst into tears.

Her father put an arm about her shoulder and held her close, murmuring soothing nonsense. Elizabeth, twisted awkwardly in her chair, clung to him for a moment. He released her to rub her back. A kerchief appeared before her face. She took it and applied it to her eyes, drawing away from him slightly.

"I'm sorry," she murmured as she lowered the now-damp kerchief. "I don't know why I'm crying now. I didn't cry once on our journey."

"Journey?" Mr. Bennet repeated. "That is a pleasant word for a horrific affair." He stopped patting her back and retook her hand. "You're crying now because you can. You're safe. During your ordeal, you had to be strong, and I know you were. You're one of the very bravest people I know, Elizabeth."

Elizabeth blinked back more tears. She didn't feel brave. She felt tired and out of place, and she missed Mr. Darcy. More than that, she ached with the fear he might no longer want her.

Mr. Bennet cleared his throat. "I don't want you to be hurt more than necessary by this." He studied her face. "I don't mean to sound like your mother, but it truly would be best for you to marry. Not for Mrs. Bennet's or your sisters' sake, though I suppose that is true. Best for you, Lizzy."

She nodded.

"I don't mean to be indelicate but, well, have you anyone in mind who might have you?" Mr. Bennet grimaced over his own words. "I can offer a thousand pounds. I wish I could give you more. Do you think, though it should humble me to ask it of him, that Mr. Darcy might add to that?"

A sound, half hiccup half laughter, bubbled from her. "Oh Papa, Mr. Darcy's a better man than that. He proposed."

"He did?" Mr. Bennet asked, tone shocked.

"Actually, he proposed before we were even kidnapped." Should she tell her father the truth? Of all people, she could most count on him to keep her secret, and she most wished him to understand. "That's why he was at the parsonage. What he was doing there."

Mr. Bennet leaned back in his chair, expression dumbfounded.

"And I declined."

He swiveled to look at her. "Did you?" For some reason, that brought a slight smile to his face.

"I did. Unequivocally." Elizabeth touched his hand. "We're not going to tell anyone, but I wished you to know. Mr. Darcy said, and I agree, that we wouldn't lie, but we would use that part of the truth, his original proposal, to allow everyone to believe we've been engaged this whole time."

"So, he didn't accept your refusal?" He frowned.

"He did, but he's since proposed again."

Mr. Bennet appeared thoughtful. He shook his head. "You don't have to do this. With any luck, I can live a few more years and force your mother to save. I don't want you to marry an unpleasant man whom you hate. You are entirely without fault. Somehow, we will get through this."

Elizabeth offered her father a gentle smile. He was a true champion to her, not like her mother. She was pleased she could offer him reassurance on the point of Mr. Darcy's character, at least. "Mr. Darcy was the soul of courtesy and honor on our journey. He treated me with kindness and respect."

"He left here as soon as your mother opened her mouth."

"I know." Her smile fell.

"And he has not yet asked me for your hand." Mr. Bennet added an apologetic look to that observation.

Elizabeth swallowed down worry. "I realize that as well, but he did tell his family and his staff that we shall marry." She thought back to Mr.

Darcy's abrupt departure. "He wouldn't go back on his word." She made the statement as much for her benefit as her father's.

"Your mother and younger sisters are a great deal to ask of a man like Mr. Darcy."

Elizabeth was aware of that, as well. "Mr. Darcy is not good in social situations with people he does not respect." She allowed with a grimace. "However, he was properly humble when begging for food. In a crisis, he was magnificent."

Mr. Bennet shook his head. "Almost by definition, crises occur rarely. Can you live with a man who will embarrass you during day-to-day interactions but does well on those very rare occasions when something goes terribly wrong?"

"I've lived with a mother and sisters who embarrass me on a daily basis and, when something goes wrong, are only worse," Elizabeth pointed out wryly.

"Enduring the failings of your family is eminently different from enduring the shortcomings of your spouse," Mr. Bennet said, tone equally droll. "You have a choice in your spouse and so must not only endure them but live with the knowledge that you brought any unhappiness on yourself."

"But I don't have a choice. Not really."

"You do." Mr. Bennet's tone was earnest. "We will get through this and, in the meantime, I will curtail your mother's tongue."

Elizabeth's lips turned up in a real smile. "That's not why I don't have a choice, Papa. Somewhere in the middle of nowhere in Scotland, Mr. Darcy captured my heart. I'm afraid, snobbery and all, I love him."

Mr. Bennet raised his eyebrows. "You're sure?"

"Yes, Papa. I am, but please don't say anything yet. I wish to allow Mr. Darcy to ask you in his own way. That's one of the reasons I haven't told Mama." Elizabeth kept her smile in place. She'd leave her father with that truth and not weigh him down with all her reasons for silence. Not with the spite that, shamefully, caused her to torment her mother. Nor with her lingering fear that, when faced with her family, Mr. Darcy had already fled Hertfordshire, never to return.

Chapter Twenty-Three

Darcy stood at a window in one of Netherfield's cozier parlors, not really seeing the well-manicured grounds. He was hiding and not even ashamed to do so. He'd no patience for Miss Bingley's sniveling. Since the harsh tone he'd taken with her upon his arrival, she'd endeavored to reingratiate herself, mostly through false compliments to Elizabeth. Darcy had only been in Netherfield a few hours, but he simply couldn't endure any more of Miss Bingley for the moment.

Footfalls sounded in the hall, too loud and sure to be Miss Bingley's mincing steps. Darcy turned in time to see Bingley stroll into the room. He crossed to proffer two envelopes. Darcy accepted them, a glance showing both bore his man Edwards' neat script.

"The first came by regular mail and the second was an express," Bingley said. "I swear, that man of yours knows where you'll be before you do. He must have been beside himself when you were missing."

Darcy hadn't considered Edwards' feelings on the matter. He supposed there would have been some concern. Theirs, though exemplary, was a business relationship. All Edwards had said on the matter was that he was pleased Darcy had returned unharmed and that, no, he hadn't received Darcy's ring or a ransom letter.

"Something important?" Bingley asked, nodding to the envelopes Darcy held.

"We'll see." Darcy waited. There was no real reason for Bingley to bring his mail. Any servant in Netherfield could have. "Well?"

Bingley cleared his throat. "Yes, well… Look, Darcy, I know what you think of her family and her connections, though you haven't a leg to stand on there any more, you know, and I know you don't think she loves me but, damn it, Darcy, I'm going to ask Miss Bennet to marry me."

"Good."

"Good?" Bingley repeated in surprise.

"Do you think she loves you?"

"I do." Bingley's reply held a bit too much bravado to be completely sincere.

Darcy suppressed a sigh. Why couldn't Bingley simply know? "Well, then, let me ask you this. Do you still want her even if she doesn't fully reciprocate your affection?"

"I do." This time, Bingley sounded sure.

"Then I say, good, ask her." Darcy offered a slight smile. "You should know, Elizabeth feels Miss Bennet does, or at least did, love you. I'm sure if anyone besides Miss Bennet knows the truth of the matter, she does."

"Elizabeth is it?" Bingley asked.

Darcy shrugged and turned his attention to his mail. He cracked open the larger of the two envelopes to find another inside, his name scrawled on the outside in Wickham's messy script. In addition to Wickham's letter, the first envelope also contained Edwards' brief description of a visit to his office by Wickham. He added that while Wickham was writing his letter, Edwards had arranged for him to be followed.

"Trouble?" Bingley asked, settling onto the sofa facing Darcy.

"Wickham."

"The man is like a bad sliver. One that gets infected."

"Indeed." Darcy cracked the seal on Wickham's letter and began to read.

Shock and anger filled him at his onetime playmate's words and demands. This time, Wickham went too far. Darcy's jaw clenched. He would…

He curtailed that thought and drew in a deep breath. He skimmed the letter again. Obviously, from his salutation onward, Wickham wished to evoke anger. Well then, Darcy would strive for calm.

"What does he want?" Bingley asked.

"Money."

"Will you give it to him?"

Darcy skimmed the letter yet again. He could. It wasn't that much. A pittance, really, compared to the joy of being rid of George Wickham forever. Somehow, though, Darcy didn't believe it would be forever. And, of course, there was no possible way he would pay Wickham to marry Elizabeth.

Frowning, Darcy snapped open Edwards' second letter. Briefer than the first, this one reported information provided by the man sent to repay the Scottish cook at the inn where they'd parted ways with Wickham. First surprise, then wry amusement, filled Darcy.

"Good news?" Bingley asked.

"Indeed." Darcy couldn't keep a somewhat malicious grin off his face. "It seems our Mr. Wickham is deserving of congratulations. He recently wed."

Bingley looked almost as surprised as Darcy had been. "Well, that ought to keep him out of trouble, at least," Bingley offered. He frowned. "Does that mean you will or won't meet his demands?"

If anything, Darcy's smile became more wicked. "No, I will not. I do need to compose some letters, though, if you will excuse me."

"Of course," Bingley said. He stood as Darcy strode from the room.

The first letter, instructions for Edwards, Darcy penned with his usual efficiency. He took longer on the second. Not because he wavered over what to say, but because he found grim satisfaction in the task. He couldn't keep a hard smile from his face as he imagined Wickham's reaction when he read it.

After finishing the letters, Darcy had a light dinner with Bingley and Miss Bingley, who continued her barrage of false goodwill toward Elizabeth. Darcy retired early, claiming lingering fatigue. He could tell from Bingley's grimace that he knew Darcy's precipitous departure after dinner was Miss Bingley's doing.

It wasn't until the next morning, as he lay in bed wishing Elizabeth was beside him, that Darcy realized he might have hurt her by leaving so hurriedly. He sat up in bed, sheet falling to his waist, feeling something akin to alarm. What did she think of his leaving? What concerns had his lack of even a nod of farewell birthed in her?

Not that she would have seen a nod. She'd been so caught up in her family that she hadn't even noticed he'd remained by the carriage. She'd jumped out and dashed away from him without a glance back.

Darcy grimaced. That was an unworthy thought. Couldn't he let her have a few moments to spend with her family? She'd been separated from them for longer than even their ordeal, having been in Kent. Of course, she would miss them, no matter how terrible they were.

In truth, leaving so she could reunite with them was a kindness.

He shook his head, doubly annoyed with himself. No, he hadn't been kind. He'd been terrible. He'd fled. There was no way around that truth.

All he need have done was tell her that he would be staying at

Netherfield Park and would return in the morning. Instead, he'd slipped away. At least he'd affirmed for Mr. Bennet that Netherfield was his destination, but that didn't mean Elizabeth knew as much. Mr. Bennet, by Darcy's candid estimation, was an often-absentminded parent.

Darcy arose and dressed without the help of his valet, who still slept despite the way the sun rested on the horizon, making it clearly no longer night. He hurried to the parlor, but discovered breakfast wasn't yet ready. Well, he'd recently had plenty of practice starting off the day without sustenance. After a brief search for a footman, he ordered his carriage, as he hadn't brought a horse.

A part of him still hoped to retrieve the one their kidnappers had stolen, a favorite. Edwards had men searching. Darcy would, of course, pay whomever had the animal, assuming they appeared not to realize they'd purchased a stolen horse.

It wasn't until he arrived at Longbourn, sun a few handspans above the horizon, that he considered Elizabeth might not be awake yet. During their travels, she'd always risen early and at Pemberley as well. Here?

He was shown into the breakfast parlor, a good sign. At least someone was awake. Hungry now, Darcy hoped he would be invited to breakfast.

His gaze met Elizabeth's as he entered the room. Hers brightened, a smile on her lips. Was her expression touched with relief as well? He couldn't be sure. His guilt might simply be placing the emotion there.

"Good morning, Mr. Darcy," Mr. Bennet said, standing.

Darcy pulled his attention from Elizabeth and bowed to Mr. Bennet. He realized, as they all stood, that Miss Bennet and Miss Mary were also at the table. The hour, Darcy quickly surmised, was blessedly too early for Mrs. Bennet and the youngest two Bennet sisters.

"Mr. Bennet, Miss Bennet, Miss Mary," Darcy greeted. His gaze returned to Elizabeth. She looked well. Rested. Calm. He couldn't help a smattering of chagrin for her sanguine attitude. He'd been restless all evening without her... and all night. "Miss Elizabeth."

"Would you care to join us, Mr. Darcy?" she asked, the warmth and hope in her tone calming his disquiet.

"Very much so, for I have not yet eaten, but first I believe it is high time I asked to speak with your father."

"High time indeed," Mr. Bennet said. "Past time, in truth. That is, assuming you want to have my permission to marry my daughter."

Miss Bennet let out a happy exclamation and ran around the table to hug Elizabeth. Miss Mary stared at Darcy as if he'd sprouted horns. Mr. Bennet sat back down and applied himself to his bacon. From the circle of her sister's embrace, Elizabeth watched Darcy with shimmering eyes.

He cleared his throat. "Yes, sir, that is the matter on which I would like to speak."

"As I said, you're too late," Mr. Bennet said. He waved toward the chair beside Elizabeth, across from Miss Mary. "Sit down. Have something to eat."

"In what way am I too late, sir?" Darcy asked.

Elizabeth looked happy. Miss Bennet appeared ecstatic, but that confirmed nothing. She might not know all. Darcy needed matters made clear before he could hope to sit, definitely before he could eat. Had Wickham somehow beat him to putting the question to Mr. Bennet? Did he lurk nearby even now? But no, what about that would make Elizabeth happy?

"Elizabeth already informed me of your offer." Mr. Bennet clarified with a glimmer of amusement in his gaze that made Darcy wonder if Elizabeth had confessed to her father about both of his offers. "I gave her my permission to wed you. It seems redundant to therefore force you to seek my permission to wed her."

Relief assailed Darcy. Giving in to a smile, he left his place in the doorway and strode into the room. Miss Bennet released Elizabeth and returned to her seat between her father and Miss Mary. Darcy hurried around the table to help Elizabeth with her chair before sitting beside her.

"That's better," Mr. Bennet declared. "It was growing difficult to eat with you hovering in the doorway, Mr. Darcy." He waved to a maid. "Bring Mr. Darcy coffee," he said before turning back to Darcy. "I believe that is your preferred drink?"

"It is, thank you." Under the cover of the table, Darcy briefly clasped Elizabeth's hand.

She offered a smile. "Shall I fill a plate for you, Mr. Darcy?"

"I can fill my own."

"I'm sure you've more to discuss with my father." She stood and headed to the sideboard, where she began assembling his favorites of the selection offered. It warmed him to realize she must have observed his likes and dislikes over breakfasts at Pemberley.

"If you mean monetary matters." Mr. Bennet aimed his words more at Darcy than at Elizabeth. "I'm not going to try to negotiate a settlement."

Miss Bennet watched the exchange with noticeable interest. Miss Mary applied her attention to her plate. The maid returned and placed a cup, saucer and spoon on the table.

Darcy raised an eyebrow, surprised by Mr. Bennet's declaration. "You aren't, sir?" Did he not take an interest in Elizabeth's future?

Mr. Bennet offered Darcy a bland smile. "Not even whether you will care for the rest of my family if they are in need after I die. From what Elizabeth has told me, I will leave it to your sense of duty. Putting it in writing will help if you predecease her, of course, but you are intelligent enough to cover that, and I daresay all other, contingencies." Mr. Bennet put a bit more butter on his bread and took a bite.

Darcy stared at his future father by marriage for a long moment. Finally, he chuckled. "You, sir, are a scoundrel. By putting it that way, you hope I will be more generous than I would be if we had an adversarial negotiation."

"Did I succeed?" Mr. Bennet asked.

"Unfortunately, yes," Darcy said, amusement coloring the words.

"Good."

Elizabeth returned to the table then and put a plate before Darcy. Conversation turned more general as they ate. Miss Bennet said little but watched everything. Mr. Bennet and Elizabeth spoke animatedly on a range of topics, sometimes disagreeing, always spurring each other on. Miss Mary offered the occasional quote, most of which weren't quite relevant to the conversation. Overall, Darcy found the meal as enjoyable as any at Pemberley and certainly more pleasant than breakfast with Miss Bingley at the table.

His only complaint was that he wished to speak with Elizbeth alone. She evidenced no displeasure with him, but he still felt she deserved an apology for his behavior the day before. Even if she didn't, he'd still wish for time alone with her. Odd though it seemed, he missed her even while seated beside her. Her shared, observed attention was not what he most longed for.

They lingered over second cups of coffee and tea when a bell sounded somewhere deeper in the house. Elizabeth and her father exchanged a look. Miss Mary grimaced. Miss Bennet let out a small sigh.

Darcy turned to Elizabeth in question.

"My mother's bell, to summon her maid," Elizabeth clarified. "She'll be down for breakfast in a short while. She'll send someone to wake Kitty and Lydia as well, so she won't have to dine alone."

"Or with us," Miss Mary said. She stood from the table. "Elizabeth, Mr. Darcy, my congratulations on your engagement." She looked about at her father and sisters. "If you'll all excuse me, I shall take a walk. I don't fancy being anywhere near when Mama hears the news. Whether in joy or sorrow, her shrieking sets my teeth on edge." She turned and tromped from the room.

Darcy watched her depart, bemused.

"Yes, well, I have letters to write," Mr. Bennet said. "Mr. Darcy, Lizzy, Jane." He nodded to them all, scooped up the paper and his teacup, and headed from the parlor.

Elizabeth looked to Miss Bennet. "Someone must tell Mama the news."

"It's your news," Miss Bennet said.

That surprised Darcy most of all. He'd never seen Miss Bennet deny anyone anything before. Then she smiled at them.

"I'm only teasing, Lizzy," Miss Bennet said. "I'll tell her. You and Mr. Darcy should take a walk. It's a lovely morning." Her expression clouded. "That is, I mean, I suppose you've walked a great deal. You don't have to walk. There's always the front parlor."

"Where Mama can still find us?" Elizabeth shook her head, eyes dancing. "I think not. I know I'm a coward and a terrible sister, Jane, but I believe we will take a walk." She reached across the table and touched Miss Bennet's hand. "Thank you."

"You'd do the same for me," Miss Bennet said.

Elizabeth cast Darcy a quick, unreadable look. "Hopefully we'll soon see if I will." She pushed back her chair. "Would you care to walk, Mr. Darcy?"

"I can imagine nothing better than to walk with you, Miss Elizabeth." He stood and offered his arm.

Elizabeth placed her hand there, her touch light. Darcy couldn't help but miss the days when no fabric stood between them. He turned them toward the door.

"Mary always goes south, toward the pond," Miss Bennet advised as they headed from the room.

It took much of Darcy's will not to set out at a near run, he was so eager to have Elizabeth to himself. Soon, he realized he needn't hold back, for she adopted a long, ground covering stride. They strode at a much faster rate than they'd ever employed in Scotland, barring the brief stretch after the failed robbery. Of course, they'd no need to conserve their energy for a whole day of walking, so there was no reason not to adopt a strong pace.

Once they were suitably alone he ventured, "I'm sorry I left you so precipitously yesterday."

Elizabeth cast him a quick, worried look. "Why did you leave? Was it because of what my mother said?"

"Yes." He wanted to be honest with her.

She halted and turned to face him, her hand dropping from his arm. "You can face kidnapping, imprisonment, cold, hunger, begging, humiliation, dirt, exhaustion, footpads and Mr. Wickham, all without, for even a moment, behaving as anything less than a gentleman, but you can't face my mother? You knew what she was when you first proposed. Were you going to forbid me from seeing her?"

"Certainly not." Sadly, gentlemen did not do such a thing. "I wouldn't ask that of you."

Elizabeth's eyes narrowed as she studied his face. "My mother constantly embarrasses me, but she is my mother. I will not be estranged from her, especially since the only practical way to do that would be to keep me from my family." Her eyes were dark with anger.

"Elizabeth," he began.

"And that's another thing," she interrupted. "My friends and family, everyone who loves me and is close to me, calls me Lizzy. Not Elizabeth."

It occurred to Darcy that she was very angry, indeed. Had her pleasantness through breakfast been a façade? Her happiness to see him and at his affirming their engagement hadn't seemed feigned. Perhaps that joy had carried her through until now, when he brought up what, really, was the only issue left between them.

He drew in a calming breath and tried again. "Lizzy," he said, deliberately. "I can change. A month ago, I would never have believed I could humbly beg for food from a poor farmer or clergyman, or endure riding the stage, or the roof of the mail. Being with you, with your unflagging spirit and unwavering good nature, that buoyed me. You made my feelings of indignity seem as nothing. Your presence alone makes me a better man."

She watched him with wide, serious eyes. Anger drained away, flickered and disappeared like a snuffed flame. A slight smile pulled at her lips. "I can't imagine taking credit for all of your good behavior on our journey."

"You should. Without you there, Wickham and I would likely have come to blows before our second night in the ship's cabin. Who knows what shape I would have been in when the ship wrecked?" He shook his head.

"You said you were doing what you must to keep a bad situation from becoming intolerable."

"I was. For you." He caught her hands, no longer able to keep from touching her. "I'm not going to pretend to be, or even promise to become, perfect, but I know what the proper behavior of a gentleman is and that does not mean excluding your relatives from our lives."

"You mean that?" she asked, the words a bit breathless.

"I do, and if you ever catch me going back on my words, feel free to remind me."

"You'll endure Kitty and Lydia, and my mother?" she pressed. "You're certain?"

"Elizabeth." He shook his head and tugged gently on her hands to bring her nearer. "Lizzy. We traveled together by wagon, boat, ship, horseback, stage, mail and carriage. We walked and we swam. All that time going through all the hardships you enumerated, you were what kept me going. You gave me strength. I'd endure ten Lydias, ten Kitties and a hundred Mrs. Bennets to have you as my wife. I love you."

He didn't have to pull her closer. She stepped into his arms of her own accord. Her hands slipped free of his to reach up and wrap about his neck. Head tipped back, she gazed up at him.

"I love you too, Fitzwilliam."

Darcy lowered his lips to hers. He kissed her soundly, arms wrapped about her. If he could, he'd stay that way forever, with Elizabeth in his arms, where she was always meant to be.

Chapter Twenty-Four

Rough hands dragged Wickham from his bed in one of the fancier inns in London. He scrambled for the knife he now kept under his pillow, but his attackers knocked it away. Two of them pulled him upright in the dark room. They held him in iron grips.

"I'll give you my money," he cried, and why not? He should have more coming in from Darcy any day now. "And everything I have."

The darkness shifted. Someone stoked the coals in the grate. The outline of a large man emerged as they glowed brighter. So, three of them, at least. The man by the fire tossed in more kindling and a few pieces of firewood. Soon, flames began to flicker inside the hearth. The room grew lighter in slow increments to reveal his silent attackers.

He gaped. His wife's brothers. The two holding him dragged him to an armchair and forcibly sat him down.

"You know," the eldest, by the fireplace, drawled in his thick Scottish accent. "Being a widow with a babe is nearly as good as being a married woman with a babe."

"I say better," the youngest of the three snarled, one hand clamped on Wickham's shoulder, pinning him in the chair.

Wickham's heart hammered. A good judge of character, he could tell his wife's youngest brother wanted him dead. "I'm only here trying to make money for your sister and the inn," he said and offered an ingratiating smile.

"Then why'd you run off?" the middle brother, somewhere behind him, asked.

"I knew Fiona wouldn't believe me." Wickham strove for a reasonable tone despite the growing pain in his shoulder where his wife's little brother squeezed it. "I was going to come back and surprise her."

The eldest snorted. He turned and lit a candle in the growing blaze, then came across the room toward Wickham.

Wickham strained back in the chair. Was it to be torture, then?

To his relief, the Scotsman put the candle in the holder on the small table beside the chair. He pulled a letter from his coat and tossed it at Wickham. It landed in his lap with a thunk. Wickham immediately recognized the precise handwriting.

"Was that waiting for me downstairs?" he said, relief pushing back some of the pain in his shoulder. "Here's the money I was after. For the inn and your sister."

"Open it," the oldest brother ordered.

Wickham pulled his shoulder free of the youngest brother's grip and opened the envelope. Inside, on thick paper, was a note in Darcy's hand.

Dear George,

My congratulations on your nuptials.

Wickham blinked. He read the line again. How could Darcy know? A sinking feeling in his gut, he swallowed and dropped his gaze to the next words.

As you well know, for many years I've covered your debts, from Derbyshire to Cambridge. What you don't seem to realize is that never, not once, have I repaid any of your debts of honor. I have, however, kept careful track of them. There are more people than the three I've sent who are looking for you, including ones who want to do a lot worse than take you home to your wife. I expect you to consider that carefully next time you even think about contacting me or those I care about, for any reason.

Darcy

Wickham stared at the letter. He swallowed. He'd left many debts of honor unpaid, some with exceedingly unsavory people.

"I don't see any money, Wickham," his wife's middle brother said.

"Ah...Things didn't work out as I hoped," Wickham hedged. Something akin to fear stole over him. Darcy would never be a source of funds again. How would Wickham get money? How would he live?

The eldest of the three came down on his haunches to look Wickham in the eye. "If our sister weren't fond of you, you'd be dead." He stood and looked at his brothers. "Get him up. We're going home."

They unceremoniously dragged Wickham from the chair. They permitted him to dress and stuff his carpet bag, then dragged him out into the night and tossed him in a wagon he recognized as belonging to the inn. He rode in the bed of the wagon, hands bound behind his back, all the way back to Scotland. Except for brief moments, like when they fed him, his hands were always bound, even when he slept. By the time they reached the inn, so much pain stabbed through his shoulders, he doubted they'd ever be right again.

They pulled him out of the wagon and dragged him inside, still bound. Fiona looked up from where she stood beside the counter, noticeably more pregnant than when he'd left. To his surprise, the smile that bloomed on her face appeared genuine.

"George," she cried and waddled toward him. "I knew you'd come home." She shot her brother's a questioning look. "Why is he bound?"

"Because we didn't know he'd come home, Fiona."

Fiona nodded. "Well, here he is, and my thanks to the lot of you," she said as her eldest brother pulled out a knife to cut his bounds. "I hope you've learned your lesson, George."

What could he say to that? Because of Darcy, he had no money and nowhere to go. "I have, my love."

She nodded and offered another smile. "Good. Now you come with me. If I know my brothers, you've had nothing but bread and water for days."

The rope fell away. Wickham rubbed his wrists. "They also made gruel."

She shot her brother's a startled look. "And which of you learned to cook that?"

The youngest ducked his head. "I did, whiles you were away."

Fiona patted the large Scotsman on the head. "Good on you." She looked her brothers over. "Off with the lot of you, and make sure you see those cousins of ours away. You'll find they've seen to most of your chores." She offered a warm smile. "Thank you for bringing my husband home."

"Yes, ma'am," they chorused and headed from the inn.

"Now, George, come into the kitchen and I'll feed you," Fiona said, turning to Wickham. "I have some wonderful news."

Wickham was a bit startled by the warmth of his reception, but the kitchen was his favorite part of the inn, and he really was hungry. If there was one thing he could say about Fiona, beyond a pleasant enthusiasm for the marital bed, it was that her cooking was superb. He'd no doubt that's why her brothers valued her so, and how she'd won recommendation from Lady Catherine. If Wickham were the sort of man to relegate himself to one woman, he truly could love a girl who cooked the way Fiona did.

Relieved to be unbound and welcome, he followed his wife into the kitchen. He took his place at the small table and watched while she served him honeyed bread and thick mutton stew, then set to preparing a pastry to celebrate his return. She even placed a cool mug of ale at his elbow.

Once the pastry was in the oven, Fiona dragged a stool over to the row of high shelves she kept the spices on, out of easy reach in regard for their expense. She took down a dull canister and came to stand beside him where he sat at the table. Opening the cannister, she pulled out a sack of spices, then another. From the second, she removed a tightly folded five-pound note.

Wickham dropped his spoon in his bowl. "Where did that come from, love?"

"Mr. Darcy."

"What?" Wickham exclaimed, stunned. "Why would Mr. Darcy give you money?"

"A man came. He said he was an agent of someone named Edwards in London. He said he wanted to talk to the cook. He was almost threatening at first. He wanted to be certain I was the cook who was here the day you showed up at the inn."

"The day I showed up?"

"The day Mr. Darcy and Miss Bennet were here," she clarified with a nod. "The man said I sent something for them to eat. He asked what it was and how I got it to them. I told him I sent Duncan to run after them with two baps filled with bacon. Then the fellow asked my name. I gave him both my name then and my name now, Fiona Mary McClintock and Mrs. George Wickham."

Wickham suppressed the curse that sprang to his lips. His own wife, his Fiona, had given him away to Darcy. Angry as that made him, he couldn't let her know. Somehow, he didn't think she'd appreciate that he might have claimed ten-thousand pounds if only she'd kept her mouth shut. All he could do was groan, "You gave Darcy food? Why would you give him food?"

Her look was smug. "I had a hunch he's the sort who takes pompous pride in repaying his debts."

"But this is many times the worth of a few stuffed rolls." And nowhere near ten thousand pounds

"I know." Fiona grinned. "And do you know the best part, George? I'll get this every year. Duncan will get a pound, for running the baps out to them."

Some of Wickham's anger slipped away as he mulled that over. No,

216

it wasn't ten thousand but it was something. Money for him and for Fiona's youngest brother. "Five pounds a year for a couple baps is extreme, even for Darcy."

Fiona shrugged. "Like as not, he means this to impress that Bennet girl." She draped an arm over his shoulder. "Proud of me?"

Her glee stole the last vestige of his pique. Wickham slapped her on the rear. "Very." He frowned. "Why would Darcy want to impress Miss Bennet?"

"Oye, you are a thick one, George." Fiona shook her head. "He's in love with her."

Wickham raised his eyebrows. "I doubt that. He'd never condescend to be in love with her."

"He was proposing the day we nabbed them," Fiona countered, eyes glinting with amusement. "I've said it before and I'll say it again, sometimes you aren't very observant, George Wickham. Why did you suppose we even took the girl?" She cocked an eyebrow. "Leverage."

"Darcy proposed to Miss Bennet?" Lines of confusion folded his brow. "Why wouldn't they simply say as much? I can't imagine any reason to keep that from me..." His mouth gaped open. "Unless... that is... she must have said no."

A woman had refused Darcy? Wickham's mind roiled with the idea. He cast an incredulous look at Fiona, who shrugged again.

"If you say so, George." She stuffed the five-pound note back into its sack and stowed that away in the bottom of the spice jar.

As Wickham recovered from his shock, a chuckle left him. Oh, that was rich. Darcy lowered himself to propose to a country miss and she refused him. Wickham's laughter redoubled. And now, thanks to Wickham's cunning wife, Darcy would be sending him money every year. Not much. Nothing, really, but it still salved Wickham's pride.

He laughed again and took a swig of ale. "That's the best thing I've heard in years."

"Oh, and I've other news," Fiona said. She went to the oven to remove the pastry.

Full as he was, the smell still made Wickham's mouth water. "It can't be better than Darcy getting refused by Miss Bennet and sending us money."

"No, but I wanted your advice on if it's a debt to settle."

Wickham turned to watch her ease the pastry from the hot pan. "Oh?" He couldn't but preen a bit at his cunning wife seeking his advice.

"A man came in the other day, one I know. You as well, in fact. The Jonesy who was sent with Mr. Darcy's horse and ring, and our ransom note." Fiona scowled. "I gave him some ale, made like I wasn't angry, and he told me how he realized he was too afraid to head to London with a stolen horse and a stolen ring. He burned the note and sold the horse." She pulled something from her apron. "He still had the ring." She tossed it at Wickham.

Wickham caught the ring. He turned it over in his hand. Darcy's ring. Old Mr. Darcy's ring. Wickham used to love this ring, covet it. It seemed odd to hold, heavy in his undeserving hand. "Maybe I'll return it to Darcy. Buy some good will."

Fiona shrugged. "Or sell it. Buy some sugar and flour."

"I'll send it to Darcy with a note claiming I ran into the smuggler and retrieved his ring. He's sure to pay more than we could get from selling it." He tucked it into his pocket. "So what advice did you need?"

"I had my cousins lock The Jonesy in the root cellar," Fiona said. She selected a long knife from the rack. "Should we let him go or shall I have my brothers kill him for being a traitor?" Her eyes met Wickham's for a moment. She turned and started slicing the pastry. "After all, running off is an act of treachery."

Wickham swallowed. Suddenly, his stomach felt a bit sour for sweets. "Ah, I'd say let him go. Everyone deserves a second chance."

Fiona nodded. She put a slice on a small plate and, knife still in one hand, brought it to the table. "You're correct, of course, George. Everyone deserves a second chance." Her smile was beatific. "Not a third, though, love. Not a third." She returned to the counter and her chopping. "Eat your pastry, George, before it's cold."

Epilogue

Darcy and Elizabeth climbed into the carriage with their three children. Always social, their middle child, Jane, pulled back the curtain to wave as they started moving. Eliza immediately opened the book her grandfather had lent her and started to read. Willy sat beside Darcy in his mother's lap, trying to chew on his sleeve.

Darcy settled back in his seat and breathed a sigh of relief. Their annual three-week visit to Longbourn was over. They would stop for a few days whenever they went to London, but those were short enough visits to be easily bearable. This single long visit each year, though, was a trial.

Glancing up, Eliza put down her book. "Is it me, or does each year seem worse?"

"Now, Eliza, that's not a kind thing to say about your grandmother," Darcy scolded, though he privately agreed.

She turned a mischievous grin, reminiscent of her mother's, his way. "I didn't say anything about Grandma Bennet, Father."

Darcy winced. He cast Elizabeth an apologetic look.

She shook her head, a smile dancing about her lips.

"You did very well, Papa," Eliza said.

Darcy exchanged another amused glance with Elizabeth. "Am I so bad that even you know it is a strain?"

"No," Eliza said. "You just aren't you. Grandma Bennet can be a bit of a trial, though, so I understand."

"She spoils you," Darcy said. "You shouldn't complain."

"Aunt Everett and Aunt Bingley never spoil me, but I like them better," Eliza said

"You should not talk about liking some relatives better than others," Darcy said as gently as possible. He liked Georgiana Everett and Jane Bingley better than Mrs. Bennet as well, and perhaps he was at fault for displaying that preference. That didn't mean he shouldn't try to raise his daughter to be a better person than he was.

"Grandma gives me what she thinks I want, not what I actually want," Eliza said thoughtfully.

Darcy couldn't think of anything to say to that thoughtful observation that wouldn't undermine his admonishment.

"She thinks sweets are what I want," Eliza continued. "But I like Grandpa Bennet's giving me Tales from Shakespeare much more."

"You can give me your sweets," Jane said. "I wouldn't want your book."

"That's because you wouldn't read it," Eliza said. "I might as well give it to Will."

Darcy looked at his one-year-old son, sitting in his mother's lap, gumming at his sleeve.

Jane glared at Eliza for a moment, then turned back to Darcy and Elizabeth. "Why does she seem worse every year?" She looked back and forth between them.

Darcy knew better than to attempt that. He turned to Elizabeth.

She marshaled a stern expression for the barest moment, then laughed. "Mrs. Bennet was in fine form this year, wasn't she?"

Darcy also knew better than to answer that.

After a moment, amused eyes daring him to speak, Elizabeth addressed Jane. "You see, each year your grandmother grows more comfortable around your father, so each year she is more relaxed and more of her true character shows."

Eliza's eyes widened. "That wasn't her true character yet?"

"Oh no, dear, not nearly," Elizabeth said. "Just wait until you're a little older. Then she'll truly start to embarrass you."

Eliza groaned. "That sounds awful," she muttered and turned her attention back to her book.

Darcy stifled his chuckle with a cough. He pulled an envelope from his pocket. The report had arrived yesterday from Edwards, but Darcy no longer felt the need to read them immediately. Over the years, Wickham had settled into his life at the inn, and Darcy had cut back from quarterly reports to annual reports. He cracked the seal to read.

As in years past, Edwards' man had little to say. Wickham had grown bald and fat. Though, by all reports, his wife was an excellent cook, which could excuse Wickham's expanding middle, Darcy felt perhaps Wickham substituted food and drink for his old lifestyle of carousing and gambling.

Still, he seemed content to work at the inn, providing the

respectability a male proprietor offered. He was charming to guests and subservient when required. He even doted on Fiona's reputedly boisterous, red-haired daughter and the three sons Fiona had given him. All in all, George seemed a fair husband to Fiona Mary Wickham.

Darcy folded the letter and smiled. He still sent money annually. Once he realized the cook, Fiona McClintock, and Mary the maid, were all the same person, he'd nearly stopped. But then, she and her brothers had done and continued to do Darcy a great service, providing a home for Wickham and keeping him there. She deserved a little compensation for that. Good deeds, even if done unwittingly or selfishly, should be rewarded.

Darcy frowned down at his ring. It had arrived shortly after his marriage to Elizabeth, along with information on where he might look for his horse, which he'd found and still had, though no longer rode. Wickham claimed to have bought the ring, as well as information about the horse, naming a price on the high end of plausible. Darcy had decided that he wasn't going to argue with that and paid Wickham the exact amount he named. He'd also sent Wickham's wife and her brothers letters telling them how much he'd paid. For a time, he'd wondered if he should have done more or perhaps less. Now, he rarely thought on the transaction anymore.

Even if he'd paid too much or owed Wickham and his new wife some sort of retribution, it didn't matter now. There was no reason to ever contact George Wickham again. Their past was finally, well and truly, past. Georgiana was happily Mrs. Everett with a home, music and children. All of Elizabeth's sisters were married, as were Bingley's, though none had caught a duke.

Elizabeth reached over and touched his hand.

Darcy realized he twisted his ring slowly about his finger, as he often did when thinking.

"Is everything well?" she asked softly.

He nodded, his gaze dropping to his son, who would someday have the ring. Master Fitzwilliam Darcy gave every sign of falling asleep. Thumb in his mouth, his eyes were gradually closing. Darcy tucked the report away. "Do you want me to hold him, Lizzy?"

"No need," Elizabeth said. Their son cradled in one arm, she slid over on the seat to snuggle next to Darcy.

He put his arm around her, where he most liked it to be. He relaxed into the comfortable cushions of the carriage, utterly content, and let out a long breath, happy to be going home.

~ The End ~

About the Authors

Renata McMann

Renata McMann is the pen name of Teresa McCullough, someone who likes to rewrite public domain works. She is fond of thinking "What if?" To learn more about Renata's work and collaborations, visit **www.renatamcmann.com**.

Summer Hanford

Starting in 2014, Summer was offered the privilege of partnering with fan fiction author Renata McMann on her well-loved *Pride and Prejudice* variations. More information on these works is available at **www.renatamcmann.com**. Additionally, in 2016, Summer was lucky enough to be asked to join Austen Authors, a great place for fans to get more Jane Austen. To explore Austen Authors, visit **www.austenauthors.net**.

Summer is currently writing solo Regency Romance works, partnering with McMann, providing content for, creating and managing websites, and is a fantasy and science fiction faculty member at AllWriters' Workplace and Workshop, LLC., an international creative writing studio. She lives in Michigan with her husband and compulsory, deliberately spoiled, cats. For more about Summer, visit **www.summerhanford.com**.

Made in the USA
San Bernardino, CA
03 November 2018